GIANT DAYS

For Robin,
my fellow Giant Days *fan*

PUBLISHER'S NOTE: This is a work of fiction. Names, characters, places, and incidents are either the product of the author's imagination or used fictitiously, and any resemblance to actual persons, living or dead, business establishments, events, or locales is entirely coincidental.

Library of Congress Cataloging-in-Publication Data
Names: Pratt, Non, author.
Title: Giant days / by Non Pratt.
Description: New York: Amulet Books, 2018. | Summary: Although very different, Daisy, Susan, and Esther become fast friends their first week at university so when Daisy joins a club and begins behaving very strangely, Susan and Esther investigate.
Identifiers: LCCN 2018009604 | ISBN 9781419731266 (hardcover with jacket)
Subjects: | CYAC: Best friends—Fiction. | Friendship—Fiction. | Secret societies—Fiction. | Universities and colleges—Fiction.
Classification: LCC PZ7.P8888 Gi 2018 | DDC [Fic]—dc23
U.K. Paperback ISBN 978-1-4197-3488-5

Copyright © 2018 BOOM! Studios
Jacket illustrations by Michael Heath
Book design by Julia Marvel
Giant Days TM & © 2018 John Allison
Giant Days created by John Allison. All rights reserved.

Printed and bound in U.S.A.
10 9 8 7 6 5 4 3 2 1

Amulet Books are available at special discounts when purchased in quantity for premiums and promotions as well as fundraising or educational use. Special editions can also be created to specification. For details, contact specialsales@abramsbooks.com or the address below.

Amulet Books® is a registered trademark of Harry N. Abrams, Inc.

ABRAMS The Art of Books
195 Broadway, New York, NY 10007
abramsbooks.com

Non Pratt

GIANT DAYS

AMULET BOOKS

NEW YORK • LONDON

I

FIRE IN THE HALL

It looked as if someone had started a small fire in a prison block. Only the prison was actually part of the student residence for Sheffield University. J-block, Catterick Hall, to be precise. Smoke wafted gently from one of the upper windows, wispy fingers caressing the bright October sky . . . and clawing at the lungs of anyone unlucky enough to be standing downwind. J-block had been evacuated, and a Saturday-afternoon assortment of first-year students littered the quad. Those still dressed in pajamas and bathrobes mixed with those already preparing for the night ahead—party clothes on, hair half-styled, and makeup in the experimental stage. In the midst of this lackluster chaos stood Susan Ptolemy, Daisy Wooton, and Esther de Groot.

The three were a mix and mismatch of aesthetics. Daisy's clothes were as bright and colorful as Esther's were dark and macabre. Susan's preference for function over fashion gave her the look of a stray dog that had been shoved inside some comfy jeans and a tattered checked shirt. The three friends were, nonetheless, united in their focus.

While everyone else on the quad was likely speculating

as to who'd started the fire, Susan, Daisy, and Esther were more concerned with working out which of their neighbors had vomited in the sink of the fourth-floor bathroom, thereby blocking it. A crime far greater than accidentally setting fire to the kitchen, which could *totally* happen to *anyone*.

"That one," Susan said, pointing across the grass. A girl with a neat blond ponytail was standing with a duvet over her shoulders, asking no one in particular if the university would compensate her for smoke damage to her signed Ed Sheeran poster.

"How do we know it's her?" Daisy's glare wavered. Accusations weren't to be thrown around lightly.

"Show your workings," Esther said.

Susan narrowed her eyes further. Her investigative instincts remained razor sharp after a summer spent honing them the hard way on the cruel cul-de-sacs and low-key criminal underworld of Northampton, her hometown. "Look at her duvet, that hideous floral pattern . . ."

"Flowers. The hallmark of a reprobate," Esther hissed.

"I like flowers," said Daisy, her voice getting smaller. "Nature's pretty."

". . . look closer, and you'll find those aren't petals but vomit splotches," Susan finished with relish as her friends recoiled.

"No!"

"She needs to *wash* that duvet."

Susan took a pack of cigarettes from the pocket of her checked shirt and lit one, an all-knowing smile emerging as she blew a thin stream of smoke between her lips.

There were some skills Esther's privileged upbringing couldn't pay for and Daisy's homeschooling couldn't teach. An education Susan was only too happy to provide.

She might want to be a doctor in later life, but Susan's employment history until now had been erratic. Like most people, she'd started with whatever job she could find, working in one of her hometown's many warehouses—until she turned whistleblower on their substandard (and illegal) business practices. Blacklisted by respectable businesses and criminals alike, Susan applied her unique skill set and keen sense of social justice as a freelance investigator. Provided she turned over the criminals, the police turned a blind eye to her lack of license.

Some people had skeletons in their metaphorical closets; Susan had accrued a plague pit of human remains.

Not that Esther and Daisy needed to know. That was the joy of university: a fresh start for everyone. Even someone as jaded as Susan. The only things her new friends knew about her were the things she'd chosen to reveal.

An awkwardly cleared throat and some shuffling alerted the trio to the presence of a new arrival: Ed Gemmell.

"Isn't that *your* kitchen that's on fire?" he said, frowning up at the fourth-floor window.

Ed Gemmell, fellow J-block resident, was a young man with the personality of a cinnamon roll and the spine of partially cooked spaghetti. He was inoffensive and perfectly tolerable, and Daisy and Esther greeted him with the kind of delight Susan reserved for finding a lost pack of cigarettes.

Nodding, Esther waved majestically at the smoke

billowing from the window. "Behold the consequences of crossing a dark princess, a baby giraffe, and sarcasm personified . . ."

"I'm the giraffe, right?" Daisy whispered.

"No, Daisy. You're the dark princess." Susan rolled her eyes and blew smoke out of the corner of her mouth.

"Cross us, and you shall *burn!*" Esther dropped to her knees and cackled demonically, raven hair cascading down her back as she tipped her head up to claw at the sky.

Her friends took a step away.

"Should you really be confessing to arson?" Ed Gemmell asked as everyone turned to stare.

"It's not arson if it's an accident," Susan said. The three exchanged complicit looks: Esther's, guilty; Daisy's, strained; Susan's, reassuring. No one was going to prosecute over a self-combusting baked potato. Even if it had self-combusted because of Esther's extreme microwave negligence.

"Anyway . . . No one's allowed back in yet, so I'm going to the library to"—Ed Gemmell edged a little away from Susan and shot her an inexplicably cautious glance—"um, to get some books out."

"I hear the library's a good place for that." Susan watched him closely, noting the irregular bob of his Adam's apple and the way his moley little eyes darted about behind the rectangular lenses of his wire-rimmed glasses.

If she wanted to, she could crack him like an egg.

Unnerved by such scrutiny, Ed Gemmell turned to Esther with a hefty dose of desperation and zero optimism. "I take it you, er, wouldn't fancy coming with me?" Like Esther, Ed was an English Literature student. Unlike Esther, he seemed to understand that this involved reading books.

"Why would you think that?" Esther said, getting up from where she was still kneeling on the ground and dusting off her knees.

"Because you never do any work?" Susan suggested.

"Because we need to stay here in case the Fire Monitor does another head count?" said Daisy.

"Because you're still dressed for bed." To his credit, Ed Gemmell was clearly doing his best not to acknowledge the expanse of long, lean, bone-white limbs that emerged from Esther's shortest of skull-print bed shorts. These were accompanied by a T-shirt bearing the slogan *Die God Botherers*, which may or may not have been a reference to the lyrics of an obscure German grindcore band, and a pair of fleecy slipper socks that belonged to Daisy.

"Counter proposition!" Esther extended an imperious finger. "We all go to the student bar for a remedial beverage."

"Ooh, they do a lovely hot chocolate," Daisy said.

"Daisy! Such extravagance!" Esther laid a hand to her chest in mock outrage.

"But . . ." Ed Gemmell waved helplessly at Esther's attire.

"Eddie, Eddie, Eddie." Esther put an arm around him and pinched his cheek. "That's the glory of a *student* bar: They won't care. Besides, I've been to lectures wearing less."

As much as Susan enjoyed this unwitting sadism of her friend, repeatedly drawing Ed Gemmell's attention to how little she was wearing, it was getting chilly, and she didn't want to have to deal with Esther's inevitable hypothermia.

Susan finished her cigarette and dropped it to the ground, placing the toe of her Converse over the butt and grinding it into the earth.

"Come on. Let's go see if the barman remembers us from last time . . ."

"I hope not," Daisy said in alarm.

Susan gave Ed Gemmell an arch look that set him further a-blither. "You coming?" she asked.

"Maybe later . . . library . . ." he said, scuttling off in entirely the wrong direction.

Giving his retreating figure a moment's further contemplation, Susan shrugged off her suspicions and turned to follow her friends.

There were several residence halls located on different sites around the city of Sheffield. The newest ones resembled all-inclusive hotels, with clean expanses of glass and easy-to-navigate gravel paths, signs marking the locations of multiple laundry rooms, dining halls, lounges, and bars. Some had on-site shops supplying emergency essentials, such as laundry detergent, plastic shot glasses, tortilla chips, and alcohol.

And then there was Catterick Hall, the kind of place vermin came to holiday.

Like everything else here, the bar had a whiff of prison about it. An impression that was enhanced by the window bars fitted to prevent ambitious students from stealing items such as beer barrels, pot plants, and, as on the occasion that had necessitated the installation of the bars, an entire coffee table. Once inside, the decor was equally dour, with the same aim of deterring petty theft. *No one* could possibly wish to steal any of the artwork—abstract paintings layered with streaks and blisters of yellow and orange, presumably created by a Jackson Pollock wannabe who worked in bodily fluids rather than paint. Even the furniture cushions defied desirability with their scratchy fabric and miserly stuffing.

The last time the trio had ventured to this bar had been during their first week of term in September. The sagging sofas had been pushed to the sides to create a makeshift dance floor, and the jukebox had surrendered the airwaves to a third-year student in possession of a laptop and a Spotify subscription. It had been here that things came to a head with a group of glossy-haired, entitled residents of J-block, plummy-voiced witches who'd been feasting on Daisy's food in the communal kitchen and trying to subsume Esther into their posh-girl clique. Words were thrown, hair was tossed, and lines were drawn, with Esther, Daisy, and Susan united on one side and the ex-private-school girls on the other.

It was the night that had forged their friendship.

"Do you think we'll be asked to leave?" Daisy attempted to hide behind Susan, which was tricky since Daisy was a head taller—and that head was topped with a voluminous cloud of blond curls.

"I do not." Susan dropped into a sagging leather chair. "Speaking as the embodiment of human rage, *no one*, not even me, can possibly stay cross with you for that long, and this one"—she jerked a thumb at Esther—"is too sexy for anyone to resist."

Before Esther could puff up too much at the compliment, Susan shooed her in the direction of the bar.

"Put that sexiness into action. A medicinal whisky for me and a hot chocolate for the evergreen floof."

It didn't take long for Esther to return.

"One of you needs to go. I don't have any money." Esther waved at her pajamas before folding herself onto the sofa next to Daisy, who exchanged a shocked glance with Susan. Esther might have been low on cash, but there were other currencies in which she could—and frequently did—trade. Her body struck the perfect midpoint between Daisy's straight lines and Susan's curves, and her face was half big gray eyes and half infectious grin.

When Daisy first met her, she wasn't sure whether Esther was so confident because she was so pretty or so pretty because she was so confident. Either way, Daisy would have laid her savings on Esther being able to sweet-talk a round of drinks from the bar on a suggestive smile and a promise to pay later.

"Can't you flirt the drinks out of him?" Susan suggested baldly.

"I can't believe a feminist like you would entertain the idea of pimping me out for alcoholic gain." Esther feigned affront for as long as she could (two seconds) before conceding. "I tried. Apparently even this"—she gestured in disbelief at her ensemble—"wasn't sufficiently persuasive.

All I got was a lecture about the gig economy, something about the price of avocados, and a suggestion that I quit my degree and start an Etsy business."

"Must have been the longest lecture you've attended all term." Susan smirked, pulling a tatty leather wallet out of her pocket and handing it to Daisy. "I'll pay if you go. The barman sounds chatty—it's too early in the day to talk to strangers."

"It's half past two in the afternoon."

"Your point?"

Glancing anxiously to where the barman was entirely ignoring their existence, Daisy leaned in to whisper, "It's *illegal*. I'm not yet eighteen."

Susan didn't even lower her voice to reply. "Yet the barman will assume you are. And the alcohol isn't for you, so you're not doing anything wrong. You can do this, Daisy Wooton. I believe in you."

Esther raised a fist in solidarity before giving a little shiver. "Mulled cider for me."

Daisy pulled off her cardigan and laid it over Esther's bare legs before turning toward the bar with the stride of someone who knew what she wanted (a whisky, a mulled cider, and an entirely legal hot chocolate). She tried to ignore the way the soles of her shoes stuck to the floor and made a tacky little *schulp* with every step. Positioning herself a respectable distance away from where an overly affectionate couple were running their hands under each other's clothes, she waited patiently as the barman prepared coffee with all the urgency of a Windows update.

The barman had just located the milk when someone barged up, jostling Daisy into dropping Susan's wallet onto the floor.

"I'm so sorry!" Daisy apologized reflexively, even as she was bending down to pick up the wallet the new arrival had knocked from her hand.

"Don't worry about it." His voice was rich and round, nourished by a diet of elocution lessons and port, and when Daisy was upright once more, she realized she knew the person to whom it belonged.

Jonathan Tremain. Geography. Ellerton Hall.

Name-subject-hall was the way everyone had introduced themselves that first week, when Daisy had encountered Jonathan queuing for the showers in a fetching silk robe several inches too short to be considered decent, with *Amelia* embroidered on the back.

Possessed with unexpected nostalgia, Daisy waved hello.

"You probably don't remember me. I'm—"

"Poppy! Of course!"

Did it count as remembering if he got her name wrong? "Actually, it's—"

"How've you been?"

She could be Poppy. That was fine.

"I've been good, thanks. What about you?"

"I've been *fantastic!*" Propping an elbow on the bar, Jonathan set down the pile of posters he'd been holding, maintaining a continuous monologue of all the things he'd been up to. ". . . hardly have time for any bloody lectures, what with all the tryouts for the rugby league, corridor parties every night, karaoke in the S.U. You know, the Student Union?" Daisy, being familiar with the concept of abbreviations, was fully aware of what the S.U. was. ". . . Jessamy's an absolute howler, couldn't carry a tune if you popped it into a rucksack and tied it on her back."

"Jessamy?" Daisy craned her neck to see whether the barman had noticed she needed serving yet.

"Jessamy Trinker? Lives in your block. Blond girl, could drink for England, arms like a nutcracker. Big feet—*massive* feet. Absolute riot. Wouldn't be a party without her. You *know*. Jessamy."

Daisy did not know Jessamy.

"You *must* know Archie Thomas and Maggie Atherton. They do Classics like you."

"I do Archaeology."

"Of course! What a runt I'm being—so you'll be friends with Navid! Nice chap, some kind of accent. Sounds a little Welsh or a little Indian, something like that."

Jonathan sounded a little racist. Or something like that.

"Um . . ." Daisy shook her head. If there was a Navid on her course, Daisy had yet to meet him.

"Seriously, Poppy." Jonathan gave her a pitying look as he casually raised a hand to wave the barman over. "Have you made *any* friends other than me?"

"I'm friends with Susan Ptolemy and—"

"Never heard of her."

Daisy pointed to where the two friends who actually knew her name were seated. "Susan's the scruffy one in the checked shirt. She does Medicine. And there's Esther?"

She looked at Jonathan for some sign of recognition. Every-one knew Esther. She was hard to miss. "Esther de Groot? Usually wears black. Very pretty . . . ?"

"Oh, *her*—the Vampire Princess! Goodness." An unread-able look passed across Jonathan's face before he turned to address the approaching barman. "All right, mate. Andrew from the Union said to leave some of these with you."

The barman looked at the posters he'd been handed, far from enthused. "I'll put them up later."

"Andrew said I had to watch you do it now."

Daisy followed the conversation somewhat helplessly. She'd been there before Jonathan; couldn't he at least let her order? But after a silent battle of wills, the man behind the bar sloped off with a grudging "*Fine* . . ." toward the back wall.

"You and Sophie—"

"Susan."

"—and Gothy the Hottie. What on Earth do you have in common with people like that?" Jonathan's voice was loud, and Daisy hoped they were far enough away that "Sophie" and "Gothy the Hottie" couldn't hear.

"Umm . . . we all live on the same corridor?" Which sounded rather feeble.

"Ha!" When Jonathan clapped Daisy on the back, her glasses slid down her nose. "See what I mean? You need to get out there, Pops. I know!" He took a poster from the top of his remaining pile and bestowed it upon Daisy as if it were the Holy Grail.

"Activities Fair?" Daisy read aloud with a frown. "Wasn't that weeks ago?"

"They had to move the date because the old venue had black mold and had to be quarantined. Come along and say hi—I'll be there with the rugby lot."

The bartender returned and waved grudgingly at the posters he'd tacked up. "Satisfied?"

"Perfect, my man. Right!" Jonathan turned back to Daisy. "Must get on. See you at the fair . . ."

Once he was gone, Daisy folded the poster into quarters and handed it to the barman to put in the recycling. There was no need for her to "get out there" when she could stay in with Esther and Susan.

"Who was that you were talking to?" Esther began her interrogation before Daisy had even set the drinks down. If it hadn't been for Susan restraining her, she'd have barged up to the bar already.

"Jonathan."

"And what were his intentions?"

"To put up a poster advertising the Activities Fair."

But Esther waved this answer away. "I meant his intentions toward you."

"I don't think he had any." Sitting down next to her on the sofa, Daisy adjusted her cardigan, which had slid off Esther's knees and exposed goose-bumped porcelain skin.

"Oh. Well. Good. I didn't like the cut of his jib."

"I'm surprised. Thought a basic model like that would have you wooed from fifty paces, Es," Susan chipped in.

Ignoring her (even though Esther did have a fondness for boys at the blander end of the spectrum), Esther continued,

"Don't trust anyone in a rugby shirt, Daisy. His sort view women as conquests, like pints to be downed, not savored. You're too precious a vintage to waste on the likes of that."

Daisy smiled, her glasses steaming a little as she blew across the top of her hot chocolate. "I think I'm immune to whatever charm Jonathan possesses, but it's very sweet of you to look out for me."

As Esther gave Daisy an affectionate little shoulder bump, Susan raised her glass as if in a toast.

"Here's to watching out for each other." She took a sip and grinned. "We're you're family now, Daisy. No getting rid of us."

Before the words were even out, Esther met Susan's gaze and watched her friend's eyes widen in horror. What would have been a perfectly innocuous thing to say took on a different meaning when addressing someone who had been raised by her grandmother because her parents had died. As in: Daisy.

"Well, make sure you watch out for me!" Esther said too loudly, trying to plaster over the moment with bluster and cheer and self-deprecation. "We all know I'm the liability here."

Susan let out an unnecessarily loud bark of fake laughter. "Our Esther—face so pretty, standards so low. I'll drink to that."

And she tossed back her whisky so fast that she nearly choked. Which Esther considered fair retribution for being so rude about her taste in men.

Disaster dodged, the three of them reverted to safe

territory, discussing the other occupants of the bar, trying to guess which course they studied based solely on their clothing. The only one they agreed on was that the student dressed entirely in black except for a scarf, sipping an espresso, must be a Philosophy student. It helped that he was lounging back, making sure the cover of Kant's *Critique of Pure Reason* was on display as he read.

When Susan returned with the next round, the three of them decided they had enough change to spare for the jukebox, thereby putting an end to what appeared to be an endless rotation of Tom Jones songs.

"So, what are we going for?" Susan asked, change in hand, peering into the bowels of the jukebox.

"Ooh. That one." Daisy pointed. "The artwork looks really pretty . . ."

"Daisy!" Esther was horrified. "That's not how you choose music!"

"No, Daisy," Susan muttered. "One must make a selection inversely proportional to the music's appeal. Let me demonstrate . . . Look, some Metallica. That's up your street, isn't it, Esther?"

Mortified, Esther hissed, "What? Those sellouts? How dare you."

"There's some Deftones?"

"I mean, the early stuff's the best."

"Black Veil Brides?"

"Mm." Esther wrinkled her nose. "Getting a bit mainstream."

"Twenty One Pilots are alternative, aren't they?"

Esther's involuntary gasp of horror was so forceful, she nearly asphyxiated. As she coughed and spluttered, Susan thumped her gleefully on the back.

"See, Daisy, this one is a connoisseur of the darkest gift humanity has given us: music that is impossible to listen to."

Esther was used to people mocking her taste in music—after all, she'd had a lifetime (well, six years) of being misunderstood. The way of the goth was a dark and lonely path, one only trodden by those driven from a heartless society, united by a love of obscure music, the allure of the grave, and the eternal problem of dealing with deodorant stains on black clothes. Esther didn't need her new friends to love the same things she did. Nevertheless, Susan's mockery was a puff of air extinguishing the little candle of hope that burned in Esther's blackened heart.

Buying three tickets to see Necrotizing Swamp next term had been a bit optimistic.

Halfway through her second drink, Susan sensed a shift in the atmosphere. Her back was to the door, but the identity of who'd entered was written in glee across Esther's celestial visage and punctuated by an alarmed flare of Daisy's nostrils.

"Ed Gemmell's here!" Esther waved far too enthusiastically.

It seemed Ed Gemmell had returned from the library with more than reading material. He had returned with a friend. Just like that, his inexplicable shiftiness toward Susan became entirely explicable.

Susan stood up. "Time to go." No explanation, no empty

excuse. Susan made straight for the door as if there was nothing in her path.

"Good day, Sus—"

She flashed a hand up, cutting the platitude short.

The point of coming to Sheffield had been to leave the past where it belonged—in Northampton. It wasn't supposed to follow her 134 miles up the M1 and transfer into the same university.

There were too many people who'd crossed Susan for her to whisper their names before sleep, like a prayer, but each one was carved into her heart and pumped through her body like blood. A towering cowboy who'd once stood in front of her for the entire set of a bluegrass cover band. The girl from preschool who'd eaten the banana onto which Susan's mum had lovingly drawn a princess riding a dragon and *clearly* labeled with an arrow that said *Susie P.* Her first boss, who had made the mistake of thinking that to be outside the law was to be above it . . .

Enemies were easy to accrue, but Susan had only ever had one nemesis, and his name was McGraw. Ed Gemmell's new best friend.

McGraw's presence had a very different effect on Esther. Ever since this mahogany-voiced vision of mustachioed manliness had transferred to Sheffield a couple of weeks into term, Susan had refused to reveal exactly how it was the two of them knew each other. Despite begging, bribing, pleading, and prompting, Esther had gleaned nothing more from Susan than a hint at shared "history."

While Esther was an open book, Susan was a locked vault, and here was the handsome, laconic key.

"Hi, well, fancy seeing you here!" Ed Gemmell popped up in Esther's vision with a double-handed wave hello.

"Actually, we're really sorry, but we're leaving." Daisy lifted Esther up off the sofa, completely disregarding the fact that Esther had yet to make significant progress with her mulled cider or her interrogation of McGraw. "Susan's right. Esther really needs to change out of her pajamas."

"What? Susan never—" But Esther could only impart a somewhat apologetic wave in Ed Gemmell's direction before Daisy frog-marched her away.

"Was it something I said?" Ed Gemmell asked, looking down at the table of half-finished drinks.

McGraw clamped a hand onto his friend's shoulder. "I suspect it's something you brought with you to the bar."

After the briefest of pauses, Ed Gemmell looked up for confirmation. "You're talking about you and not making some oblique reference to extreme body odor or an over-abundance of social insecurities. Right?"

"Two out of three. You smell lovely, Ed."

Susan's rage-fueled steps had propelled her almost to J-block by the time the others caught up.

Within three seconds, Esther said, "Soooooo . . . you and McGraw?"

"Nope." Susan wasn't in the mood.

"Fine. If you're not going to tell us, then we'll have to draw our own conclusions, won't we, Daisy?"

"We will?"

There was nothing that could stem the tide, and Esther dogged Susan's every step with wild and inaccurate theories about the nature of Susan's history with McGraw. Trudging up the stairs, Susan was bombarded with speculation. They were ex-lovers whose passion had been torn asunder by a misunderstanding. Their families were engaged in a blood feud so ancient, none knew where or when it had taken root. McGraw was a hapless, lovelorn sap who'd followed his indifferent object of affection all the way to higher education. He was a robot sent from the future . . .

And on. And on.

But the harder Esther pushed, the tighter Susan's lips drew. Her mouth had narrowed to a short, tense, little line by the time they reached the fourth-floor fire doors, which were adorned with a certificate declaring the corridor safe.

"This is me." Susan pushed open the door to number 13, walked inside, and locked it behind her before her friends could follow. She couldn't take any more. Not now. Not ever. Past and present were two different countries, and she'd burned her metaphorical passport the second she'd set foot on the train.

Homeschooling had prepared Daisy for a lot of things. She knew everyone in her village by name and could do all kinds of things that the national curriculum never thought to address, such as tend a vegetable patch, change the oil in a car, and reprogram a broken Freeview box. But being practical in these areas didn't help when it came to solving people problems. You didn't need to talk to vegetables, cars, and Freeview boxes to work out what was wrong with them. (Although Daisy often did.)

There were some things that only mass exposure to one's peers could prepare you for, and the vagaries of friendship were among them.

"Do you think Susan's all right?" she asked Esther.

"No. I think she's pathologically secretive." Esther sighed. "And it's killing me."

Daisy folded Esther into a gentle hug. It must be hard for someone who wore her giant, generous heart on her sleeve to understand why anyone would want to keep her own counsel.

"People are different," Daisy said.

"But we're her friends. She should tell us everything. All in one go. Like transferring all your photos to a new phone."

Daisy hugged Esther a bit more, not quite sure what to make of this metaphor, since all her photos were stored in the cloud.

"Come on, let's go see how bad the kitchen is . . ."

The kitchen at the end of their corridor was small but functional. Or it had been until Esther had decided to cook everyone lunch, only to fall down a BuzzFeed quiz hole, lured in by a quiz that promised to tell her which Romantic poet she should date, based on her favorite cooking utensil. By the time she'd ascertained the answer to this (Byron, obviously) and what type of pasta/deep-sea creature/interstellar vessel/Sam Raimi film she was, the potatoes she'd put in the microwave had burst into flames and tried to take the kitchen with them.

Despite the faint, lingering odor of scorched earth and hot metal, the kitchen seemed relatively unscathed. Whiteboard, breakfast bar, oven, and sink looked no different, and apart from some smoke stains, the cabinets had survived intact.

There was, however, a note on the fridge, signed by the site manager.

All foodstuffs have been removed to avoid the risk of contamination.

Esther opened the fridge and took out another note.

(Yes. Even the stuff from inside the fridge.)

It was hard to see how the smoke was supposed to have contaminated any of the food inside a sealed metal box or, indeed, any of the unopened tins that had been in the cupboard above the toaster. Well, at least, where the toaster *had* been, because there was a note there, too.

All electric appliances have been removed for testing. (Except the fridge. Fine, be pedantic.)

A very un-Daisy-like growl issued from her throat as she pictured the site manager sitting in his office, boiling endless cups of tea and toasting the crumpets she'd been planning on having as an afternoon treat.

"Come on . . ." Esther gave her a rallying hug. "Let's work out what we need and treat ourselves to ordering it online— that'll cheer you up."

* * * * *

Cocooned in her duvet, Susan stared long and hard into the eye sockets of the skeleton propped drunkenly on the floor next to her.

She could hear the others in Daisy's room next door. The walls in J-block were thin, and Esther was loud. Really, Susan should be in there ordering the online shopping with them, insisting on food that could be eaten straight from the package to avoid future calamity and dissuading Daisy from paying for everything because she felt responsible for what had happened just because she'd let Esther cook.

"I need a cigarette," Susan told the skeleton.

There was a mostly empty pack in her hand and a mostly full ashtray on her pillow. Paying scant regard to the risk, Susan lit up and bathed her lungs in blissful death.

The skeleton watched her through tendrils of smoke.

"Stop judging me."

You're only judging yourself.

"Susan Ptolemy judges no man."

That is a woeful lie. Besides, you're a woman.

Susan scowled. "Sod off."

They stared at each other a while, the cigarette burning lower as ash dropped onto the pillowcase.

"I'm not going to tell you."

Fine. See if I care.

"It's none of your beeswax."

You've made your point.

"So stop looking at me like that."

I have no eyeballs. I'm not looking at anything.

"Am I supposed to be impressed by such arrant pedantry?"

Susan, I'm a skeleton onto which you are projecting your own internal dilemma. Any pedantry is your own.

Susan twitched her eyebrows in concession. It was probably time for her to get up before this got any more *Lord of the Flies*.

The question was, how insatiable was Esther's need to pry? Before McGraw arrived, there had been no need to worry. But now, if Susan remained silent, there was another source to whom her friends could turn. A source that Susan needed to shut down.

Susan flexed her fingers before curling them into a fist and rapping twice on the door. At the sound of footsteps beyond, Susan took a step back from the threshold, crossed her arms, and adopted the look that had forced confessions from criminals before they'd even contemplated the crime.

The lock snicked, and the door opened, the hinges making a barely audible squeak of protest. There, stooping slightly as if too languorous to hold his own body weight, was her nemesis in all his mustachioed glory. Susan forced herself to meet his eyes. A dark, muddy green to match his sweater.

The scent of sawdust wafted gently into the hall.

"Susan." McGraw opened the door a little wider, and she caught sight of a workbench in the middle of his room, wooden planks of various lengths propped up against his bed. "Would you like to—"

"None of that," Susan growled, and McGraw looked a little taken aback. "I'm here to talk terms."

She produced a sheaf of papers from her back pocket. After a brief hesitation, McGraw accepted it.

"Terms of conduct agreed between the undersigned and Susan Ptolemy . . . What, no middle name?" The look McGraw swung her was tinged with amusement. A challenge.

Without hesitation, Susan snatched back the paper, scrawled a barely legible addendum, and handed it back.

"Such a pretty name, Xanthipe . . ." McGraw murmured, reading on.

1) J-block, Catterick Hall, is considered out of bounds to the undersigned at all times.

2) Information relating to all events outside the space and time of university is to be revealed on a strictly need-to-know basis to no more than two personal friends accrued in the last month. Names to be cited below. Any transgression of this clause will be considered "gossip" and will be dealt with accordingly.

3) Human beings are considered neutral territory guided by their own agency and shall be turned neither for nor against either party. Any transgression of this clause will be considered "bitching" and will be dealt with accordingly.

4) Contemporaneous occupation of the same space is not permitted, with the following exceptions:

a) Environments in which basic human needs come first, including but not limited to locations listed in schedule A.

b) Group scenarios.

Should either named party come across the other, reasonable measures must be taken to avoid any and all contact—eye, verbal, and physical. Any transgression of this clause will be considered "engagement of the enemy" and will be dealt with accordingly.

5) Romantic alliances are not to be flaunted and are subject to Clause 2.

I hereby declare that I [insert name]

"You haven't even filled in my name!" McGraw looked up in affront.

"Chill your bristles. It's a boilerplate document that I've adapted."

"You have boilerplate contracts for things like this?"

"Don't act like you don't know." Susan crossed her arms and watched as McGraw flipped the page to read schedule A. "It's a fair deal. Stay out of my way, and I'll stay out of yours."

"Romantic alliances . . ." There was the faintest air of interest. "Have you been making any of those, then?"

"None of your beeswax."

But McGraw barely drew breath before countering, "Any undisclosed information pertaining to one of these clauses is very much my beeswax."

"I have made alliances," Susan muttered unwillingly. "None of them significant enough to affect our terms." Then, after a brief pause, she ventured, "How about you?"

For the first time since he'd opened the door, McGraw edged a little closer, his hand reaching up to her face as if to brush her hair behind her ear, but even as Susan opened her mouth to invoke Clause 4, McGraw withdrew, holding up the pen he'd taken from behind her ear.

"May I borrow your pen?"

"How about next time you verbalize your intent before violating my person?" Susan narrowed her eyes, imagining how satisfying it would be to telekinetically prune that magnificent mustache by plucking it from his face, hair by manly hair.

McGraw rested the paper on the wall, added only Ed Gemmell's name to his list of chosen confidants, and signed and dated both copies before returning them to Susan to sign.

"I've not made any romantic alliances, and I've no intention of doing so," McGraw said quietly. "I've let that spoil things for me before."

"Mm." Susan folded one contract up and tucked it back into her pocket before giving McGraw the other. "You still have my pen."

The pen changed hands in silence.

"OK. Well, then," Susan said, "since we're currently violating Clause 4, I think I should . . ."

"Is all this really necessary?" McGraw put his arm up as he leaned on the doorframe, and Susan felt an alien stab of something like nostalgia for the friendship they had once had. There had been a time when Susan had thought she'd need no other friends in the world as long as she had McGraw.

How wrong she'd been. Better not to have any friends at all than ones who betray you.

"Yes, McGraw. All this is very necessary."

And with that, Susan turned on her heel and walked away, down the long, cream-colored corridor, back to the life she'd been so keen to make for herself before McGraw had come along to ruin it.

2

THE INSPIRATIONAL IMPACT OF *NATIONAL GEOGRAPHIC*

When faced with a life-changing event, Daisy focused on the practical. Within her first week of university, she had registered with a new doctor and dentist, arranged insurance for her room, and updated her address for all the most important correspondence, such as bank statements, the quarterly village newsletter, and postcards from her Peruvian pen pal, Frida, to whom she'd been writing since she was six.

Nonetheless, when she went down to the mailroom on her way to breakfast, Daisy found a large envelope addressed in Granny's familiar looping handwriting, forwarding a stash of letters and magazines that had arrived in Crickleton.

The faint scent of home that emerged from the envelope —whether real or imagined—and the sight of the latest issue of *National Geographic* conjured a rush of homesickness so acute that Daisy had to take a moment to sit on the bench outside and gather herself.

The magazine in her hand was a yellow-framed window into the past. Daisy could see herself as a little girl, perching on the faded chintz of Granny's favorite armchair, looking with fascination at photos from across the world, from inside the human body, and of outer space. It was afternoons sitting at the kitchen table, reading about unearthed Iron Age habitations and pterosaur remains, that had awakened her interest in archaeology and led her all the way to Sheffield. Yet here she was, wishing with everything she had that she was back home, eating breakfast with Granny, so engrossed in whatever debate this particular issue would prompt that their tea would grow cold and intellectual repartee would shift seamlessly into bickering over who should make a fresh brew.

It didn't matter that she was on her way to a J-block breakfast with her friends—the only company she craved right now was Granny's. Taking her phone from her pocket, she dialed Granny's number.

No answer.

Frustrated, Daisy tried again.

No luck.

Before the dam could burst, Daisy stood up purposefully, tucking her mail into her backpack along with the things she'd need for her morning lecture. She made a great fuss of zipping it back up, tightening the straps, and striding toward the canteen, as if she could outpace the sadness at her back, whose arms were slipping around her, squeezing her chest in an unwelcome embrace.

Just as she reached the entrance to the dining hall, her phone buzzed.

"Granny!"

"Hello, my darling. Sorry I missed your call. Been wiring

a new socket into the living room. Had half the floorboards up last night and found next-door's cat down there this morning . . ."

Daisy's lip trembled at the thought of things changing without her. Sure, it was just a new socket, but then what? Finding a better home for the vacuum cleaner? Painting the front door?

". . . had to drag him out by the tail. Don't think Nancy's going to be too pleased at the state of him, but if she brings it up, I'll tell her it was either that or bury the stupid thing alive. They did that, didn't they? Put dead cats in the walls? You'd know all about this sort of thing from your course . . ."

But Daisy was lost in a nightmare vision of returning home to find everything in the house ever so slightly different from when she'd left. Door handles turning the other way. Hot taps that now ran cold. Armchairs moved six inches to the left, so that they no longer aligned with the television . . .

"Daisy?"

"Don't replace the microwave!" Daisy squawked in response.

There was silence on the other end of the phone before her granny started up in a gentle tone, "Is everything all right, petal? You don't sound quite yourself."

Daisy opened her mouth, ready to tell her grandmother how lonely she felt sometimes, how homesick . . . But then she stopped. This was *her* problem; sharing it would make it Granny's problem, too, and she already had enough of those. Daisy might feel lonely, but Granny really *was* alone, and what was she doing? Was she moping around the place feeling sorry for herself? No. She was out there wiring in electric sockets and relocating the vacuum cleaner and (possibly) painting the front door.

"I'm fine, Granny." To distract herself, Daisy walked over to the bulletin board outside the dining hall, concentrating very hard on keeping her eyes wide open. "I just called because the *National Geographic* arrived, and I wanted . . ." What she wanted was to be able to share it with Granny. "I wanted to call and thank you for sending it."

As Granny chatted happily on the other end of the line, Daisy felt tears brimming behind her eyes, and she swallowed, glaring furiously at the poster in front of her nose.

Activities Fair—Wednesday, October 18th, 3:00 P.M.–6:00 P.M.—Find your tribe. The same poster Jonathan had given her in the bar.

"Are you going out and meeting lots of new people?" Granny asked. "Joining clubs and starting new hobbies is all part of the university experience as I understand it."

Looking straight at the poster, tears in check, she replied, "There's an Activities Fair this afternoon. I'm sure I'll meet tons of new people there. Got to go, Granny. I'm meeting Susan and Esther for breakfast."

Sadness didn't suit Daisy; action did.

Any visit to the canteen was accompanied by a soundtrack of murmured and half-shouted conversations, the clink of Sheffield steel, and the sharp scrapes of crockery. Clumps of students were distributed unevenly down the long tables: foreign students held together by the shared confidence that comes from being brave enough to go to university in another country, the lads who thought that supporting a football team counted as playing on one lounging about in casual sportswear, friends united by subjects or corridors or a mutual distaste for almost everyone else.

"I don't want to be here." Susan stared balefully at her tray of limp bacon and partially solidified beans. "I want to be in my bed, tricking my brain into thinking it's asleep."

"You have a lecture," Daisy reminded Susan, ushering her further along the queue.

This only served to make Susan grumpier. Mornings were not her favorite, and breakfast was usually a cereal bar and a flask of black coffee on the way to the medical school. But today, Esther had hammered on Susan's door as she passed by on her way to an early-morning HIIT workout, and Susan hadn't been able to fall back asleep.

Esther was waiting for them by the cutlery station, the picture of irritating good health with her shower-damp ponytail and tray of muesli.

"Ugh," Susan muttered. "You're exhausting me just by existing."

"Schadenfreude isn't the only way to release those endorphins, you know. You should try a workout with me sometime."

"Absolutely not. All that bouncing and music and energy."

"You could do yoga with me," Daisy suggested.

"Work up much of a sweat when you're stretching, do you?" Esther said a little loftily.

"Sometimes. Things can get pretty intense when you're in the zone."

"Let's move this conversation along to where Kully's waving us over . . ."

Down at the far end of the table, a hand extended in a casual wave from a crisp white cuff.

Kulvinder Singh was in Susan's Anatomy group, and their friendship stemmed mostly from the fact that he appreciated a little organ-based dark humor. Handsome and preppy, he sat in stark relief to the girl slumped next to him, whose eyes were bloodshot, skin the pallor of a mausoleum's masonry.

"Daisy, Esther, you know Kully," Susan said. "And this is Grace Latter. The work-hard–play-hard variety of medical student."

If Kully's beam was the trademark of a man who knew exactly how good he looked, Grace's crease of the lips was the dying effort of someone far too hungover to care about anything other than not being sick. She had a heart-shaped face and pretty blue eyes, with lilac hair pulled back in a scraggy ponytail, and she appeared to be wearing clothes three times too big for her judging by how far she'd had to roll back the cuffs of her sweater.

"Hi." Grace took a single, delicate nibble from a slice of dry toast. Every finger—even her thumbs—had an interesting-looking silver ring on it. "It seems I woke up in hell."

"Clearly you're not familiar with the city of Northampton,"

Susan said. "Legend has it that if you see a bus depot and say the name backward, a portal will open to spit you out through the hellmouth and into the city."

"And do those of us with a Young Person's Railcard get a third off?" Esther inquired.

"Of course." A malevolent grin crept across Susan's face. "A third off your *life*."

"Erk." Grace slowly folded over, like a balloon from which the air was escaping.

"So, anyway . . ." Kully pushed a glass of water closer to Grace. "What are you doing up so early? I thought English students just stayed in bed all day."

"Not when there's a seven A.M. class down at the gym." Esther put her spoon down to poke her bicep speculatively. "I'm going to hurt so much tomorrow . . ."

"Stop it. Your good health is making Grace ill." Susan nodded across the table to where Grace was struggling up from the table to make a bolt for the toilets.

"I think that might have more to do with her hangover than Esther's gym talk," Kully said as they all watched Grace barge through the students still queuing for food, scattering them like bowling pins. "She drank the corridor party dry last night. Wasn't in a fit state to get back to hers, so she slept on my floor." A frown drove two straight lines between Kully's brows the way one might Photoshop "consternation" onto the face of a male model. "I hope she isn't about to be sick on the clean clothes I lent her."

✗ ✗ ✗ ✗ ✗

As Susan and Kully moved on to talk about their subject the way everyone did if they had a quorum of two, Daisy carefully quartered her apple. Not having participated in much of the discussion meant she'd already eaten her granola and yogurt, and she was trying to slow herself down so she didn't have to just sit there with an empty plate and an interested expression.

Next to her, Esther's attention was bounding around the room like a puppy at a barbecue, as if she believed there was something more to discover.

Maybe there was.

"Um," Daisy said.

No one heard her.

"Esther?"

No response.

Daisy tried to think how her friends went about commanding attention when they wanted it.

"*Actually* . . ." Daisy said in as confident a voice as possible, "I was thinking about going to the Activities Fair later."

Esther redirected her attention, and Susan looked up from her conversation with Kully, who said, "Wasn't that weeks ago?"

"Black mold. Health and safety," Daisy said, remembering what Jonathan had said. "It got moved to today. I thought maybe we could all go together?"

She looked hopefully from Esther to Susan, who issued a disgusted snort.

"Clubs and societies are enforced fun for people who

don't have anything better to do with their lives than waste them." Seeing how crestfallen Daisy was, Susan added a little more kindly, "Sorry, Daisy. I'm not much of a joiner."

Esther was holding her fingers to make a crucifix and leaning away in fear. "Nuh-uh. I've had my brush with organized socializing, thanks, and all I got was a tattoo and an overwhelming sense of foreboding."

Daisy had forgotten about that.

As they went to offload their breakfast things, Daisy reasoned that it shouldn't matter whether her friends came with her. As a freshly hatched social butterfly, she would just have to spread her wings on her own.

Even if she still felt more like a caterpillar.

On her way out of breakfast, Esther had found Ed Gemmell. Somehow they had ended up in the library.

"I can't believe you're doing actual work," Esther said, giving a slightly demonic expression to a skull she'd just drawn on the back of her hand. "The whole point of university is to learn to develop our own theories through experience and contemplation, not by copying out other people's ideas."

"I think the point is that we have to know what theories already exist; otherwise we won't know whether our ideas are original," Ed Gemmell said without looking up from the book he was studying.

Esther reached out and flipped the book over to a black-and-white photo on the dust jacket. The man in it was wearing a turtleneck and a stern expression, wiry hair cascading down either side of a shiny bald head.

"If Rupert Chalfont-Debray's theories are so original, how come he looks exactly like all the other dusty white male academics? You could have subbed him in for the man who gave that lecture."

"By 'that lecture,' do you mean the series of six compulsory lectures we've had on early twentieth-century prose?"

"Yes. Six. Totally what I meant." *SIX?!*

"That would be because they're one and the same person. Rupert Chalfont-Debray is the head of the faculty."

"And *how* compulsory were those lectures, exactly?"

"They didn't check attendance, if that's what you mean."

"Right." Esther returned the book to its original position. "But . . . I should probably read this, then?"

"Probably," Ed Gemmell admitted, then cleared his throat. "You could study it with me now if you'd like?"

But Esther had returned to doodling on her hands. "No thanks. I'm someone who works best under pressure. No prep until five minutes before I have to prove I've done any."

Esther hopped off the window seat on which she had been lounging to drift around the stacks, idly picking out titles and taking selfies in the same pose as the author in the photo before putting the best on Instagram and sending the rest to Daisy and Susan with the message: *A Study in Being Studious.*

She didn't like to admit it, but Esther was lonely. She had friends—good ones—but she also had a lot of free time. Back home, for all she'd bathed in the melancholy of being misunderstood, she'd also been busy. The Tackleford Academy timetable hadn't allowed for much wallowing. Attending lessons was mandatory, and everyone's extra-curricular time followed the same schedule. There had been little opportunity for the free time that she'd craved like a drug so she could be alone with The Boy. (Once she'd secured him. High school romances seemed to move at a glacial pace.)

Now that she had oodles of alone time and the privacy of her own room in which to spend it, Esther no longer saw the appeal.

Not when she no longer had someone to share it with.

Everyone back home had told her how hard a long-distance relationship would be to maintain, but her stubborn, can-do attitude had inured her to reason.

Eleven days she and The Boy had lasted, and it had been Esther who'd pulled out. Or, technically, she'd pulled a shady character called Steve Shields in a dingy nightclub and ended up in his bed. Whatever. The result was the same.

Since then, she'd been free to explore the alien landscape of university as a free agent, unfettered by her ties to Tackle-ford. And yet, university wasn't proving quite how she'd imagined it. There had to be more to this alien landscape than lectures and libraries and laundry (not that she'd done much of any of those things). University was unchar-tered territory, and already it felt as if she'd mapped out the essentials without making any exciting new discoveries. Where were the lofty intellectuals who stayed up all night drinking three-hundred-year-old wine and debating posh cheese? Or the secret societies that guaranteed you a job in an FTSE 100 company just because you'd once jumped off the roof of a lecture hall?

Drifting back to where Ed Gemmell remained hunched over his book, Esther slumped down next to him.

"Are you planning on using your laptop?" She nudged him with her foot.

"Probably not."

"Can I?"

That got his attention. "For work?"

"For solitaire. Susan made me delete all the games off my phone because she bet me I couldn't go a week without playing any."

"Won't this mean you lose the bet?" Ed Gemmell typed in his password and pushed the computer over.

"You're not the sort to kiss and tell." Esther leaned over and gave him a distracted kiss on the ear as she opened up her game.

Even solitaire, chosen sport of the professional procrastinator, wasn't doing the trick, and Esther's attention kept drifting out the window. This side of the library faced one of the city's many parks, where some tiny toddlers were hurling bread with unnecessary aggression at the ducks in the pond.

She missed the days when life had been that simple, when feeding the ducks occupied a morning and it was socially acceptable to nap in public and throw a tantrum when presented with anything unpleasant. Growing up was over-rated—all it seemed to involve was taking responsibility for stuff that you didn't want, like actually having to manage your own time and work out what to eat and when and how you were going to last the week on only the dregs of your wardrobe because no one had done the laundry.

Just as she was about to turn back to her card game, a girl walked right past the window in front of her. Her head was down as she concentrated on her phone, streaks of white layered through a sharply styled beetle-black bob. She wasn't tall—although the thick-ridged soles of her boots gave her an extra couple inches—and she gave the impression of a spun-sugar delicacy, with slender legs in shredded jeans leading up to a black bomber jacket with a red fur collar.

There was a ring on every finger and a scowl on her face, and Esther thought she was *magnificent*.

Here, at last, was someone who understood the struggle of the outcast, who wouldn't mock her esoteric taste in music, who would have an infinite capacity for hearing about heartache.

Someone exactly like Esther's old friends. Only new.

Without turning away from the window, Esther dragged Ed Gemmell over. "Who's that?"

"Who's what?" But he was too slow, and the girl had passed.

"That vision of gothic perfection."

Ed Gemmell glanced uncertainly at Esther, then at the window. "Are you . . . admiring your own reflection?"

"What? No. I'm not *that* vain."

Ed Gemmell turned crimson. "No. Of course not."

But Esther wasn't paying him any attention; she was disentangling herself from her chair and pulling on her jacket.

"Where are you going?" Ed Gemmell's plaintive voice called after her, but Esther didn't even bother looking back as she bellowed, "To find my new best friend!" much to the irritation of everyone else in the building.

Especially Ed Gemmell.

The S.U. was busier than all the previous Wednesdays, on which Daisy had used the four-hour window between Emerging Europe and the Celtic West (a thousand-year window, archaeologically speaking) to treat herself to a hot lunch there followed by a bit of note consolidation and essay planning in the library. A schedule that was starting to fall into the comfortable pattern of a routine, in much the same way that her "new" slippers had ceased to be a novelty now that they had molded themselves to the shape of her feet. Daisy liked routine. She liked plans and schedules and boundaries. Nice, solid walls keeping her safe from the kind of chaos on which Esther thrived.

But that was the problem, wasn't it? Daisy had been so good at setting up her life at university that the riskiest thing she'd done since arriving in Sheffield had been to use the "disabled" bathroom in Starbucks when she couldn't find the regular one. (She'd been desperate.)

Even her friends had been made within an hour of stepping off the train, falling into the kind of companionable little group that suited Daisy best.

All because they lived on the same corridor.

For all Jonathan Tremain's scorn, Daisy didn't see the problem with that. Sure, Susan refused to open up, and Esther was so preoccupied with what was happening *next* that sometimes it felt as if *now* barely existed for her. And, OK, any inadvertent reference to parents or family or death was inevitably followed by an awkward pause and a rapid tiptoe out of the past and into the present.

Friends didn't *have* to show an interest in how Daisy came to be orphaned and why she lived with her grandmother.

Did they?

"That's enough!" Daisy was so stern with herself that the boy in front of her, who'd been reaching for a third packet of ketchup, retracted his hand and gave her a somewhat nervous glance before hurrying away to his friends.

Daisy had played it safe long enough. This afternoon, she would break from the comfort of her routine, and she would go to the Activities Fair. Alone. She could do this.

After she'd had a hot lunch.

Before she'd started, Susan hadn't known exactly what to expect from studying Medicine. She knew she was smart, but there were bound to be elements of the course she'd struggle with. Maybe histology or embryology or something as seemingly simple as taking a blood pressure reading. But nothing she had watched, googled, or imagined had prepared her for the intricacies of the first-year medics' timetable.

There was no regularity to any of it. They might have lectures nine to twelve every morning, but the afternoons were anyone's guess. Last Wednesday, there'd been a rogue cardiovascular lecture. The Wednesday before, she'd spent all afternoon doing a placement in the hospital next door. Each week followed some kind of mystical rota written by the Gods of Spreadsheets and distributed to mere mortals to paper across the walls of their bedrooms.

According to the list she'd copied from today's schedule onto the back of her hand, Susan's afternoon would be spent at the health center over on the other side of the city. Parting ways with Kully, Susan met up with a marginally revived Grace at the bus stop, where students outnumbered regular passengers three to one. Gossiping amenably about the morning's lectures, they squashed into what standing space remained on the first bus.

"Excuse me . . ."

Susan tensed. She knew that voice. As Grace stepped aside to make space, McGraw set down what looked like a cupboard door, propping it gently against a folded stroller with more care than if it were an actual child.

There was no avoiding him. Susan was held immobile between Grace's backpack and a woman a little older than her mother who was muttering a constant stream of obscenities under her breath, possibly at Susan.

Surprise and wariness rippled across McGraw's expression when he saw her.

"Susan."

"Mm." As she avoided his gaze, her attention flickered to the cupboard door by his feet, which McGraw mistook for interest.

"To replace one that disappeared from our kitchen in the

night." McGraw ran his hand over the grain. "Better quality than the university deserves."

He looked at her again then, dark eyes beneath thick dark brows.

"You're violating the contract," Susan said, so reluctant to speak that she hardly moved her lips. McGraw issued a barely discernible sigh and turned away.

They rode for six stops before McGraw picked up his stupid cupboard door with his stupid sinewy arms and took his stupid unnecessary self out the doors and off the bus.

"Who was *that*?" The question exploded from Grace's lips barely before the bus doors hissed shut. She stood on tiptoe, neck craning to get another look as he crossed the road.

"No idea."

"Don't lie—he knew your name!"

"A lucky guess."

Grace looked at her askance, not yet calibrated to Susan's level of sarcasm. "Well, next time can you tell him *my* name? And my address, e-mail, and availability."

"Don't you have a boyfriend?"

"Well, yes, but he's in Plymouth, and I need a crush to pass the time." Grace gazed thoughtfully at the spot where McGraw had been standing. "That particular gentleman was *lush*."

"If you say so," Susan replied, pulling her jacket tighter and lowering herself gently into the seething hot waters of resentment.

The distance between the S.U. and the Octagon (the boxy redbrick building where the fair was located) was small, but the number of overly enthusiastic students distributing flyers between them was large. By the time she made it inside, Daisy had acquired a pretty blue balloon with a tree on it and a perforated page of drinks vouchers from every pub, bar, and nightclub in town.

"Welcome, friend!" A round, gregarious young man opened his arms to reveal a T-shirt with *FREE HUGS!* written on it. As he approached, Daisy skittered backward, tripped over the tail of someone dressed as an enormous blue kangaroo, and fell back, scattering flyers like confetti.

The Free Hugs guy reached down and offered her a hand.

"Not interested in joining the Free Huggers, then?" he said.

"Not really. Is there a Preserve Personal Space Society?"

"You could try the Young Conservatives. No one ever hugs those guys . . ."

A group of people so posh they could have been mistaken for a shooting party were offering people a tray of Pimms and pin badges that said *Too Rich to Tax*.

"I'm not sure they're really my type of people," she told the Free Hugger, but he had already abandoned her to launch himself enthusiastically at someone else.

The Octagon was huge inside. Banners and posters lined the walkways and hung from the beams, and all the booths were festooned with freebies. New blood was at a premium, and Daisy's combination of vulnerability and good manners made her an appealing target. Five steps into the room, and she was accosted by a barbershop quartet, who sang her a jaunty little tune detailing what she could expect if she just wrote her e-mail address on the bottom of their sign-up sheet.

When she asked if they knew any Enya, they burst into an a cappella version of "Orinoco Flow," delighting Daisy so much that she signed her name with a flourish and moved on to the next booth.

As Daisy worked her way through the press of eager students, it seemed to her as if there were a book club for every language, a society for every sport, and so much more. There was no hobby in the world that wasn't catered to, each with a crack group of enthusiastic participants hawking their passions to a receptive crowd.

"Come test your tiddlywink skills . . ."

"Can you tell your feta from your cheddar?"

"Sign up for squash!"

They made everything sound so *enticing*—no, she'd never considered writing a comic before—yes, it *did* sound fun—pigeon fancying? Yes! She'd just adopted an orphaned chick who lived in the nest outside her window, his name's Baby Gordon, only maybe he's a girl and—oh, of course she'd sign the mailing list . . . A pin badge? Thank you so much . . . Sign here to petition for UK students to maintain access to the Erasmus scheme? I don't know what that is, but—ooh? A pen. Of course. Sign here? Right?

It was impossible to say no. Everyone was so charming and friendly and smiling, and they all had such exciting merchandise. By the time Daisy had reached the far end of the room, her hand was cramped from all the mailing lists she'd signed up for and her *Totes a Fan of Totes!* bag was stuffed to the seams with swag.

As she turned the corner, Jonathan's familiar voice boomed across the crowd. Daisy saw him thrust a clipboard forcefully at a group of passing girls and cajole them into signing up for women's rugby. Panicking, not wanting to become his next victim, Daisy dived behind the nearest booth so fast that her tote bag slipped from her shoulder.

The contents cascaded across the floor, pin badges and coasters and pens and sweets and key rings all skittering and bouncing and rolling everywhere.

"I'm so sorry!" Daisy yelped to no one in particular, falling to the floor in an attempt to scoop everything back up, somehow scattering things farther afield.

"Don't worry about it." Someone was crouching down next to her, a slim, perfectly manicured hand resting on Daisy's wrist. "There's no need to panic."

Which was all very well for this stranger to say, but she wasn't the one in danger of signing up for women's rugby.

"Hi," the stranger said, lips parting in a wide smile that crinkled the corners of her deep brown eyes. "Do you need a hand?"

Daisy wasn't capable of anything more than nodding and staring. This woman was possibly the most intimidatingly beautiful person Daisy had ever seen. She had glossy black hair and a face of clean lines and cute curves, with the kind of light Mediterranean-brown skin that Susan might have had if she bothered with things like exercise and healthy eating and sunlight.

When the woman reached forward to pick up a handful

of badges, the bare skin of her arm brushed Daisy's hand, leaving Daisy feeling as if she'd been warmed by the sun.

Turning the badges over to read what they said, the newcomer raised her eyebrows, which were strong and dark and sharply angled at the apex, like the outstretched wings of a seabird.

"Are you trying to collect a full suite of acronyms?" she asked, pressing one into Daisy's hand. "What's H&S?"

"Hide-and-Seek," Daisy managed.

"LGBTQA . . ." She flicked a curious glance up at Daisy, who flushed and muttered, "Yes. Well. Um . . . they were really friendly," while shoving the badge into her bag.

"Is this one of yours? Black and Minority Ethnic?" The stranger didn't hand the BME badge straight over to Daisy, clearly thinking there had been a mistake.

This time, Daisy didn't mumble or blush.

"Actually, my granny's black. She's from Jamaica, but she moved here in 1957." She took the badge and pinned it to the outside of her tote bag. "But my grandad's white, and so was my mum."

"Was?"

"Both my parents died when I was two. I grew up with my granny." It was the most she'd ever said about her family since she'd arrived in Sheffield, and she didn't even know this girl's name. Maybe a name mattered less than a calm and interested expression, something Daisy was unaccustomed to. Susan's face relaxed naturally into a scowl, and Esther only left pauses in conversation when she got distracted by something outside the window.

As friends went, they didn't exactly invite quiet, meaningful sharing.

Still. Knowing someone's name was always nice.

"Hi. I'm Daisy." Daisy held her fingers up in a cautious wave, and her companion smiled.

"My name's Elise."

Aware that it was long past when she should have eaten, Esther scuffed her way miserably in the direction of the S.U. It was the nearest, cheapest place she could think of to get a hot meal, and after more than an hour of wandering in the cold, Esther was desperately in need of warming up.

She had looked everywhere. Or at least, everywhere in the vicinity of the park. She'd walked the paths like someone looking for a lost dog or, judging by how many people had stopped to ask, like someone who might have been selling drugs, which had her reconsidering today's choice of distressed fishnets and giant hoodie.

It had all been fruitless. Goth Girl was gone. Disappeared like a graveyard shade that could only be seen at three minutes to midnight every third Sunday.

So much for finding her new best friend . . .

Esther indulged in a fantasy of bumping into Goth Girl on her way to a gig—something obscure and angry—only to find that they were both on their way to the same concert. Crowd-surfing and headbanging and hijinks would ensue, and Esther would finally have someone with whom to share makeup tips and music and (potentially, maybe, one day . . .) secondhand Victorian ballgowns.

Walking under the bridge toward the S.U., Esther had to push through a more purposeful crowd than usual. Besides the usual milling-about-ers under the bridge, sitting on the raised flower beds, chatting and smoking and messing about, there was a swell of people handing things out.

"You look like a considered connoisseur of crossover cyber grindcore." A young man shoved a flyer into Esther's hand.

"Er . . . this says it's for something called 'Rock Night,' and you've listed . . ." Her face contorted in horror. "*The Killers???*"

The man shrugged within his duffel coat and pulled a wry smile.

"Thought I'd try to give it a positive spin." He ruined it by winking. "Just for you, sweetheart."

"No, thank you." Esther handed the flyer back, but she'd barely walked another step before she was accosted by someone asking if she'd ever considered becoming a Mathlete.

She had not and would not.

"What is all this?" she asked.

The math enthusiast pointed across the forecourt to the squat red building next to the union. "Activities Fair. In the Octagon."

Of course. Daisy had said something about that at breakfast and—now that she was here—Esther considered trying to find her. It might be fun to sign up for something safe. Something that didn't involve the words *Black* or *Metal*. Or a tattoo gun. Maybe something like tiddlywinks or origami . . . Who knew? Maybe she'd find Goth Girl queuing up for a bit of Minecraft action.

That made her smile.

As if someone that cool would go to an Activities Fair.

As if *Esther* would. Turning away, she went in pursuit of hot food.

Elise was as easy to talk to as she was hard to look at, a confusing combination that left Daisy flustered and jittery. Once the two of them had collected all Daisy's things, they walked together down the next aisle. This time, Daisy found herself so distracted by Elise that she barely noticed any of the booths they passed.

". . . it's not that I'm looking for new friends, it's just . . ." Daisy paused, not quite sure how she'd stumbled into this line of conversation.

"Of course not," Elise said, her offhand smile warming Daisy's cheeks and easing her conversational anxieties. Daisy watched as Elise drew a strand of glossy black hair behind her ear, painted nails smoothing it into place before she said, "But it's natural to want to belong somewhere— and you don't feel that way yet."

"I don't?" Daisy hadn't realized she'd said that. She'd been too distracted by the perfect shell of Elise's ear, wondering how everything about her managed to look so neat and precise and *finished*. Like she knew exactly who she was and what she was doing.

When Elise laughed, it was low and husky and made Daisy's skin prickle with excitement.

"If you did, would you be here?" Elise waved at the booths around them. "Your friends didn't come with you because they've found their groove already."

Daisy wasn't so convinced. She had the distinct impression that Esther was a skipping record, the needle not yet aligned with the right track, and Susan . . . well, she wasn't someone who found grooves so much as carved her own path without worrying about whatever was in her way, like a plow churning through a football field.

"I'm mostly here because Granny said I should get out and try new things." Daisy took her glasses off to polish a smudge that wasn't there, thinking of the rainbow letters of her LGBTQA badge lodged in the bottom of her tote.

She wasn't sure what Granny would make of that.

She wasn't sure what *she* made of that.

All Daisy knew was that this was the first time she'd been exposed to so many people her own age, and it wasn't the boys who drew her attention. It wasn't exactly that many of the girls did, either . . . just one who sat across from Daisy during Information and Information Studies and drew on her hand for most of the lecture while still managing to ask the most incisive question at the end of it.

And Elise. Maybe.

Elise, who had laid a hand on Daisy's shoulder and was now giving it a gentle, sympathetic squeeze.

"Don't worry, I remember what it was like when I first started." Elise registered the question in the way Daisy's eyebrows shot up and added, "Third-year Philosophy student. I know exactly where I belong."

"Oh. So, um . . . How come you're here?"

"To meet people like you," Elise said. She drew to a halt

by one of the stands and said, "You know you've missed out on the best society going, don't you?"

"Are you going to try to get me to sign up for rugby?" Daisy's eyes narrowed warily.

Elise let out another one of those inside-twisting husky laughs and shook her head. "Quite the opposite. I was going to ask if you like yoga."

She stepped aside to give Daisy a better view of the yoga mats that were laid out on the floor next to them. There was a bedsheet backdrop with a hand-drawn image of a lotus flower. All the overlapping leaves had been painted in different colors and made to look like eyes. There were a couple of people there already, sitting in casual Hero poses and sipping tea from fancy clay cups.

"I *love* yoga!" Daisy's voice was squeaky with enthusiasm as she took it all in.

"Well, this is something a little different. We're the Brethren of Zoise." Elise took a small card from the pocket of the sports top she was wearing. On one side was the lotus flower symbol, on the other, an address and the times and dates of when there were meetings. "It's a new form of yoga. Holistic. There's a big focus on community, in case you couldn't guess that by the 'brethren' thing. I think it's what you came here looking for."

Daisy thought she might be right.

"Do you have a mailing list I can sign up for?"

3

A LEISURELY SATURDAY

Susan's room was not one in which to step lightly. Or, indeed, heavily. Or at all, if you wanted to avoid breaking your neck. The floor was carpeted in clothes, and Daisy secretly held the theory that Susan simply rolled out of bed and across the floor and emerged in whatever wrapped itself around her before she got to the door. It was the room of someone whose brain was too busy to bother with something as frivolous as hygiene.

However, Daisy found herself there because someone had hacked into her university e-mail account and sent disturbing e-mails to everyone in her contacts list. (It was a toss-up as to which was worse: sending her grandmother a ransom demand or the Vice Chancellor a link to some NSFW fan fiction.) There was only one person Daisy could turn to.

"Does your skeleton have a name?" Without moving from the safe spot on the bed, Daisy knelt so she was level with the skull, squinting into its eye sockets as it leered out of the wardrobe.

"If you can guess, it'll spin straw into gold for you."

"Rumple-skeleton!"

"Nope."

Daisy looked crestfallen for a moment, then brightened up. "The Duke of Skellington?"

"Wrong again."

Daisy opened her mouth, then shut it. "I'm going to think about this."

"You do that"—without looking up, Susan cocked her finger at Daisy—"or the skeleton will eat your firstborn."

Daisy side-eyed the skeleton and whispered, "You wouldn't do that to a friend."

Her gaze drifted around the room and settled on the jar of teeth Susan used as a paperweight, an item that Esther coveted with overwhelming intensity.

"Where did you get—"

Susan turned abruptly, cutting her off. "Daisy, I love you, but this kind of work needs silence. I'm going to give you a golden five-minute window of opportunity, and then you're going to leave me in peace."

"Oh." Daisy drooped.

"Don't look so downhearted. Esther would do literally anything for an offer like this, and I'm giving it to you." Susan held up the timer on her phone and pressed start. "Five minutes. Go."

"Name the skeleton."

"Indiana Bones. A fellow archaeologist."

Daisy's expression darkened. "Indiana Jones is a very bad archaeologist. You're not meant to meddle with mystical objects like that."

Susan's attention drifted to the jar of teeth. "Probably best you don't ask me about those, then."

Since that had been her next question, Daisy cast around the room for another prompt. She'd never been good under pressure.

"Tick-tock, Wooton." Susan waggled her phone.

In desperation, Daisy just started pointing at things, Susan firing back the source. The reading lamp had been purloined from the British Library; a fraudulent mystic had been using that blanket as a tablecloth . . . everything had an origin story worthy of a two-hour superhero film.

"The fairy lights!" Daisy wasn't sure what possessed her to point at those.

"Elmswood Garden Center," Susan replied. A surprisingly mundane answer for someone so interesting, only then she added, "They were strung across the entrance to Santa's grotto. I had a man on the inside help me extract them."

There was something about the guilty flicker of her gaze that looked familiar. It was the same shifty look she got whenever McGraw's name came up. The golden five minutes were nearly up, but Daisy had to ask.

"Was that inside man McGraw?"

Susan nodded.

"So . . . you were friends?"

There was a moment in which Susan appeared to wrestle with herself, ingrained secrecy battling with honoring a promise to answer Daisy's questions.

"We were best friends. Secondary school. McGraw was . . . well, we were a team. A good one."

"What happened?"

"I made a mistake."

Daisy waited.

"I . . . I thought maybe we could be something more. And he didn't."

"Oh, Susan . . ."

"Yeah, well . . ." Susan picked at a loose thread on the hem of her T-shirt. "It didn't have to be the end, but it was."

"I'm sorry." When Daisy reached out a comforting hand, Susan didn't flinch but, rather, let Daisy's hand settle on hers and give a gentle squeeze.

"These things happen to the best of us. You know that." The smile Susan gave her was small and rueful and yet managed to speak volumes. "How's Information and Information Studies been this week?"

It was a subtle nod to Daisy's first—disastrous—attempt at addressing her feelings for the girl she'd been crushing on since the start of term. One wild night out as friends hadn't turned into anything more, despite Daisy's having plucked up the courage to ask. Fortune did not always favor the bold.

"I've not been," Daisy said, ducking her head. She hadn't intended on telling her friends this, but when she managed to drag her gaze up to meet Susan's, all she saw was sympathy.

"You do what you need to survive, Daisy. That's all any of us can do." The alarm on Susan's phone sounded, and she sat up, patting Daisy's hand dismissively. "Now leave me alone—there's a dear."

✳ ✳ ✳ ✳ ✳

It took Susan another hour and a half before she was satisfied that Daisy's account was secure, any unopened e-mails recalled, and the mystery hacker identified and neutralized. For good. As often happened when she was singularly focused on something worthy of her skill set, Susan had been oblivious to what was going on around her. She'd missed a call from one of her six older sisters (not the good one, so it wasn't like she had to return it) and several messages from her friends back home. Shrugging, Susan popped her phone into her pocket and went to return Daisy's laptop. She watched over her friend's shoulder as Daisy turned it on and checked her e-mails, just in case something unimaginable had happened.

It hadn't, but Daisy was frowning at the screen nonetheless.

"Umm . . . Susan? Why does it say I have 203 e-mails in my spam folder?"

"Because you have 203 e-mails in your spam folder. Just a wild guess."

"And that's nothing to do with the hacker?"

"Nope." Susan met Daisy's glance of trepidation with a reassuring smile and watched as her friend reached out a trembling finger to open her spam folder.

Dedicated follower of fashion? Calling all catwalkers, FASHION FIRST will be meeting in Catterick bar at 7:30 P.M. Friday for vogue-ing and vodka . . .

CIRCUS SOC NEEDS YOU! Drawing from all levels of the talent pool, from trapeze-walking fire-breathers to anyone *who can make a passable shadow puppet, Sheffield Circus Soc invites *you* . . .*

Ever feel like the world would be better if speech bubbles emerged from your mouth and someone else had control over your facial expression? Here at Comic Club we appreciate the magic that happens when words and illustrations collide . . .

DEBATING: for or against? . . .

"It's all the clubs I signed up for at the Activities Fair!" Daisy squeaked, darting a guilty glance in the direction of her desk, which was littered with candy wrappers, a miniature croquet set, pin badges, and a Student Union–branded mug overflowing with promotional pens and pencils, rulers, and what looked like a magic wand.

Susan's phone buzzed *again*, and she slipped it out of her pocket to check. Yet another message from her friend Beebz. A picture . . .

"What do I do?" Daisy asked, scrolling in panic through her spam folder. "There's so many of them!"

Had Daisy looked up, she would have been one of only seven (living) people to witness Susan Ptolemy having her own brand of server meltdown.

"So many what?" Susan looked up, the screen of her phone pressed to her chest in case Daisy was tempted to look.

"Clubs . . ."

"Excellent. You should try some of them."

"Really?" Daisy's voice rose in surprise. "I thought they were 'enforced fun for people who don't have anything better to do with their lives'?"

"Yes, well . . . what *are* you doing with your life? Today,

I mean. It's a Saturday. Day of leisure. Go . . . be leisurely."
Susan backed hurriedly out the door. "Right now, in fact.
You'll have a great time. Send me a postcard. Bye. Love you.
Take a packed lunch."

Slamming the door shut, Susan collapsed back against
the wall and stared down at her phone in abject terror.

Esther was restless. She'd been sitting at her desk for more
than an hour, and she'd barely managed a chapter of *The
Moonstone*. Or rather, the York Notes on *The Moonstone*.
They couldn't possibly expect her to actually read all these
books. That'd take forever.

Maybe if she'd still been with The Boy, she could have
wasted time sending him sexy messages—or, wasn't it the
weekend? Not bothering with lectures meant that it was
hard to tell what day it was sometimes. Esther checked her
phone.

Yes. It was the weekend. Which meant he could have
caught the train down from Tackleford for a little sexy real-
time—

Only he wouldn't have, would he? That had been the
problem.

There were no traces of him in her room. The same day
that they'd broken up, someone had put up a poster in the
stairwell advertising a swap shop, and Esther had gone
there to trade a laundry basket's worth of memories for a
set of six different-sized scissors, a secondhand collection
of York Notes, and a funky notebook that said, *You're weird.
I like it.*

No regrets. The notebook was cool, the scissors sharp, and, well, she'd just read half a chapter about *The Moonstone*.

Emotional baggage, on the other hand, wasn't so easily swapped, and Esther had decided to drop hers on the floor and run as far away from it as she could.

Maybe if she hadn't run quite so far, quite so fast, then she could have tried giving one of her friends from home a call to catch up, but she'd left it too long now.

A message from Daisy or Susan, even from Ed Gemmell, got answered within the hour, but the last message from Sarah Grote, her best friend back home, had come in six days ago. It was the sort of heartfelt, kind message that demanded a more meaningful reply than a silly selfie or a blithely chirpy emoji.

So she hadn't sent any reply at all.

Before she could plummet any further into the abyss, Esther yanked herself up with the thought of an impromptu night out. A cheap one—the end of the month was fast approaching, and Esther was running on fumes. Raking through her brain, she recalled something about a rock night down at the S.U.—that would do. All she needed now was to rally the troops. Skipping across the corridor, Esther rapped a jaunty rhythm on Daisy's door just as it started to open.

"Daisy!" She flung her arms open and enveloped Daisy in a hug, only to get tangled up in the yoga mat hitched over Daisy's shoulder. "I didn't know you did yoga on Saturdays."

"You know what day it is!"

Ignoring Daisy's delight, Esther spun her around and bundled her back into her room so she could get changed into something more lively. "Exactly. It's the weekend. Time for a bit of fun."

"Yoga is fun!"

"Not as fun as a wild night out. Me, you, Susan—"

"I have plans!" Daisy slipped out of Esther's grasp and laid a firm hand on the door, preventing further ministrations.

This was unexpected. Daisy was supposed to be the compliant one.

"Couldn't you change those plans?"

Daisy's frown was not of the familiar confused variety, and it took Esther a moment to understand it was because she'd annoyed her. "No. I can't."

"Not even for me? Please?" Esther dropped to her knees, eyes widening into pools of pure hope, hands clasped in supplication. "I'd cancel my plans for you . . ."

It was supposed to be persuasive, but, judging by the look Daisy was giving her, it was anything but. Esther rose to her feet, awkward and uncomfortable under Daisy's stern stare.

"Being a good friend isn't just about canceling your plans when someone needs you—it's about respecting plans that have already been made. I'm going to yoga, and you're welcome to come with me—"

Esther's derisory snort was reflexive, and she regretted it instantly.

"You don't like yoga. I understand." Daisy laid a hand on Esther's shoulder, and her voice wasn't without kindness when she added, "But you need to understand that I don't like crowded dance floors and loud music."

After giving Esther a reassuringly affectionate squeeze, Daisy left. Never one to be deterred, Esther decided to try her luck with Susan, thumping insistently on the door to number 13 before trying the handle.

Locked. Getting her phone out, Esther dialed Susan's number, ear pressed to the door, but when the call connected, the room remained silent.

One ring . . . two . . . *three*? No answer. Esther hammered out a message.

Where are you???

Out, came the reply.

You're never out!

Fake news, gothy. Daisy's birthday? Last week? She attached a photo of the three of them, taken in the pub the week before, their faces aglow from the candles on Daisy's cake.

Stop whatever you're doing. There's a rock night down at the S.U. You're coming with me.

Not interested.

Please . . .

Begging is undignified.

I WANT A NIGHT OUT, AND NO ONE WANTS TO COME WITH ME!!!!!!!!!!

A tantrum. Much more on brand.

Another message followed that.

Sorry. Really I am. I'm out with the medical lot. Try Ed Gemmell. You know he'll take any excuse to make you happy.

Esther looked with disgust at the little winky face with which Susan had punctuated that sentence and wondered whether her friend was feeling all right.

Susan was very definitely *not* feeling all right. The friends sitting at a corner table of the pub were very definitely *not* medical friends and they were very definitely *not* supposed to be in Sheffield.

It had taken some very quick thinking on Susan's part when she'd received a horror story in three photos from two of her closest friends from back home:

Tiny little Beebz, her dreads squashed under the hood of a bright orange anorak, jerking a thumb at the departures board of Birmingham train station and looking delighted.

Madeleine, all silk scarves and a Cossack hat, pressing a red-lipped kiss onto a train ticket from Leeds.

The two of them, united, outside a sign welcoming them to Sheffield, looking utterly delighted with themselves and the caption *SURPRISE!* As the midpoint between where the two had moved since leaving their hometown, Sheffield was the natural choice for a reunion.

One that had been kept secret from Susan, because her friends knew she'd never have agreed to it. That was the problem when people knew you too well—which was exactly the reason Susan had wanted to keep them away. If there was one thing being a private investigator taught you, it was that knowledge was power. No need to share it with more people than necessary.

Still. They were only here for the day.

And Susan was resourceful. Picking up three glasses, she made her way back to their table. No one was going to turn down an all-day boozing session, not when Susan had cracked open her emergency stash of fifties and tucked three of them into her bra.

Daisy stood on the driveway that led up to the House of Zoise and looked at the address on her phone doubtfully.

The houses on this road weren't typical of student accommodations. They were tall and redbrick—Edwardian, maybe—with high windows and gabled roofs, the kind of house a parent or a grandparent might live in, but not someone Daisy's age. Maybe it was a ploy? Maybe someone had hijacked the mailing list for the Brethren of Zoise? A serial killer who lured yoga fans to his house and murdered them halfway through a Sun Salutation?

Maybe she should skip this and have a bite to eat before attending Late-Night Pool Club . . . but she was still stuffed after having afternoon tea with the misnomered Ladies Who Brunch, and, having walked all the way here, it seemed a shame to give up. Approaching the front door, Daisy was reassured by the paint flaking off the window frames, the algae in the mortar, and the weeds poking up through the paved driveway. And wasn't that a Che Guevara poster she could see in the front room?

Daisy took a fortifying breath. She was good at doing things on her own, but that didn't mean it was easy. Especially not when she'd conceded the possibility of getting murdered.

Grasping the satisfying heft of the lion's head knocker, she announced her arrival.

The door opened to reveal a young man about Daisy's

height with shaggy ginger hair and bare feet. Daisy thought he might have been with Elise at the booth. He wore a dressing-gown-like black robe and a slightly bemused expression.

"Hi, my name's Daisy. I'm here for the Zoise meeting?" She gestured at her mat.

"Of course, come in. You must be here for the taster session. My name's Jasper." Jasper's hair curled up over his ears and onto his neck, and he had a splatter of freckles across the bridge of his nose and the tops of his cheeks. As Daisy stepped past him, she had the feeling that this was exactly the sort of boy Esther would find very attractive indeed.

"This house is really nice," Daisy said. "I didn't realize there was any student housing this far out of town." Daisy followed Jasper down a hallway. The floor was hardwood, and fairy lights wound up banisters that looked like an original feature of the house. Coving on the ceiling, picture rails . . . if it weren't for the socks drying on the radiator and the pizza boxes and take-away trays littered about, she could have stepped into the last five minutes of *Property Brothers*.

"Yeah, we're really lucky. This place came up for sale a few years ago, and my dad bought it so me and my brother would have somewhere to live."

"Does your brother do yoga, too?"

Jasper laughed. "Finn spends ninety percent of his time getting high in the attic—says yoga's too energetic. And there's Mei, but you'll never see her—she basically lives with her boyfriend these days."

"And Elise?" Daisy said, trying not to sound too hopeful, although Jasper gave her a curious look when he said, "Oh, you'll see a lot of Elise. She and I, we're the yoga buffs. Through here . . ."

Jasper waved Daisy toward the back of the house, where the smell of baking—earthy and nutty and delicious—intensified. The room into which Daisy stepped was so far from the bubbled plasterwork and linoleum of Catterick Hall that to use the word *kitchen* to describe both rooms would be blasphemous.

The floor was tiled in terra-cotta, the walls painted the same lush creamy white as the wooden cabinets, and the counters were wiped clean enough to gleam. On the far side of the room, beyond the chunky farmhouse table, Elise extracted a tray of biscuits from a sprawling range oven. When Elise stood, petite and perfectly curved in a loose vest and tropical print leggings, Daisy felt as if she'd stepped into a photo shoot for some trendy lifestyle magazine.

"This is Daisy," Jasper said. "I think she could use a beginner's infusion if you've any left?"

"Oh, I know Daisy."

Under the beam of Elise's smile, Daisy disappeared inside the neck of her sports cardigan, almost relieved when Elise turned away to set things on a tray—enamel-lined clay cups and plates heaped with warm cookies. As Jasper turned toward the sink, the Eyes of Zoise embroidered onto the back of his black dressing gown twinkled happily at her.

Elise nodded toward a door that Daisy had thought was a pantry. "We're down in the basement," she said.

Opening the door, Daisy found stone steps leading down to where a pool of warm, wavering light welcomed her. The steps were cool beneath Daisy's feet, but on reaching the bottom, she stepped onto a thick, plush rug. The basement was huge—the house must have been built on a hill, the front higher than the back, because the entire back wall was nothing but glass-paneled doors looking out onto what Daisy presumed was the garden, although it was too dark to see more than a hint of a greenhouse and some trees. The floor was so densely layered with rugs and mats that when she stepped forward into the studio, it was as if she were walking on a spongy cloud. Spotlights in the ceiling were turned down low, and all around the walls, jars and vases with candles burning inside hung from nails embedded in the brickwork.

The smell from the kitchen permeated the room, mingling pleasantly with the low murmur of friendly voices and whatever was burning in a gently smoking stone basin. Something about the room, the people in it, and the prospect of some social yoga made Daisy feel at ease.

As she took a sip of the brew that Elise had given her, she realized this felt a lot like coming home.

Esther remedied rejection the way she remedied everything: with loud music and a lot of makeup. Who needed Susan and Daisy when Ed Gemmell was around? All Esther needed to do now was locate him.

Where are you?

Nanoseconds later: Catterick bar.

Excellent. See you in 5.

Not bothering to read whatever he'd sent in reply, Esther grabbed her coat and hurried across the quad. The bar was busier than when they'd been there last, which wasn't surprising, given the time of day, and Ed Gemmell was hard to find in a crowd. McGraw, however, was not, and Esther wriggled her way to where the two of them stood by one of the barred windows.

"Gentlemen!" Esther flung her arms out in ecstasy, squeezing a wheeze of welcome out of Ed Gemmell and turning uncertainly to McGraw. "Do we hug?"

McGraw looked at Esther, then at the full pint of beer in his hand. "Another time, perhaps."

Probably for the best.

"Right. Well, Ed Gemmell, I'm here to hijack whatever plans you have for the evening and whisk you away to Rock Night."

She'd already looped her arm in his when Ed Gemmell made a strangled noise that sounded like, "I can't."

"What?"

"I—er—not sure—I can—"

"Of course you can."

McGraw, who had been standing there silently like a sexy statue, chose that moment to clear his throat.

"McGraw! Why don't you come, too?" So what if she was fraternizing with the enemy? Susan only had herself to blame. If she'd been there . . .

"No, thank you. I have plans. With Ed."

"To come dancing with me." Esther snuggled closer and gave Ed Gemmell a hopeful pout.

"I . . . maybe . . ." He swayed a little as if hypnotized before peeling his eyes from hers and mouthing a desperate "*Help me!*" at McGraw.

"Stop this black magic." McGraw put his pint down, covered his friend's glasses with one hand, and extracted him from Esther's grip with the other. Once free, Ed Gemmell glanced desperately between them like a dog torn between two owners, and McGraw fixed Esther with a stern stare.

"The man said no."

"No, he didn't." Technically, he'd said, "I can't," which wasn't the same thing at all. "Come on, Ed Gemmell, come on . . ."

"This is beneath you, Esther." McGraw drew Ed Gemmell away from her reach. "Leave him be."

Esther's Hail Mary was a Fail Mary. Storming back across the bar, bruised by her lack of success, Esther turned to shout, "Susan was right about you!" at McGraw. "You *are* an awful human being!"

But McGraw just gave her a cheery wave, one arm still clamped on Ed Gemmell's scrawny form.

Susan decided to switch pubs. It was a risk, but the one they'd been in didn't do food, and they needed something other than liquid sustenance.

"Why can't we see where you live?" Madeleine asked, sounding peevish as she wound her scarf tightly and tugged her Cossack hat farther onto her head. "I want to see this famed student lifestyle I'm missing out on by actually gaining relevant experience in the workplace."

"And meet your *friends*!" Beebz added before giving Susan a doubtful look. "Assuming you have any . . ."

"What do you think?" Susan shot back, playing into her friend's expectations with a little misdirection before hurrying in the opposite direction of Catterick Hall.

"The old Susie P would have been perfectly happy for us all to hang in her room, smoking her way through a bottle of whisky in her PJs," Beebz muttered.

"What kind of host would I be if I didn't show you the sights of Sheffield? Look"—she pointed down a nearby alley—"a fox dragging a trash bag across the street. Bet you don't get that kind of wildlife in Birmingham."

Susan *knew* that Beebz and Madeleine would love Esther and Daisy just as much as she did. Well, actually, probably not; Susan was a lot fonder of those two scamps than she liked to admit. But that wasn't the point.

Beebz and Madeleine had known Susan a long time—and with a long-shared history came long-shared memories. With Esther's unquenchable thirst for gossip and Daisy's innocent charm, it would take all of five minutes of shared conversation for Susan's past to spill over into her present, muddying everything up and making things messy.

This was her shiny new life, and for a while at least, Susan wanted to keep it that way.

As they passed a crowd standing outside one of the chains, Madeleine—conspicuous in her tall boots and bright clothes—drew a chorus of wolf whistles. In perfect synchrony, Susan and Beebz flipped the boys off.

"Good to know Sheffield has its fair share of skeevy lads

for you to wreak vengeance upon," Beebz said with an impish grin.

"*Mate*. You have no idea . . ." Susan slung an arm around her friend's shoulders, ready to regale her with what had happened when a disgusting group of tosspots had posted Esther's picture on a website called Bantserve, when Madeleine slowed her pace and turned to give Susan a shrewd look.

"And I hear that a certain Graham McGraw is one of them?"

Susan didn't miss the look that passed between her two friends.

"How's he doing these days?" asked Beebz.

"Don't know."

"You know he broke up with Kylie Traynor, right?"

"Don't care."

"It's a shame you and he never—"

"*Don't.*"

Ushering Beebz and Madeleine into the first pub she could find that advertised food, she hoped that the crush of the crowd and the stress of finding a table might prove sufficiently distracting, but once they were sitting down, food ordered, and drinks in hand, the conversation continued in the same hateful direction.

"Don't think you're getting away that easily." Madeleine clinked her glass against Susan's and nudged her in the side. "Not when we've come *all the way* here to find out the gossip on your love life."

"There is no gossip. Me and McGraw hardly have anything to do with each other. Which is exactly how I like it."

Beebz's eyes lit up. "Interesting how Madeleine was asking you about your love life, and you went *straight* to McGraw."

"Shut up." Susan's grip on her tumbler tightened, her knuckles turning white.

"So, what I'm deducing from this"—Madeleine indicated the scowl that had blackened Susan's expression—"is that *if* there were any juicy liaisons, then those liaisons would not be with some new and sexy foreign student, but with a tall and taciturn gentleman you've known since you were a scrappy little tween."

"Stop talking now."

Beebz picked up where Madeleine had left off. "Someone who already knows all your darkest secrets. Someone who knows where the bodies are buried because he helped dig the graves . . ."

Susan slammed her tumbler down so hard that the whisky slopped out and onto the tabletop.

"What *did* go wrong there, anyway?" Madeleine asked, and the two leaned over the table in a remarkably good impression of Esther.

"I need the loo." Susan stood abruptly and shoved her way through the crowd.

It wasn't until she was leaning over the sink and glaring at her own reflection that Susan realized that when Esther had last looked at her like that—only a week previously—Susan hadn't stormed off in a huff.

She'd told her the same thing she'd told Daisy earlier that morning.

Not *quite* the full story, as such. She'd let her friends assume that the rift arose from wounded pride, but that wasn't it, not really. It was that she'd thought McGraw was more than just some cute boy. He was her friend, her ally; yet he'd left her to battle with her feelings on her own.

It wouldn't be this way if McGraw had called Susan just *once* two summers before . . .

God. Even silently admitting this to her reflection in the privacy of the ladies' bathroom was excruciating.

And yet there was a part of her that could imagine how easy it would be to tell Esther and Daisy. After all, she'd already told them things about herself that she'd never told anyone else.

A most discomfiting thought. And also . . . kind of a nice one.

Friendship: so bloody confusing.

When Esther pulled the door open, expecting the sweet aural embrace of angry music and a vision of sweaty bodies, she was met with a roomful of people seated around many small tables, lights bright and voices low.

"Hello!" A boy wearing a long fake beard, a pointed hat, and a sparkly muumuu waved from the stage, microphone in hand and a stuffed bird on his shoulder. "I see we have another Death Eater! Put your entry money in the Goblet of Fire and pick a team!"

Esther looked down at her T-shirt in confusion. The skull and snake logo was that of a band called Victuals, who had a reputation for throwing rubber snakes into the crowd during the chorus of their cult hit "Snake-rifice."

Death Eaters, goblets . . . She took another look around the room, at the scarves and broomsticks and cloaks and preponderance of people in round glasses.

This was not Rock Night. It was Harry Potter Quiz Night.

It was Ed Gemmell's fault. Tapping someone on the shoulder while they're getting money out is never a good idea.

Still, Daisy was profuse in her apologies as she followed the map on her phone to Late-Night Pool Club. After her fiftieth variation of "Sorry," Daisy switched to reassuring. "You'll be able to breathe in a minute—a chop to the wind-pipe is more about shock than damage."

Ed Gemmell gave a small, nervous nod and pointed along the road before miming a very strange dance.

"Ooh, are you going swimming, too?" Daisy gave the small record bag he was carrying a doubtful look. Hopefully the fancy leisure center that the Pool Club used would offer their patrons towels. Walking along, Daisy wondered aloud about what to expect. Was this going to be competitive? Or perhaps it would be like one of those parties with inflatables? That would explain why the meeting was being held so late . . .

All the while, Ed Gemmell made frantic flapping gestures that betrayed a very poor technique.

The leisure club was so exclusive that there wasn't any of the usual ostentatious glass, just a set of plain black doors under a backlit sign indicating the entrance to The Club.

"Two for the pool, please," Daisy said. The man behind the desk was an unorthodox but effective advertisement for whatever personal training was on offer, since he looked as if he regularly ground bones to dust. "And can you tell me where the changing rooms are?"

"Change is through there."

Concluding that despite his Yorkshire accent, English must not be his first language, Daisy thought better of correcting him and pushed open the double doors.

At which point it became abundantly clear that it was Daisy who'd gotten things wrong.

Ever one to make the best of what appeared to be a disastrous situation, Esther had embraced Harry Potter Quiz Night with all the enthusiasm that she would have embraced Rock Night. In seconds, she'd been assimilated onto a team of misfits captained by Susan's friend Grace and including a girl called Noor, whom Esther recognized as someone from her course from her pink headscarf and dimpled smile, and a mountain in a Hogwarts T-shirt who was introduced as American Chad.

They were terrible.

As Esther and Grace drained pitcher after pitcher of Harry Potter–themed cocktails, the others seemed to get equally drunk on hysteria as their team, the "Mugglebloods," crashed into last place through every round with increasingly far-fetched and fanciful answers, referencing magical creatures from all the wrong mythologies, made-up spells, and ever so slightly rude variations on character names.

"Who knew A-level Latin would come in so useful?" Noor collapsed into Esther, giggling as they staggered their way out of the Union.

"That look on Dumbledore's face when you yelled out 'haemorrhoidus explodus' as the spell Harry used on Draco Malfoy!" Esther couldn't breathe, she was laughing so much.

"You guys are crazy!" American Chad leaned forward to put his arms over their shoulders and squeezed them so tightly, Esther felt as if her head would pop. "I've never had so much fun *losing*."

"Let's go dancing!" Grace swung around and pointed in the direction of town, swaying unsteadily so that Noor gently shrugged Chad off and hurried over to her.

Esther frowned, thinking back to how many pitchers they'd had, with Grace topping up Esther's glass of "Marga-Rita Skeeter" faster than Esther was drinking it. She felt merry and fuzzy but in full control of her faculties, unlike Grace, who was having a heated and slightly hysterical argument with Noor.

"Is she OK?" Esther asked Chad.

Chad shrugged. "Who knows? She veers between nights of partying as hard as she works and days of sitting in her PJs eating nothing but cereal."

For a moment, Esther wondered why he knew this, before remembering Grace had said he was one of her housemates. "The only decent one," she'd said, although Esther hadn't exactly known what that meant. Not for the first time, she felt grateful to have been housed on a corridor with Daisy and Susan.

She watched Grace lean forward to hug Noor, crying onto her shoulder.

"Is this about her boyfriend in Plymouth?" Esther asked. He'd come up a few times during the quiz.

"I guess. They talk a lot on the phone, but I think she's finding it hard."

Esther nodded, thinking of how it had been when she was still with The Boy—the constant ache of not being with him and yet not being free, anchored in the water, pulled back and forth with the tide. It wasn't hard to see how Grace was struggling to get the balance right.

It had been difficult, but with a little distance, Esther thought that perhaps what had happened to her had been for the best.

A salacious "Ooooooooh . . ." rippled around the table, and a few last-minute bets exchanged hands before someone took up the chant, "Dai-sy! Dai-sy! Dai-sy!"

Scrutinizing her options, Daisy chose her spot and bent over. The baize was soft beneath her fingertips as she splayed the fingers of her left hand, the wood of the pool . . . pole? brushing against her chin. Drawing air into her lungs, Daisy channeled a little Zoise learning to summon a yogi-like calm amid the clamor of the pool hall. In one smooth motion, she struck the cue ball, and the room fell silent.

The white rolled the length of the table and gently kissed the black.

Almost before it was sunk, the room erupted into a cacophony of cheering and whooping. Ed Gemmell grabbed Daisy's arm and swung it high into the air.

"The undisputed champion—Daisy Wooton!"

Overwhelmed at being the focus of so much good cheer from so many strangers, Daisy edged away toward the vending machine, hoping that no one would notice.

But one person did: her opponent.

"An excellent match and a worthy victor." McGraw held out his hand, and they shook. For all that her loyalties lay with Susan, there was no denying that McGraw was one of the most considerate, polite, and downright *chivalrous* people Daisy had ever encountered. He had the manners of a Regency gentleman, the mustache of a middle-aged man, and the youthful twinkle in his smile of someone who looked at the world and liked it.

Which was probably exactly the reason Susan found him intolerable.

"Do you fancy another game?" McGraw asked, but before Daisy had a chance to excuse herself, his phone rang. Looking down, McGraw frowned at the name onscreen before answering. "Hello?"

This wasn't supposed to have happened. Susan wasn't someone who drank too much. *Ever.* It must have been something in that tapas platter.

It certainly *smelled* like something in that tapas platter.

"I'm not drunk. I'll be fine." Susan groaned at the patch of tarmac she was staring at, sitting on the curb, her elbows propped on her knees, hands supporting her head. "You've got to get your train."

"We're not leaving you on your own . . ." Beebz said from somewhere above.

Susan spat despondently, wondering how much more she could possibly throw up before she turned inside out. She didn't know where Madeleine had gone, probably somewhere out of splatter range. Susan really was more worried about them getting the train than anything else. She couldn't afford for them to stay over. Couldn't afford having to explain to Esther and Daisy who they were or why they were there . . .

There were some scuffled footsteps and murmured conversation, and then Beebz was crouching in front of Susan, nose wrinkled as she said, "Cavalry's here. Forgive us our trespasses and all that. It was good to see you, Ptolemy."

"Bye, you, feel better." Madeleine was back again and kissing the top of Susan's head, which was almost certainly the only safe place to kiss.

And then someone was hauling her up. Someone strong. Someone familiar.

Someone against whom Susan would have invoked Subsection B of Clause 4 of their contract, if she'd felt a little less feeble.

It was a bright and cheery morning, but only Daisy was up to see it, lying in bed and checking her e-mails to find one from Jasper.

Welcome, Brethren.

Thank you to all those who attended last night. Please find attached the MP3 file for this week's Zounds of Zoise—20 minutes a day is all it takes. See you next week!

Remember: The path to enlightenment reveals itself to those who share. Bring a friend, and reap the bounty of the Brethren.

Daisy looked over to where her own velvety black robe hung on the back of her door. The robe was on loan. Daisy was free to attend up to three sessions as an honorary member, after which point she was expected to make a contribution to the group and become a full acolyte. When Daisy had asked what kind of contribution was expected, Elise had recited the same line as at the bottom of the e-mail: *The path to enlightenment reveals itself to those who share.*

"Yes, but share what?" Daisy had frowned.

"You can introduce friends to the group or share worldly possessions."

"You mean money?"

But Jasper had overheard and stepped in. "Cash holds no meaning for one who wants for nothing. It is not the worldly value of your gifts that Zoise desires, but the *emotional* value of the transaction."

Which hadn't exactly cleared things up, but he'd gone on to explain about the belt system, and Daisy had gotten caught up in the thought of progressing to her first full belt. It was a bit like being back in Girl Guides and working toward a badge, and Daisy welcomed the feeling of purpose that came with it.

Her smile faded as she heard noises from next door. Susan was awake.

It was safe to say that Susan did not have the healthiest relationship with sleep. Last night, it had reached a new low as she plummeted into a fractured reality, with Beebz and Madeleine face-swapping with Esther and Daisy, McGraw's voice asking over and over, "Are they going to sign a contract, too?" mixed through with lucid recollections that she *wished* were dreams and also, horrendously, more vomiting.

When she woke, fully and finally and mercifully restored to something like health, Susan knew that there was worse to come, and it had nothing to do with the aftereffects of the tapas platter. Or seven neat whiskies.

"Susan?" There was a knock on the door before Daisy pushed it open and, seeing that the inhabitant was conscious, tiptoed across the room. She opened the window and lay a plate of toast and a cup of black coffee on the bedside table. "You should eat."

"Thank you," Susan whispered, not able to meet her eyes.

The silent reproach that flooded into the room after Daisy left was suffocating. After a restorative shower, a change of clothes, another round of toast and coffee, and a short stroll, Susan paused outside Esther's door and listened to the murmur of conversation within before knocking and entering. Esther and Daisy were sitting on the bed, caught in a tableau of what looked like a game of gin rummy.

"Hi," Susan said.

"How are you feeling?" Daisy asked gently, setting her cards down.

"Terrible."

"Do you want me to make you something?" Daisy was already half off the bed when Susan raised a hand to stop her.

"Not that sort of terrible." God. This was hard. "I feel bad about what happened yesterday."

"You mean blowing us off to go and hang out with your real friends?" Esther's words stung.

"Yes. That."

The two of them were looking at her expectantly, but when Susan remained silent a moment too long, Esther spoke. "Are you ashamed of us or something?"

"Of course not." But her protest had no effect on either of their expressions. "The only thing I'm ashamed of is me."

Humility. It hurt.

"Go on," Esther said.

"Look. I just—I didn't plan for my friends to come here. It was a surprise visit, and . . . I panicked."

"Why?" asked Daisy, her voice, her expression a little softer than Esther's.

"I'm just not ready for things to . . ." She meshed her fingers together. "Mix. You know?"

Daisy glanced at Esther, then said, "I'm not sure we do."

Closing her eyes, Susan tried to put words to something that she'd never tried to make sense of. Opening them again, she knew that if they didn't understand what she said now, there'd never be a way to explain it.

"I have . . . trust issues." Esther snorted at this, but Daisy settled her. "I don't want you to get to know me through someone else. I want you to get to know me through me."

"You do?" Esther's eyebrows shot up.

"I do." Susan managed an almost-smile. "But . . . I'm not like you. It takes time."

Susan looked across the room at her two friends—the two people who had started to matter the most—and wondered whether it was enough to *want* them to understand.

Esther shrugged, glanced at Daisy, and said, "OK."

Picking up the cards, Daisy looked over at Susan. "Want me to deal you in?"

Over in F-block, McGraw returned from a pleasant Sunday lunch with Ed to find a Post-it Note on his door.

1) J-block, Catterick Hall, is considered out of bounds at all times.

Last night, I believe you breached our terms. Consider this a warning.

4

J-BLOCK UNITED

Esther was painting yellow cobwebs on her black-varnished nails when she heard someone step into her open doorway.

"Hard at work, then?" Susan asked.

"I think I missed my calling." Esther splayed her fingers and took a photo of her handiwork. There was always a swell of appreciation for dark nail art in the run-up to Halloween.

She watched Susan perch on the end of the bed and clear her throat.

"Are you hinting that you want me to give you a dark magic manicure?" It was too good an opportunity to miss, but as soon as Esther snatched Susan's hand, she recoiled at the sight. "Eurgh! Wait, no, this is far more horrific than anything I could achieve."

Ragged cuticles, split nails, scabbed skin—Susan's hands looked like those of a zombie that had just clawed its way out of the grave.

"Achievement unlocked. I am officially too slovenly for a makeover." The malevolence in Susan's grin was dimmed beneath a veil of caution. One day on, and things were still a little tender between them. "Anyway, I'm not here to enable your time wasting."

She took a card out of her top pocket and handed it to Esther.

"Grace gave me this. We're all invited."

Esther looked down at the card, the words *HALLOWEEN PARTY* in what looked like fake blood catching her attention.

"But you hate parties." Esther looked up in confusion. "Parties mean people, and you hate people."

"Not all people." Susan studied the nubs of her fingernails before muttering, "There's a couple I think are all right."

But the last word was barely more than a squawk as Esther barreled in to give Susan a hug.

"Steady on," Susan said, wriggling her way out of Esther's arms. "Don't think I'm going to dress up."

The door of room number 12 was wedged open, revealing the extent to which Esther had embraced her favorite festival. Bat-shaped bunting swooped from corner to corner, and fake candles glimmered inside skull-shaped lanterns and the occasional hollowed gourd. Susan's skeleton had been temporarily relocated and arranged by the door, one arm offering a bowl of gobstopper "eyeballs" bobbing about in a bowl of bloodlike black-currant cordial. Esther had somehow managed to rig up a motion sensor so that when anyone passed, the skeleton would emit a recording asking whether they would like to make a sacrifice.

Susan approached, skirting outside the range of the sensor, just to be contrary.

"This is your five-minute warning—WHAT THE HOLY HELLFIRE HAVE YOU DONE TO DAISY?"

Susan was a medical student. She was familiar with blood and viscera; in preparation for her degree, she'd indulged in some pretty extreme Google-image exposure therapy. It was safe to say that Susan had Seen Things.

But she had never before Seen This Thing.

Esther sat back on her heels and studied her handiwork. Daisy herself remained still, glasses folded in her lap, eyes closed, breathing slow and shallow.

"Doesn't she look amazing?"

That was one word for it, but there were several that were much more appropriate: *Terrifying* and *grotesque* and *disturbing* sprung to mind.

Susan waved a hand in front of Daisy's face, but there wasn't so much as a flutter behind her eyelids.

"Did you hypnotize her? Daisy?" Susan snapped her fingers—no response. "Daisy Wooton, you're scaring me."

"That's the whole point." Esther rolled her eyes, then said, "Oh, you mean the meditation. She's been going to some yoga club where they give you MP3s to help with your meditative cycle. Zeus or Zorb or something. She popped her headphones in and has been like this ever since."

The two of them looked at Daisy speculatively.

"She said to tap her on the nose when we wanted her to come out of her meditative state." Esther leaned in and tapped Daisy three times on the nose.

Daisy's eyes opened slowly, pupils coming into focus.

"How do I look?"

Daisy hadn't been convinced she was Halloween party material, but in the hands of her self-appointed fairy goth-mother, she certainly *looked* the part.

When she emerged from her meditation, Daisy marveled at how Esther had turned a pair of tights into sleeves that were painted to look as if the skin of Daisy's arms was peeling away to reveal rotting muscle fibers and clotted blood. Beneath wild green-and-gold-sprayed curls, half of Daisy's skull had been face-painted away to expose teeth and tongue, while the other half had been made up so beautifully that even her huge round glasses didn't detract from the effect. If Daisy only approached people from the left, they'd think she was gorgeous.

While Daisy looked like something that had emerged from the grave of a ritual sacrifice, Esther had gone for the sexually promiscuous vampire aesthetic. Her hair was straightened into two thick black curtains, framing long-lashed eyes with yellow irises, courtesy of a pair of contact lenses that Esther had spent at least fifteen minutes trying to put in before Daisy pinned her down for Susan to do the honors. The corset she wore was so tight that her breasts had been plumped into plush round cushions, as if two oversize marshmallows had decided to nestle on her chest for the night. A thin dribble of fake blood trailed from one corner of her shiny red lips down her neck and into her eye-popping cleavage.

If it weren't for the trapper hat that Esther had rammed firmly over Susan's ears moments before they left, Susan would have looked exactly the same as she always did: boots, jeans, and a checked shirt.

When the third person they passed actually stopped to poke Daisy in the rotting side of her face, Daisy resolved to give Susan creative control over her outfit the next year.

Not all of Sheffield University's first-year students lived in halls. A few, like Grace, shared houses on the city's many little side streets. Cheaper but riskier. What if you didn't like your housemates? What if you ended up living with people who left dirty plates under the settee, or insisted you go in on a Sky Sports subscription even if you never watched TV, or walked through the house in nothing but their slippers?

The thought had been too much for Daisy, who preferred to know the people who had the opportunity to murder her in her sleep.

Daisy, Susan, and Esther followed the bloody footprints from the gate of Grace's house to the doorstep, admiring the effort that had gone into spookifying the front of the building, which was bedecked with cobwebs and bouncy rubber bats and snakes and . . . bunnies.

"Who's scared of bunnies?" Daisy whispered to Esther, who shrugged.

"Takes all sorts, Daisy. Let's not judge."

Before they even had the chance to knock, the door swung open, and they were greeted by American Chad, huge and hulking and wearing nothing but an artfully arranged American flag and a monocle. Arms spread as wide as his grin, he ushered them into a crammed little hallway and squeezed out to get more plastic cups from the corner shop.

"Why is it that all the girls' outfits are sexy?" Susan muttered, side-eyeing a Puss in Boots whose rakish hat and rapier were teamed with a single-button waistcoat, spray-on hot pants, and patent thigh-high boots.

"Some of us can't help it." Esther's reflexive hair toss whipped Daisy in the face.

"You're missing the point. Sexy's fine, but it should be a choice, not a rule. I mean look . . ." Susan pointed through the door to the front room. "Sexy witch, sexy car mechanic, sexy sentient tree, sexy crayon, sexy mobile phone . . . sexy tin of beans. But the boys . . . gross zombie, gross swamp monster, gross monk, gross rugby player . . ."

"Hey!" The boy whom Susan had none-too-subtly pointed out last took offense. "I've just come from the rugby social. I'm not in costume."

"Even more horrific." Susan shooed him off.

"What about that hunk over there? Looks like a pretty sexy nurse to me . . ."

"That's just someone in scrubs. All the nurses look like that."

"I'm clearly doing the wrong course," Esther said, fanning herself and giving the male nurse a little more attention.

"My point is: Why are the men fully clothed and the women in their underwear?" When Susan failed to get any response from Esther, she turned to Daisy. "You're with me on this, right?"

"Umm . . ." Daisy's attention was bouncing around the room like a pinball. "Many bras. So objectionable. Much patriarchy."

"Daisy!"

"Sorry, Susan. Maybe it's just that men aren't as nice to look at, whatever they're wearing?"

The smile Susan bestowed upon her was both indulgent and knowing, and Daisy blushed beneath her face paint.

As Esther made a beeline for the press of rhythmically flailing bodies in the front room, where the music was loudest, Susan gave Daisy a subtle nod toward the back of the house.

"Everyone knows the cool kids hang out in the kitchen."

"Cool kids?"

"Us, Daisy." She gave Daisy a gentle pat on the arm and steered her farther down the hall.

The dance floor was crammed with chisel-chested boys and loose-limbed girls writhing and whooping to the music.

"ESTHER!" someone screamed, and she found herself facing a big grin beneath a black headscarf, eye mask, and penciled-on mustache.

"NOOR!"

The two embraced like long-lost sisters rather than two casual acquaintances who had spent no more time together than the length of an ill-fated Harry Potter quiz. Within seconds, they were joined by Grace—dressed as a ghost in a faded old T-shirt and bleached-out jeans—and there ensued a flurry of compliments as each commented on the others' outfits.

"Less talking, more dancing!" Grace yelled at the two of them, and Noor bowed. "As you wish . . ."

Halfway through the song, Grace waved them closer, pulling them in for a series of selfies.

"Which one shall I post?" She scrolled through them, Noor and Esther looking on, pointing out minor flaws in their own pictures and telling one another how amazing they looked.

"Stop, wait, go back . . ." Esther grabbed Grace's phone and peered at the screen. In the last picture, just over Noor's shoulder, she could see a familiar black bob streaked with white, the owner casting a disinterested look across the people on the dance floor from under her bangs as she sipped some punch.

"It's her!" Esther whispered reverently, whipping to look over her shoulder in case Goth Girl was still there.

"Who?" Noor asked.

Esther zoomed in as best she could.

"Oh. Her." Noor's expression soured a touch. "Yeah . . . she does English, too."

"She does?" Esther seized her by the shoulders. "Why did I not know this?"

"Well, it's not like I've seen you at that many lectures . . ."

"What's her name?"

"I don't know! She doesn't really talk to anyone."

"Grace!" Esther turned to show her the screen, but Grace wasn't paying any attention.

The big hit of the summer was playing, poppy and peppy, something Esther could dance to at a nightclub but only permit herself to enjoy ironically. A few girls leaped onto the sofa in a coordinated move, and people surged into the middle of the room, arms aloft and voices loud, reliving a younger, simpler life that they'd had only months before.

But not Grace. The verve with which she'd hauled them onto the dance floor had faded away, replaced by an appropriately ghostlike melancholy as she stared into some distant memory, eyes misting over.

Esther touched her friend's arm. "Grace? Are you OK?"

"This song reminds me of Tony." Grace didn't seem to be talking to Esther at all until she said, "Actually, I need the loo. See you in a bit."

As Grace slipped through the crowd, Esther and Noor exchanged a glance.

"What was all that about?" Esther asked.

"Tony, I guess." Noor reached into a nearby bowl and picked up a supply of strawberry laces; then with a sigh, she said, "Same old. They're long distance, and yours truly is long-suffering." She gave Esther a rueful smile and nodded after Grace. "I'd better go make sure she's OK. You all right on your own?"

Esther nodded fervently. She wouldn't be on her own for long. Noor had said that Mystery Goth didn't talk to anyone, but that was only because she'd yet to meet Esther de Groot, mistress of the eldritch and yet-to-be bestie.

Contrary to all expectations, Daisy was having an *excellent* time. Everywhere she looked, she came face-to-familiar-face with someone she knew. After waving hello to a couple of people she'd met yesterday at the Origami Soc, she'd bumped into one of the more affable Ladies Who Brunch, been briefly swallowed up by some pool players who wanted to know her "secret," and when she'd passed the Doritos to a sexy ghoul, the ghoul nodded at Daisy from under her hood and said, "Zoise thanks you, Sister."

Finally settling in a far corner of the kitchen with a couple of people from her course—Reggie with the cool T-shirts and Nikki, whose Boudicca costume had started an excellent conversation about the Celts, druids, and ritual sacrifice—Daisy felt as if she'd finally blossomed. Her jokes were funnier, her conversation wittier, and even though she had long since lost sight of Susan, she felt that maybe she wasn't just Halloween party material on the outside but on the inside, too.

Out in the relative safety of the stairwell, Susan could see through to the front room, where Esther was tossing her hair at a group of generic boys, and out to the kitchen, where Daisy was perched on the counter with a couple of people who'd come out for her birthday the other week. She'd shoved a set of fangs under her top lip to do impressions of someone, and the three of them were in hysterics.

Her two charges making their merry way in the world, forging new friendships all on their own.

Leaning back against the wall, Susan lifted her freshly cracked can of dark ale to her lips. A taste of home, memories of sitting in the pub after a shift.

It didn't taste great.

Yet again, her attention wandered back to Daisy, to Esther.

So much for a J-block night out.

Before Susan could take another sip of tepid misery, someone crashed into her from the side, sending the can flying. Whipping around, ready to unleash her ever-present anger, Susan came face-to-face with the sexy sentient tree, whose branch had thwapped her in the back. For several seconds, there was a standoff, and then . . .

"Oh, my god, I'm so sorry—"

"No, totally not your fault. Your branch—"

"Here, look, have my rum and Coke."

"No, no, that's fine . . ."

"I insist!" Then came the comment, "I'm so sorry about this stupid outfit. I mean, who the hell thinks trees are sexy?"

Susan's pupils turned into little hearts. "I KNOW!"

Eventually, Daisy had to make a break for the loo. Small talk seemed to require a lot of sipping of one's drink, and Daisy had drained four cups of lemonade already. Following the makeshift sign that said BOGS THIS WAY, Daisy slipped out through the back of the kitchen, past a washing machine, and ducked down under the fake cobwebs someone had strewn across the light fixtures to a door marked THE BOGS, whose handle didn't turn when she tried.

Dancing a little dance of desperation, Daisy counted to fifty before reaching out to knock.

"Um . . . hi, sorry, I just want to check if you're going to be long? Which would be fine! But I'll go and find—"

The lock clicked, and the door opened.

"Free now," murmured the girl who emerged. Her eyes

were down, but Daisy instantly recognized Grace. Everything about her was drained and drooping, and for a moment, Daisy fancied that she really was looking at a ghost.

"Grace? Susan introduced us at breakfast the other week . . . Is everything all right?"

"Uh-huh. Yup. Fine." But her phone was clutched tightly in her hand, and she sounded as if she'd been crying. No matter how desperate Daisy was for the loo, the thought of leaving Grace feeling that her misery had gone unnoticed was too much.

"I know we're not friends—"

"None of us are." Her words weren't spoken sharply but murmured fast and low. She looked up at Daisy then, her smile sad and crooked. "I don't mean to be snappy. I'm just not in a party mood tonight."

"That's OK. You don't have to be."

"It's the only way I know how to get through." Grace's ghostly visage ducked and bobbed in Daisy's vision as Daisy danced the Dance of the Desperate Bladder. "Toilet's free. Go pee."

It didn't matter how quick she was. When Daisy emerged once more, Grace had disappeared.

Susan and the sentient tree had been joined by a Hobbit. Apparently there'd been a whole fellowship thing going on, but they'd lost the others. Susan, the tree, and the Hobbit found this hilarious and had been giggling about the Mines of Moria and how treacherous Boromir was.

"I mean, he's gone off with someone dressed as Aslan, and, y'know?" The Hobbit was aggrieved. "That's just *not on*—mixing the magic like that. Something bad will happen."

"Tolkien and Lewis were friends, though . . ." Susan was losing the thread of her thoughts—she'd had a *lot* of rum and Coke. "So that makes it all OK. I'm sure. Boromir can get it on with Aslan, and everyone's happy."

"What is it you're dressed as, anyway?" the tree asked. "Davy Croquet?"

"That's not right." The Hobbit wagged a finger. "It's Davy Croquette. Like the little potatoes."

"I'll give you a clue . . ." Susan set her trapper hat straight and reached out to pluck a weapon from the hands of an axe-wielding murderer, which she then swung about, miming chopping wood.

"A LUMBERJACK!" Susan's companions bellowed in unison.

"A *sexy* lumberjack!" Susan corrected, unbuttoning her shirt to an almost indecent level, the other two girls cheering and smashing their plastic cups together to shower themselves in a fountain of Coke.

"No, no, no, no, no . . ." The Hobbit slung an arm around Susan, eyes a little fuzzy, speech a little slurred. "Now, *that's* a sexy lumberjack."

Susan followed her finger and tried to focus on the person at whom the Hobbit was pointing. Big workmanlike boots. Pale blue jeans, scuffed, and a fitted checked shirt, the sleeves rolled up to expose a pair of strong forearms. A woolen hat, the rim turned up.

It was the beard. That's what tricked Susan into what she said next.

"Yup. That's a sexy lumberjack, all right."

And then, with the kind of horror that washes in a second after one has done something unimaginably regrettable, Susan realized who it was.

On any other night, Esther could have asked a group of students if they'd seen someone who looked like a fairy in mourning, and they'd have known exactly who she meant.

Tonight, however, that description was getting her exactly nowhere.

Esther stopped by the drinks table just as "Like a Prayer" came on, and a murmur of nuns got overexcited, forming a circle around someone who'd come dressed as Madonna. There was no way of crossing the dance floor now—she'd just have to wait.

"Lads, lads, lads!" A giant in a rugby shirt and token devil horns standing next to Esther slapped a nearby boy on the back with a hand the size of a Frisbee. "I know who she is!"

Esther wasn't sure how he knew whom she was looking for, given that she'd not actually asked him . . . until she realized he wasn't talking about Goth Girl. He was pointing a giant sausage finger right at Esther.

"It's *you*! Off that website! Shaggable number 3—quick!" He reached into the crowd of dancing nuns and pulled out a set of rosaries, beads bouncing across the floor from where the string had snapped. "I've got a crucifix—let's tame the beast . . ."

He lunged forward, aiming the cross at Esther's left breast as if to brand her.

But weeks of an afternoon Boxercise class hadn't left her defenseless. A step to the side, and he missed, the momentum sending him crashing face-first into the drinks table. Cries of outrage and groans of disappointment erupted from the dancing nuns and nearby drinkers.

Almost immediately, his friends—a groom whose heart had been ripped from his chest and a barista with a coffee cup that read *[You're name hear]*—closed ranks.

"I'm so sorry about him," the barista said.

"Keeps his brain cells in his bollocks, that one," the groom added.

"What, all two of them?" Esther said, turning her back on where their friend was floundering in a puddle of punch.

The boys turned with her, arms crossed, heads shaking, identical frowns of disapproval.

"Sexist brute."

"Toxic masculinity."

"Product of an institutionally sexist society."

"Dismantle the patriarchy."

"Down with men."

"Oh, I don't know . . ." Esther fanned her face with one hand, flustered by all the feminism and appraising her companions. Uninspired outfits, tidy haircuts. Exactly to her taste. "Some men are all right."

"We're all dogs, love." The barista reached out to rest a hand on her shoulder, stopping an inch short. "Sorry, is it OK if I touch your shoulder?"

Too used to having to swat off unwanted paws, her deeply ingrained Britishness had her rewarding such good manners with an automatic nod of consent.

On her other side, the groom cleared his throat and handed Esther a fresh drink. "Amends?"

"Thanks, but I'm actually looking for someone." Esther waved the drink away. "Short girl, black hair, really cool . . ."

It was a frustratingly vague description, but the barista was nodding along, eyes flickering between Esther and the groom next to her. "Yeah. I think I know who you mean—saw her go upstairs a few minutes ago."

"Oh. Yes." The groom joined in. "Why don't we help you look for her?" He pushed the drink into Esther's hand once more. "You can bring your drink."

Daisy had been scanning the crowd for Grace when she saw Esther emerge from the front room and head upstairs with a couple of boys.

Which seemed odd. Boys often flocked like moths to Esther's beautiful moon-face, but Daisy had never seen her do anything more than make suggestive eye contact and shimmy provocatively in their direction. She never actually *engaged* with any of them.

(Except that one time—which all of them, Esther included, had put down to an extreme lapse of judgment due to emotional trauma.)

What if Esther was emotionally traumatized *now*?

As Daisy fretted, she saw the two boys high-five each other behind Esther's bodiced back.

That didn't seem right, but Daisy felt woefully out of her depth. There should be something on the national curriculum that dealt with these situations, with convenient multiple-choice options. Socializing had rules, but they weren't ones Daisy understood.

A fleeting glimpse of a checked shirt through the crowd presented Daisy with the solution: Ask Susan. She knew *everything*.

It was even harder to move through the house than it had been earlier, but eventually Daisy reached the point where Susan had been. Only she wasn't there. Glancing up the stairs, toward where Esther had disappeared, Daisy caught sight of the familiar red check halfway up in the shadows.

"Excuse me . . . sorry . . . oof . . . my face got in the way of your elbow there . . . please could I . . . ?"

But by the time Daisy had squashed past all the people sitting on the steps, she discovered this wasn't the lumberjack she was looking for.

"Daisy!" McGraw looked pleased to see her. "You're here. I just saw—"

"No, not you!" Daisy cut him off.

McGraw's face fell, but it was herself that Daisy was cross with—*of course* this wasn't Susan! His height had been obscured by the branches of a sexy sentient tree.

"Sorry, McGraw, you're a perfectly lovely lumberjack, but I was looking for Susan . . ."

"You mean the awesome little feminist with the ridiculous hat?" asked the tree. An unlikely but accurate description. "She kind of bolted that way . . ." The tree extended a branch down the stairs toward the front door, the opposite direction to Esther.

They'd made their way upstairs, and although Esther had registered some vaguely familiar faces (had that been McGraw behind that beard?), none of them had been the one she sought. It wasn't a big house, or a long climb, but for some reason, Esther's limbs felt loose and rubbery, and she kept stumbling into her companions.

"I think this is the room . . ." The groom, who'd introduced himself as Eric, knocked on the door as he pushed it open.

First glance was promising—there were novelty candles dotted about on the shelves and bookcase and windowsill, and a pentagram was scrawled on a bedsheet on the floor—but when Esther looked a little closer, the rest of the room didn't match the details. The bed was rumpled and unmade, the duvet was half out of its candy-striped cover and on the floor, next to an assortment of lads' mags, inside-out jeans, balled socks, and boxer shorts. The posters on the walls weren't of brooding bands but of busty ladies glistening in swimwear, and there was a huge *Take Me to Your Dealer* poster tacked to the back of the door that the barista—Nick—had just pushed shut.

Eric the groom had said this was the room, but for what?

For all Esther could absorb information, she couldn't quite decipher what any of it *meant*, thoughts incapable of pushing through the cotton wool that clouded her brain. Esther looked down at her cup and frowned. She'd been alternating punch with lemonade, and she was certain she'd not had much of either.

"Oh, my god! Look! A Ouija board!" The words that came out of Barista Nick's mouth were as scripted as the stage was set, and his friend was lighting all the candles as if he owned the place.

No matter what state she was in, Esther was always up for a Ouija board, and she flung her arms up enthusiastically, spilling whatever was left in her cup as she cheered, "Dead things love me!"

"I've never done one of these before . . ." Barista Nick had set his grammatically incorrect cup on the shelves and was gently holding Esther by the shoulders, helping her down to rest with her back against the bookcase.

"Don't worry. You shtick . . ." The slurred words caught Esther by surprise. "*Stick* with mmme."

Her tongue was Velcro, the words so fuzzy, they kept getting stuck.

"Even the dead are frightened of . . . Living Dead!" She nearly knocked over a candle as she swung her arms forward and swayed like a zombie, before remembering she was dressed as a vampire.

Eric the groom took a seat on her other side and pulled the board closer. They should really be sitting in a ring, but Esther lacked the wherewithal to explain, simply falling forward to rest her fingers on the glass set in the middle of the board. The gothic-script letters swam around the edge of her vision.

"I'll keep you safe." Barista Nick had his arm over Esther's shoulders.

"*We'll* keep you safe." Another arm draped across her.

"Spirits . . ." Esther mumbled.

"I've got some vodka . . ."

". . . of the other world!" Esther forced out, her eyelids heavy. "Hear our . . ."

Her trance was so intense that her head flopped to the side to rest on Eric the groom's shoulder before a noxious burst of his cologne revived her.

"Hear our calls."

The glass swept quickly across the board, which was odd, because they hadn't asked it any questions yet.

"Oh, my god!" Barista Nick gasped. "It's saying it's angry!"

"Wha . . . ?" The letters were coming too fast for Esther to read.

"Why are you angry, spirits? What have we done to upset you?" Eric the groom asked, the glass completely out of Esther's control.

"It says your corset reminds him of the one his wife wore when she . . ." Barista Nick gasped, eyes wide with horror. "When *she murdered him*."

"Quick, take it off!" Eric the groom reached across for the knot at the top of Esther's bodice.

"What? No!" Esther tried to move away, but with Barista Nick on top of her, it was hard to move. "I didn't see that . . . Spirit, show yourself!"

The glass remained at rest for a second, and in that briefest of pauses, there was a faint, unmistakable knock.

Rap-rap.

Barista Nick and Eric the groom exchanged a glance across Esther. All three of them had one hand on the Ouija board. Barista Nick's other arm was around Esther, and Eric the groom's left hand was in plain view, still reaching hopefully toward Esther's corset.

"Spirit?" Esther said in surprise.

Rap-rap-rap.

And then a disembodied voice, quiet and muffled.

"I'm looking for Esther de Groot? Is she there?"

The scream from behind the door was bloodcurdling in its enthusiasm.

"I'M HERE, SPIRITS OF THE OTHER WORLD! COME IN!"

Daisy tried the handle and opened the door. There was a lot of information to process in the tableau presented inside. A Ouija board, candles . . . an enraptured Esther, and two boys whose expressions were slowly climbing their way from terror into shame.

"Who are you?" one of the boys said, aiming for aggressive and coming off sulky.

"Daisy!" Esther leaped up, trampling over the Ouija board to fall forward into Daisy's arms. "The spirits, they spoke to me!"

"They did?" Daisy battled an excess of limbs. Esther's eyes were wide, and she seemed incapable of standing. "What did they say?"

Confusion clouded Esther's face. "They told me to take off my corset . . ."

"Did they now?" Daisy gave the boys a long, wary look over Esther's shoulder. "Sounds to me like those spirits were"—Daisy lowered her voice to a whisper—"*perverts.*"

The two boys shrank away a little, shuffling awkwardly about and making as if to tidy away the board.

"I'm feeling sleepy," Esther said, drooping farther and nuzzling in closer. "You smell like pine cones and vanilla, Daisy."

"I think that's the novelty candles," Daisy said, steering Esther out of the room without a backward glance. "Let's find Susan and go home."

Susan was smoking a cigarette in the front garden. Her last one. God*damn* McGraw, tricking her with a sketchily drawn-on beard . . .

She was drunk. That was all. Drunk makes you stupid.

Goddamn that sexy sentient tree and her willingness to share her drink . . .

But it wasn't the tree's fault. It was Susan's. She should have stayed close to her friends.

What happened to her plans for a J-block night out? Wasn't that why she'd come to this stupid party in the first place? Not to make new friends she didn't need, but to cement memories with the ones she already had. The ones who *mattered*.

There was a burst of noise from behind her as someone pushed open the front door.

"Woo-oo, I'm boneless. Flippy, floppy vampire . . ."

Susan whipped around at the sound of Esther's voice.

Something had happened to her. It was like watching Daisy wrestle a giant jellyfish down the front steps.

They tripped the motion sensor for the security light, and Esther flung her arms up. "Sunlight! It burns!"

"It's eleven o'clock at night—you're fine," Susan said, flicking her unfinished cigarette over the fence and hurrying toward her friends. She registered the relief in Daisy's face as she slipped under Esther's other arm to help.

"I'm not sure if someone didn't spike her drink . . ." Daisy said.

"You think?!"

Esther passed out at the end of the road, and they resorted to carrying her like a sack of potatoes. Her enormous boots made her at least twice her natural weight, and Susan would have taken them off if she'd been able to work out how they unbuckled. As it was, she had the heel of one biting into her hip with every other step.

"I found her in a room with two boys and a Ouija board."

"Of course you did." Susan narrowed her eyes. "Tell me what they looked like, and I'll exact some appropriate revenge."

"Are you going to publicly shame them in a zine like you did with McGraw?"

Susan had forgotten about that little episode.

"I've wound the zine up, Daisy. Wielding the might of the media was too great a strain. There are other ways to make scoundrels pay." Like making them believe their house really *was* haunted by an awakened and vengeful spirit . . .

They struggled on a few more paces before they came to

a bench where they could lay Esther down gently and have a bit of a breather. Through the heavy breathing and gentle sweating, Susan closed her eyes and thought of McGraw. She shouldn't have let his presence at the party unsettle her like that. Maybe if she'd stayed inside the house, she'd have seen what Esther was doing, been able to stop her before she'd gone into those sleazy lads' bedroom.

Susan looked across at where Daisy was standing, hands on hips, head tipped back to study the sky. There were times when Susan wondered whether she underestimated how capable Daisy really was . . .

"Do you think maybe those boys really were just trying to get some help with their Ouija board?" Daisy asked.

Esther woke after midday. There was a little care package of foodstuffs and drinks with a note from Daisy at the foot of her bed, and she delicately picked the lot up and returned to bed. Gazing out her window, Esther watched some people kicking about in the leaves that had gathered in the corners of the buildings and thought of all the times she'd grumbled at being forced to help her parents clear leaves in the garden. Squabbles that turned into rows and door slamming and hours spent muttering how she couldn't wait to move out.

She never thought she'd be sitting here at university dreaming of moving back.

"Hello?"

"Dad. It's me."

"Sorry, who's this?"

"Er . . . the only person who calls you 'dad'???" Esther shot the phone a disgusted look.

"Might be a wrong number."

"It's not a wrong number. It's your daughter." Then, even though she was the only child they had, she added, "Esther."

"I know your name."

"Well, apparently you don't know my voice."

"Maybe because it's been so long since I've heard it." But the tone Esther's dad used was gentle, and Esther—puffed up and ready to be difficult—held back. "How've you been, love? Tell me all about it."

No mention of The Boy. No mention of the fact that her parents had been right. Just straightforward parental interest.

"I'm fine."

Esther's dad left a pause long enough for Esther to elaborate before he prompted, "Have you been going to all your lectures?"

"Uh-huh."

"Finding them interesting?"

"Yup."

"Anything you want to talk about?"

Esther frowned down at the foot she'd propped on the windowsill and picked at a loose thread on the seam of her sock. "Not really."

It wasn't like she was going to tell her dad anything about the random she'd gotten together with, or her photo appearing on that website, or what had happened with the

Ouija boys. All of a sudden, Esther wasn't so sure that she really *had* wanted to ring home.

"Well. I'm pleased your mother and I found the money to send our only child away to . . . what was it? 'Reach her full potential not only as a unit of productivity in the capitalist society but as a soul in need of sustenance.' Because you sound positively overwhelmed with excitement about it."

"My generation isn't supposed to be good on the phone. I'm the living embodiment of society's expectations."

When her father next spoke, Esther could hear the smile all the way down the line. "Now, there's the precocious little sulk bag I know and love. I was getting worried for a moment there."

Esther nodded. "Me, too, Dad."

"Love, I know I already asked this, but . . . are you really going to your lectures?" When Esther didn't respond, her dad went on, "It's just, I remember what is was like—those first few weeks—which I know seems improbable, because I'm so old, et cetera, et cetera, but . . . so much is changing for you at the moment, with moving away and . . . everything, that sometimes having a little routine really does help."

"Thanks, Dad," Esther whispered, then held her breath for a second so that her dad wouldn't know she was crying. "I think focusing on my courses might be a really good idea right about now."

Besides, hadn't Noor said that Goth Girl did English, too?

Daisy was just heading out to her first Stand-up Comedy Club social when an anguished cry stopped her in her tracks. Susan was out buying milk—when Daisy had offered her soy milk as a substitute, Susan had narrowed her eyes and hissed—but Esther was in.

"Hello?" Daisy knocked on the door and pushed it open to find Esther lying prostrate on the floor next to her open laptop.

"Help me," Esther said, words muffled by the rug as she waved a hand at her computer.

Crouching down, Daisy saw the familiar university crest in the corner of the screen. Not daring to believe it, Daisy whispered, "Esther . . . are you trying to work out which lectures to go to?"

"I don't even know what modules I'm doing . . ." Esther rolled over to click through the multiple tabs she had open on her browser. "There's so many ways to study books. Who knew?"

"Didn't you look through any of this before you applied?"

"Was I supposed to?"

"Yes." Daisy dipped her head to give Esther a very stern look, but she took enough pity on her to check her watch before lifting the laptop onto her knee and reading through the information. She could miss the first five minutes of her social if she had to. Setting Esther on the correct academic path was much more important than having fun.

"These are for second and third years, and these are only for the next two semesters. You can worry about those later . . ." She doubted Esther had the capacity for worrying about more than one semester's worth of work. She handed the computer back to Esther and clicked on the first page.

"These are the options for this term. I ran a keyword search in your e-mails, and apparently you're signed on for Biblical Studies and Creative Writing. Have you really not been to any of the lectures or seminars yet?"

"Er . . . some of them. I think." Esther brightened a little. "Does listening in the bar to other English students grumbling about how everyone in *Titus Andronicus* gets stabbed count?"

"No, it does not!" Daisy stood to grab a pad and pen from Esther's desk. "Let's make a timetable. I'll read, you write."

"Technically, this degree is about doing both."

Esther met Daisy's eyes and gave her a small yet resolute smile.

5

COMMUNITY-MINDED

Some days, Susan almost liked Sheffield, with its vast parks and tree-lined roads, resplendent in their autumnal livery. She liked the homeliness of the houses and the overabundance of pubs and kebab shops frequented by people who didn't look quite as haunted and grim as the ones she was used to seeing back home.

And then there were other days. Like this one.

Susan had never experienced rain that was so persistently *wet*. Curtains of water fell in swaths from great, moody clouds, lashing at her cheeks and chest and thighs as she battled her way down the road, fingertips shriveling in the dank depths of her pockets, the material now soaked too stiff to get them out. It was like walking in clothes made of cardboard.

She had stubbornly walked past the bus stop, pitying those who waited, crammed under the shelter, knowing that even a long walk in torrential rain was preferable to gently steaming among strangers, breathing in the mustiness of over-warm, overcrowded public transport. Besides, with a bus, there was always the risk of running into McGraw.

By the time she reached Catterick Hall, she was too wet to bother going up to her room and made straight for the nearest showers. Shivering and miserable, Susan unearthed her phone from the waterproof pouch in her backpack and dialed Esther. Esther might have developed a new academic zeal over the last couple of days, but she was still an English student. It's not like they had many lectures.

"Hello. I'm very wet. Please send help in the form of a thousand towels, delivered to the ground-floor showers."

It was amazing how effective the promise of gossiping through the shower curtain could be. Esther couldn't have been faster if she'd parachuted directly down the stairwell.

"So, where've you been to get so wet?" Esther asked.

"Outside. In the rain." Susan pressed her fingers so hard into her scalp as she lathered up that it felt as if she were cleaning her brain.

"Yes but *why?*"

Susan twisted the hot tap up another notch, wondering whether she would ever feel warm again. "I've been feeding my CAS patient's neighbor's cat."

"What's a gas patient?"

"CAS—Community Attachment Scheme. Me and this single-purpose tool called Milo have been assigned to an outpatient called Mrs. Doherty. She's pregnant. We have to interview her to find out what it's like being a patient, rather than just reading about it in a book."

"Sounds like your version of hell."

It was. "Yeah, well, patients are kind of a thing if you want to learn how to treat them."

"So why are you feeding her cat?"

"The cat next door—cat feces are bad for Mrs. Doherty's unborn child." It was an unorthodox arrangement.

"Aw, Susan, you're so community-minded."

Feeling had returned with a vengeance to her toes, and Susan was ready to get out. Turning the tap off, she held an arm out beyond the curtain. "Towel, please." The one Esther handed over was thick and warm and smelled of expensive fabric softener. Not one of Susan's, which were all ratty and thin and never quite dry.

"Actually I'm getting paid twenty-five pounds a day." Susan ruffled her hair and thought about apportioning some of the profit to purchasing a set of new towels.

"And just like that it became seedy."

"What? I'm feeding an overly affectionate cat called Tibbles for three days. I've stooped lower." Susan cocooned herself in the towel. "Besides, seventy-five pounds is exactly the right amount for a new winter coat."

Almost the second she said it, Susan shut her eyes in regret. There was the squeal of the shower curtain being flung aside, and when she opened her eyes, there stood Esther, starry-eyed and breathless with euphoria.

"SHOPPING TRIP!"

There was a missed call from Esther on Daisy's phone. At the time it came in, she'd been sprinting as fast as she could through the Botanical Gardens, away from a shattered pane of the Glass Pavilion, and answering her phone hadn't been a priority.

Anarchic Croquet was a much more extreme sport than she'd been expecting.

Regrouping at the rendezvous point, shoulders bristling with an assortment of "mallets" (baseball bats, hammers, a golfing umbrella, and a plastic flamingo), Daisy wondered about asking what would happen if they'd been caught on security camera, but someone bellowed out "Nachoooos!" and the group moved off toward a nearby pub.

Daisy dithered. She did that a lot these days—not that the word *days* really meant anything to her. Every waking hour—and some of the ones she usually reserved for sleeping—was taken up attending all the clubs and socs and groups she'd joined. What had started as a manageable trickle had turned into a deluge of commitments, her phone screen flashing like a social stock exchange.

She could be halfway through a conversation with someone over a cup of tea and her phone would beep to inform her that she should be on the other side of the city attending drinks with the Circus Soc, or that she was supposed to be drawing up a petition for the Campaign in the Arse Association. There were times when such commitments overlapped, and Daisy found herself walking one way, then doubling back, over and over, caught in a frenzy of indecision and obligation, until her phone beeped again with a message asking where she was.

In what could have been three days or thirty, it felt as if she'd gone from being entirely anonymous to almost universally recognized. The Halloween party had been but the tip of an iceberg large enough to sink the *Titanic*. People kept giving her those little chin-nods of acknowledgment as she passed them on the street, and her phone was crammed with messages from unknown numbers as part of the various group chats she'd been assimilated into.

This was the university dream, wasn't it? Drinks every night and a friend in every corridor.

Only that wasn't quite how it felt. Like Jonathan Tremain, Daisy spent most of her time calling people by the wrong name. And shouldn't she know more about all these new friends than the fact that *Adaptation* was so-and-so's favorite Nicolas Cage film or that girl had singed her eyebrows after trying to juggle with fire? She'd had the same conversation about the best cartoon theme tunes so many times that her nightmares were haunted by out-of-tune renditions of the theme song for *DuckTales*. Daisy felt overloaded with so much inconsequential information that at times she struggled to remember anything significant about herself.

She was floating in a sea of newfound friends, untethered from anything or anyone of significance.

Daisy looked down at the phone in her hand. Something about a missed call . . .

But then two overdue reminders blooped up in quick succession.

Assassins Association said the first—there was a time and a place listed with it.

The second simply said: *shopping.*

As she stared at the word, she felt a dim pang of longing for a half-remembered life, and faces of people she actually wanted to see swam before her eyes . . . but then her phone buzzed with a message on yet another of her groups, reminding her there was somewhere else she needed to be. Esther's missed call and the reminder Daisy had set for their shopping trip was swallowed up by the behemoth of obligations eating Daisy Wooton alive.

The card issued by the National Union of Students promised a world of discounts, from 10 percent on clothes purchased at Forever 21 to 25 percent off cinema tickets and probably some other things in which Esther had no interest. She was crooning over hers, stroking the passport-booth photo of her own face.

"You have a problem," Susan said, giving her a disgusted look and edging a little farther away from where Esther was sitting on the lip of the water feature outside Sheffield town hall.

"Says the woman incapable of quitting smoking."

"Don't go there unless you want me to go home and order myself a coat online without your input."

"No!" Esther flung herself across Susan's lap as if she really had been about to leave. "I bow down to your superior willpower. All hail Susan, queen of iron."

"Off!" Susan waved her away and checked the time on her phone. "I don't think Daisy's coming."

Not that Susan blamed her. If she'd had even a shred of confidence in Esther's judgment, she'd have handed over her measurements and tasked Esther to buy her a coat while she applied her 10 percent student discount to something more enjoyable. Like bulk buying a load of tampons.

"But I put a Post-it Note on her door . . ."

". . . and did you try sending one via pigeon post? Baby Gordon's a bit young for that." But Esther had that slightly wounded air about her, to which Susan was gradually growing sensitive. She laid a hand on Esther's shoulder and gave it a squeeze. "Come on, let's go get me a parka so I can pretend I'm proper Northern while you spam Daisy's messages with pictures of all the ridiculous outfits you can't afford to buy."

The Assassins Association wasn't for her, Daisy decided as she slithered through a cubicle window and swung onto the drainpipe next to it. She was a lover, not a fighter. A healer, not a hit man. When they'd put a hood over her head and asked her to swear fealty to the Mercenary Code, she'd pretended to be desperate for the toilet, and now here she was, shimmying down three stories' worth of drainpipe, unable to check any of the messages she could feel buzzing through to her phone.

If she hadn't been so averse to killing people, Daisy suspected she might have made a very resourceful assassin.

They'd found an Army Surplus store. Even the fact that it didn't offer a student discount hadn't deterred Esther from purchasing half the stock. Struggling back to their hall, she was weighed down with bags stuffed with a rifleman's jacket, desert boots, and weird strapping and belts and holsters with which she'd said she would modify some of the more tired items in her substantial wardrobe.

Susan was wearing a grotty arctic jacket and carrying a

single expensively branded bag containing towels so luxuriously thick that they could have doubled as a mattress.

"Can't you at least give me a hand?" Esther said, dropping her bags for a moment and staring at her bloodless fingers while they waited for the traffic light to change.

"No. I said I wouldn't help you back in the shop, and I am a woman of my word—"

But Susan's sanctimonious sentence was cut short when Esther body-slammed her into a bush. As Susan fell awkwardly, protecting her towels while spitting and cursing, Esther peered out between autumn-sparse fronds at something up ahead.

"There she is . . ."

"Who?" Susan hated whoever she was without even having set eyes on her.

"The Goth Girl," Esther breathed, her whole face as reverent as if she'd seen a dark angel. "Look at her."

"Thought I already was." Susan shot a wry look in Esther's direction before following her gaze.

She knew who Esther meant the second she saw her. Shorter even than Susan but delicate, like a twiggy little doll. The enormous headphones that rested around her neck looked especially out of proportion on someone that petite. She was walking with a group of smiling girls, all of whom chattered brightly while Goth Girl's face remained impassive, a marble statue amid a flock of starlings. She had a permafrost expression and a pinched, pretty little mouth pursed in a perfect purple cupid's bow.

"Why are we hiding from someone you want to be friends with?" Susan asked, starting to stand up. "We could just go and talk to her."

"One does not simply approach a dark goddess!" Esther hissed, yanking Susan back into the bush. "Not looking like this."

Susan cast a critical eye over Esther in an attempt to see what was wrong, but she looked as effortlessly chic as Susan did disheveled. It was like seeing a single beautiful bloom shying away from the sunlight.

"You look perfectly glorious. As always."

"To you . . ." Esther said dismissively.

Smothering a twinge of hurt, Susan waited until Esther's quarry was farther away before emerging from the foliage. Not bothering to say anything, she trudged toward Catterick Hall, regretting she'd ever mentioned that she needed a coat.

Daisy's door was open when they got back to their corridor, but she wasn't there. Half an hour after Esther had forced her purchases into spaces they were not designed to occupy, she checked Daisy's room again. Gently swirling golden light from a glitter lamp bathed the room in honey, the radio, turned low, played soothing world music, but there was still no sign of Daisy.

Esther took one look at the scene and went to find Susan.

"I'm worried about Daisy."

"When are you not?" Susan was lying on her bed beating her laptop at chess and didn't bother looking up.

"I'm serious. She doesn't have any lectures this late, and her door's been open since we got back."

Susan shoved her laptop aside and sat up in alarm, slapping an overly dramatic hand to her face. "Oh, my gosh! Do you think she's been abducted by aliens?"

But Esther wasn't playing. "I think we should check the showers in case she's fainted and cracked her skull open."

"A vivid and disturbing image." Susan dropped the act and stood up. "One that I now can't get out of my head."

Although there were showers on their floor, one had a broken shower head, another's thermostat couldn't be coaxed above room temperature, and Daisy swore that the third was haunted, so it was to the floor below that Esther and Susan hurried, their pace getting quicker with every step, so that they were sprinting by the time the door was in sight.

Steam rose from behind the first shower curtain.

"Daisy! Is that you?" Esther prodded at the curtain.

"Do you mind?" A girl's head emerged from behind the curtain, shortly followed by a boy's. "Some of us are trying to get clean here."

"You say that . . ." Esther hurried past before nudging Susan and whispering, "Looked more like they were getting dirty to me."

There was no one in the second shower, but the curtain was drawn across the third—although there was no sign that the shower was on.

"At least there's no blood," Esther murmured, glancing at Susan before she raised her voice. "Daisy? Are you in there?"

A groaning kind of sigh sounded from behind the curtain, and the girls looked at each other in horror.

"Pleasedon'tbenakedpleasedon'tbenaked . . ." Susan yanked the curtain aside.

There, still in her bathrobe, slumped against the wall, her forehead resting on the taps, was Daisy. And she was sound asleep.

Once Daisy was showered and dried and clothed in the outfit she'd laid on her bed before she'd gone down for a shower, she accepted a mug of cocoa from Susan and sat at the kitchen table.

"It's six o'clock on a Tuesday, Daisy," Esther said. "You really should *not* be this tired."

"Unless you're an insomniac." Susan pointed both thumbs at herself, then gave Daisy a doubtful look. "Which you're not—are you?"

"I don't think so." Daisy blew across the top of her drink, watching the ripples. "I've just been a bit busy."

"Doing what? Digging trenches and carbon-dating human remains?" Susan asked.

"Ooh, or you've uncovered some kind of cursed medallion that possesses you during the night, so that you wake more exhausted than when you went to bed, dirt under your fingernails and a taste for blood . . ." Esther stopped talking when she realized how the other two were looking at her. "What? Like you weren't thinking that, too."

"I definitely wasn't," Susan said.

"Nor me." Daisy studied her fingernails. "Although it's

good to know what signs I should watch out for. No, I'm actually a bit behind on my course."

"What?" Susan was aghast. "I mean, I expect this from Esther—"

"Hey!"

"—but *you*? Daisy Wooton, I would never have you down as a slacker."

"I'm not usually." Tracing the pattern on the side of her mug, she reluctantly met Susan's eyes. "It's just, you know, you said I should try out some of those societies I signed up for at the fair?"

"I did . . ." Susan was wary.

"I might have signed up for a few too many."

"A few, like, how many? Five? Ten?"

Daisy replied, but it was too quiet for either of the others to hear.

"Sorry, what?" They both leaned in.

"A few like . . . thirty-two?"

It was remarkable how quickly one could stage an intervention—especially when you had exactly the right outfit for the occasion. Esther marched back and forth in front of the enormous whiteboard in the kitchen in her new rifleman's jacket, feeling incredibly important and trying not to get distracted by the tiny little jizzing penis in the bottom corner of the whiteboard that a long-ago J-block occupant had drawn in permanent marker. Drawing a grid with long, swooping lines so that everything was on a slight slant,

Esther mapped out a week planner, while Susan and Daisy sat at the table, Daisy's laptop open and her out-of-control inbox on the screen.

"Daisy, please write in your course commitments." Esther held out a red pen imperiously, and Daisy jumped up to write in five lectures, one seminar, and a lab session before returning to her seat.

"And you actually go to all these . . . ?" Esther asked doubtfully.

Daisy nodded in earnest, and Susan smirked. "Good to see that the de Groots are getting value out of those tuition fees . . ."

Ignoring that dig, Esther switched to a green pen and stepped up to Monday.

"Club me up."

Daisy ran a search for the date, and four separate e-mails showed up.

10:00 A.M. Comic Club

12:00 P.M. Ladies Who Brunch

3:00 P.M. Paper Clip Fanciers

6:00 P.M. Snap Soc

As Susan read out each entry, Esther added them to the board. Moving on to Tuesday, she wrote in five more meetings, two of which clashed.

"Seriously, Daisy, how, exactly, did you plan to attend two different clubs at opposite ends of the city scheduled for exactly the same time?" Susan asked. "Were you planning on splitting yourself in two like a sociable amoeba?"

A faint whimper emerged as Daisy shrugged. "I thought maybe I could FaceTime the Debating Society while doing origami."

"If there's anyone in this world capable of delivering a speech in favor of"—Susan leaned across to check the e-mail—"compulsory pasteurization of Continental cheeses while folding a paper strawberry, it's you."

"Actually, I was only going to listen. Apparently my debating style is too feisty for those thin-skinned public-school boys."

Susan cast Daisy an affectionate look. "That's my girl."

Three meetings scheduled for Wednesday. Six on Thursday . . . three, four, and *seven* on Sunday.

"Written out like this, it does look like quite a lot," Daisy admitted.

"You think? I'm exhausted just reading it." Susan took the pen from Esther and stepped forward. She crossed out anything that interfered with Daisy's course, which eliminated Comic Club and Marble Enthusiasts. "Now for anything that clashes. Go with your gut. Debating or Origami?"

"Origami," Daisy said without hesitation, and Susan put a line through *debating.*

"Esther, unsubscribe Daisy from the list."

"On it." Esther hammered out a polite request to be excused from further meetings and clicked the unsubscribe button, looking over Daisy's shoulder as she removed herself from the group chat.

"Tiddlywinks or Beekeeping?"

"Ooh . . . that's a hard one . . ." Daisy pondered for a few seconds. "I mean . . . I like bees, but am I ever going to own a hive . . ."

Esther started playing the *Countdown* theme on her phone, and Daisy grew increasingly flustered before exclaiming, "BEES! I CHOOSE BEES."

They eliminated two more clubs this way, but that still left Daisy with an impossible twenty-six memberships. After an hour discussing the merits of each, all three of them had lost the will to live, and an alarm sounded on Daisy's phone.

"I've got to go!" She started gathering her things and pointed at the 9:00 P.M. meeting scheduled for Tuesday. "I've got a Nicolas Cage Club meeting to attend . . ."

"No, Daisy!" Esther leaped in front of her to bar her exit. "You've got to break the cycle. You don't even know who Nicolas Cage *is*."

"Yes, I do! He's the man who wrote *The Notebook*."

"No, you're muddling him up with the Nicholas *Sparks* Club. That's not till Friday."

"BUT I NEED TO GET TO MY MEETING!"

No sooner had she sounded the battle cry than Susan had launched herself across the room to wrap herself around Daisy's knees while Esther remained resolute in barring the doorway. The struggle was intense but brief. Daisy was no match for Susan's tenacity or Esther's strength. Defeated, Daisy sank back down on her stool.

They needed a distraction, and the only one Susan could think of was to put the kettle on. Daisy asked for a fruit tea.

"I really appreciate what you're doing," she said, giving Susan a wan smile when she took the tea.

"It's for your own good," Susan said, feeling like a horrible Victorian patriarch, not helped by the fact that Esther was still stalking around in her ridiculous military regalia.

"It's a bit hot to drink just yet." Daisy set her mug down. "Can I just nip to the loo while it's cooling?"

Stopping her from going to the toilet seemed a step too far, but when Daisy had been gone for five minutes, Susan exchanged a worried glance with Esther. As one, the two sprang up, hurrying down the corridor to Daisy's room. The window was open, and the leather coat that had been on her bed was gone.

Susan rushed to the window and looked out into the wild October night. Esther looked over her shoulder at the corridor behind them and wondered why Daisy hadn't just snuck down the stairs.

"She's in deeper than we thought," Susan said. "We're going to have to extract her from each society, meeting by meeting."

"You mean . . . ?"

"One of us has to go with her to Nicolas Cage Club."

Daisy had already crossed the road and was heading in the direction of Halifax Hall, where the Nicolas Cage Club was holding a showing of *Con Air*. All members had been instructed to come dressed as their favorite version of Nicolas Cage, and Daisy was wearing a hideous silk shirt she'd found in a charity shop and a brown jacket borrowed from McGraw. She did not really know whether *Snake Eyes* Nic Cage was her favorite, but it was certainly the easiest to dress up as.

There was a tap on her shoulder, but when Daisy turned, it was her assailant who yelped in terror.

"Esther?"

"Daisy?" Esther reached out to touch the round glasses that Daisy had set over her mask. "Where the hell did you get the mask from?"

"They attached it to the e-mail. You get a new mask for every meeting." Daisy glanced at her watch. "I'm going to be late . . ."

"You don't have to go."

"But what if people who really like Nicolas Cage are my type of people?" Daisy hurried up the path to the front door.

"Then you'd probably already like Nicolas Cage, too . . ."

"Maybe I do, and I just don't know it?" Daisy pressed the buzzer for Room 34, and almost immediately a voice came out of the intercom.

"Password."

"Put the bunny back in the box."

"Oo-er . . ." Esther was so busy nudging Daisy that she almost missed the door buzzing open. "Are you sure this isn't some other kind of club?"

"Esther!" Daisy was glad her mask hid her blush. "It's a quote from *Con Air*."

"A film that you've never seen . . ."

"I'll see it tonight."

"You are *very* determined to like Nicolas Cage, aren't you?" The two of them spotted the door to number 34 at the same time, and they ground to a halt. Plastered across the wood was a range of Nicolas Cage faces, googly-eyed and shouting, each more manic than the next. It was almost impossible to pick out a single face, and one was left with the overwhelming horror of being swallowed up in a vortex.

"And you're determined to give this club one last go before you decide whether it's for you?" Esther asked, eyes averted from the many faces of the Cage.

Daisy nodded.

"Well, then." Esther looped her arm through Daisy's. "If it were anyone other than you, I'd have jumped out that window and run all the way home by now. Let's go put this bunny in that box. And get you *out* of this club."

6

THE FINAL HURDLE

The plan was going well, and, between them, Esther and Susan had successfully extracted Daisy from almost every society she'd signed up for. Esther had been in charge of any meetings during the morning or early afternoon—Susan's course didn't allow time for daylight hobbies—and Esther's shameless ability to make a spectacle of herself was working out well. There were few people one could rely upon to willfully misunderstand the ethos of the Paper Clip Fanciers by loudly declaring a sexual attraction to stationery and rubbing herself up against a display of pastel-colored bulldog clips, moaning sensuously and shouting, "Daisy! Thank you so much for enabling my erotic predilections by inviting me to this orgy!"

Daisy had been ejected from the club, and an e-mail with Esther's photo attached had been sent out to every stationery store in Sheffield warning employees not to let her in.

Leaving embarrassment to Esther, Susan favored overly competitive involvement and anarchy. She'd entered the opening game of the Snap Soc meeting with such aggression that she'd broken someone's finger and started a bar fight, from which she and Daisy were forced to retreat through the beer cellar and out onto the street. Shortly after, Daisy received notification that she had been removed from the Snapchat group and would not be privy to the locations of further meetings. The same technique had worked flawlessly for Pokémon and Anarchic Croquet. Apparently, anarchy didn't stretch to Susan dousing a croquet ball in gasoline, setting it alight, and attempting to smash it through the window of a nearby bank while screaming, "TAKE THAT, CAPITALISM!"

That morning, Daisy had sung her last four-part harmony with the Barbershop Babes, played her last chip at the Poker Soc, and supped her last goblet of mead over lunch with the Medieval Reenactment Org. A few things she would miss, like the excuse to wear a straw boater and the feel of crushed velvet, but some things were better enjoyed as a fleeting memory, rather than a weekly commitment. (Plus, she wasn't entirely sure the members of the Medieval Reenactment Org would let her back in after one of the less noble knights had suggested that Susan had the comely shape befitting a serving wench and had promptly been informed of exactly where he could relocate his lance.)

Only one society remained, one that both Susan and Esther would attend that night. Apparently, they didn't trust Daisy's judgment even when it came to yoga. It didn't matter how much Daisy waxed lyrical about the two beginner sessions she'd attended; they were skeptical. As Susan had pointed out, a society called "The Yogic Brethren of Zoise" was distinctly on the strange side, and all Daisy's arguments trying to persuade them otherwise somehow only seemed to cement her friends' conviction to extricate her.

Daisy's afternoon had been spent pleasurably enough contemplating Iron Age settlements. As she took her time packing away her notes, Reggie shuffled over to lurk at the end of the row.

A moment later, he coughed.

"Reggie, if you want to talk to me, just say, 'Hey, Daisy.'"

"Oh, er, hey, Daisy." When Reggie smiled, his whole face creased up, and you couldn't help but join him. Sliding her notes into her bag, she zipped it up and slipped it over her shoulder, falling into step with Reggie on her way out of the lecture hall.

"I like your T-shirt," she told him. Daisy always liked what Reggie wore. He seemed to have an inexhaustible supply of humorous slogan T-shirts. Today's said: *Archaeology? I dig it.*

"I was thinking about starting a regular post-lecture social," he said. "Would you like to be the first member of the Beer Time Team?" He held the door open for her, and Daisy followed the rest of the class down the stairs.

Daisy *did* fancy it, but Susan and Esther had made her swear on Baby Gordon's life that she wouldn't accept *any* social invitations until she'd freed herself from the clutches of the ones she'd already accepted.

"Sorry, Reggie," Daisy said, giving his arm a consoling pat. "I'm trying to scale back my socializing at the moment. Maybe next time."

* * * * *

That afternoon, Esther had Creative Writing. It was a module that she'd been approved for at the start of term, but the first scheduled seminar had fallen during one of her many personal crises, and when the tutor had asked everyone to hand in what they'd been working on, she'd been forced to submit a page crammed full of lovelorn song lyrics and doodles of broken, bleeding, pulpy hearts.

An inclination to idleness wasn't the only reason Esther had been reluctant to return.

So far she'd missed five out of six classes, but the whole point of this module was to leave students plenty of time to explore their own writing, and she'd *pffted* away Ed Gemmell's concerns that she might have been taken off the course.

Dressed in her sports gear, ready to work up a mild perspiration doing yoga, Esther stopped by the university bookshop to grab a copy of her favorite book for the purposes of discussing "the nature of the reader experience," then made her way to the seminar room. Strictly speaking, her favorite book was *Lady Boss* by Jackie Collins, but that wasn't exactly *literary*, and she'd liked *Frankenstein* well enough when they'd read it in school. Besides, there was no author more extra than Mary Shelley.

The building in which the seminar was held was about as inspiring as a block of offices. Esther could almost feel her muse withering with every step she took up the three flights to get to the right floor, then dying completely when she turned down a corridor lined with fluorescent lights and linoleum. When she pushed open the door to room 31B, it took a second for her eyes to adjust to the relative darkness within before she saw that thirteen students and one proper grown-up had turned to stare at her.

"Ah, er . . . hello?" The tutor was Dr. Cordoba—dad age but pretending not to be in a V-neck sweater and scruffy hair kind of way. "If you're looking for fourteenth-century Spanish literature, that's one floor up. Don't let the name Cordoba confuse you."

There followed an echo of a chuckle among the students, as if they'd laughed louder the first time he'd said this.

"Actually, I'm here for Creative Writing." Esther closed the door behind her and searched the room for a seat that didn't exist. "Esther de Groot? I was approved for this module at the start of term."

"I see." Dr. Cordoba raised eyebrows as shaggy as his hair. "And yet this is the first time you thought to attend?"

It was unusual for anyone to forget Esther, but she wasn't exactly rocking the usual full-gothic aesthetic (although her leggings had a token ram-skull print).

"Actually, I came to the first seminar, but I've had some, er, personal issues . . ." Her voice trailed off as something clicked in Dr. Cordoba's recall. His eyebrows dropped, and a look of mystified horror washed across his face as he no doubt recalled her paper. ". . . issues that have since been resolved," Esther continued. "No more drama for me."

"Well, the drama department's loss is our gain, I'm sure."

Esther laughed exactly one second before she realized it wasn't a joke.

When Cordoba started talking once more, Esther sat down gratefully in a chair that one of the boys had pulled in from the side of the room and took stock of the people sitting around the U-shaped arrangement of tables. A couple of people she vaguely recognized from the Prose lectures looked at her with all the welcome that antibodies might bestow upon an invading virus. Someone she and Ed Gemmell referred to as "Thesaurus Boy" for the ridiculous way he phrased questions during lectures gave her a nervous smile, and next to him . . .

Esther's heart stopped.

It was a long walk back from visiting her CAS patient, Mrs. Doherty, but Susan had missed the bus, and it would be quicker to walk than wait for the next.

Also, walking would mean she didn't have to spend any more time with the student she'd been paired with. Milo was the sort of person who thought he knew everything and didn't shut up about it. Susan had been forced to endure ninety minutes of him going on about the various genetic factors linked to gestational diabetes instead of listening to Mrs. Doherty, who actually *had* gestational diabetes. As Susan had to point out to Milo when Mrs. Doherty had left the room to make them a cup of tea, the point of students visiting patients wasn't to pontificate about their clinical knowledge but to interview *the patient* about what it was like to live with a diagnosis.

It was supposed to be a civil warning but had ended with Susan threatening to give Milo a taste of what it might be like to live with a diagnosis of having been punched so hard in the testes that they retreated back into his body cavity.

Hurrying through a gap in traffic, Susan narrowly avoided getting hit by a cyclist with an impressively profane vocabulary. The streets were lethal, and even if she *ran* all the way into town, she'd still be late.

And with her lungs, running wasn't exactly an option.

Not wanting to hold the others up, Susan took her phone out to message Daisy.

In the last half hour, Esther had developed reader relationships with *The Catcher in the Rye*, *Keep the Aspidistra Flying* (who knew George Orwell has written something other than *1984* and *Animal Farm*?!), and *The Lord of the Rings* without ever having read a single sentence. None of them were relationships she wished to pursue, and she'd spent most of her time pretending not to stare at the girl next to Thesaurus Boy. Although there was *so much* for Esther to stare at. The perfect fade of her green eyeshadow and the precise taper of her eyeliner. The skull-and-crossbones stud in her tragus and the line of sharp black studs, like rotted teeth, nibbling the length of her ear. The wolf print of the knotted scarf holding her hair off her face. Her shirt, her nails, her jewelry . . .

Esther had never seen anyone so cool in her life.

Despite Noor's assurance at Halloween, Esther hadn't seen Goth Girl in any of the lectures she'd managed to attend in the last ten days, and she hadn't anticipated seeing her now. If she had, Esther might have worn something a little more lively (or deadly) than a plain black hoodie, minimal makeup, and no jewelry. If she wanted to impress, she'd have to do it with her mind.

When a boy called Da Vinci, who clearly considered himself to be edgy, started reading out loud from *American Psycho*, Esther yawned. Loudly.

"Sorry," she said, sounding anything but when everyone turned to look at her. "Conditioned response to anything that considers itself shocking."

Edgelord Da Vinci looked set to explode.

"Dude. It's been made into a movie. I'm not saying it's not great literature, but if your only relationship with *American Psycho* is the desire to be shocked, then how are you really engaging with what the author intended?"

There was a stunned kind of silence in the room, the kind Esther reveled in. She'd forgotten how much she enjoyed the role of provocateur. Back when she was an amateur, she might have played the *American Psycho* card, but Esther had long since turned pro.

"Interesting that you should bring up the notion of authorial intent when this discussion is focused on the reader," Dr. Cordoba said, but he didn't look displeased. "Does it matter what Easton Ellis intended? *Should* it matter?"

There was a murmur in the room as Da Vinci closed his book and gave Esther a mutinous look. She blew him a kiss.

"Esther"—Dr. Cordoba reeled her into the conversation—"it's clear from this that you're someone who places great importance on the nature of the author-reader relationship."

She hadn't until then, but Esther could work with that. After all, she'd brought Mary Shelley to the table.

"Surely all literature is a communication from the author

to a reader, and therefore every reading, whether we wish it to be or not, is a tacit acceptance of this contract?"

Back in Tackleford, a casual "tacit acceptance" might have been enough to impress the rest of the class into agreeing, but had Esther attended more of her course-mandated seminars, she would have discovered that university debates were not so easily concluded.

From the far end of the table, with a voice like soil scattering over a coffin, Goth Girl spoke up.

"Surely one can hypothesize that literature is a construct of lies, and therefore one cannot trust the concept of authorial intent? Even if one were to argue that an author can make a statement of their intent—in a foreword or an interview—the truth of such a statement is in and of itself a lie."

Esther had been *in and of itself*-ed!

"Would you care to expand on that, Vectra?" Cordoba said.

Her name was *Vectra*. Could she be any more awesome?

"The mechanics of intent, action, and reception are complex, but you're asking us to draw a straight line from intent to reception without taking into account how a person goes about writing. Any examination of our reaction to a book for the purposes of finding our identity as readers should be taken in isolation."

So many words arranged in such complicated syntax. Esther was out of practice and could no longer translate intellectual doublespeak fast enough to provide a counter-argument.

The discussion was over. Vectra had won, but maybe that was for the best. People felt happy when they won, right?

Esther met her eye and gave an "all's fair" kind of smile that wasn't returned.

"Vectra makes a compelling point. From now on, we will disregard whoever authored your favorite books. I want to hear about how *you* interacted with the *story* only. And where better to start than with a book that was famously published anonymously by the author herself, arguably because she knew that the perception of who she was would negatively affect the critical reception . . ."

Everyone was looking at Esther, who in turn looked down in despair at the cover of *Frankenstein.*

"Esther, please tell us what is so special to you about your relationship with Mary Shelley's seminal novel."

Esther wished she'd been honest enough to bring Jackie Collins.

Having secured an empty table with nothing more than a mug of fruit tea, a book, and her phone for company, Daisy had presented too vulnerable a target amid the post-lecture frenzy of the coffee shop. Her spare chair and 80 percent of the table surface had been annexed by a group of History students, one of whom kept turning to glare at the side of Daisy's face as if she were the interloper.

Daisy looked wistfully at the message on her phone from Susan asking for the address of the yoga place and saying she'd meet Daisy there. If Susan were sitting here, those

History students would have yielded the table for six and offered to buy them fresh drinks in reparations.

As it was, Daisy was faced with the dilemma of eking out the last cold mouthfuls of her tea or risk losing her seat if she stood to order another.

She'd have to find a way. Esther wasn't due out of her Creative Writing seminar for fifteen minutes. If Daisy needed to defend this table for longer, she could do it. For Esther.

"Excuse me?" Daisy used her quietest and most polite voice. "Could you save my seat for me while I get another drink?"

The History student she asked nodded, and Daisy wondered whether she hadn't been unkind in her judgment. But when she came back to her table, all her things—the book she'd been reading, her hat and gloves—had been heaped on her chair, and the table had been shuffled across the aisle and assimilated into the History students' territory.

"Saved your seat!" the student she'd spoken to said with a smirk.

So that would be a 100 percent fail rate at Creative Writing. Esther pushed out of the door, wanting to get away from the humiliation, but it followed her down the stairs.

"How did you even get in?" Vectra laughed as she fell into step with Esther. "*Everyone* knows Frankenstein's the name of the doctor, not the monster."

"Aw, that's not true. I didn't until I read it." Thesaurus Boy was jostling along next to them, beaming at the side of

Esther's face so that she couldn't tell whether or not he was being sarcastic.

"Good point." Vectra nodded, giving Esther a sly look. "Most of us have read our favorite books. And those of us who consider ourselves sisters of the night would know our gothic literature."

Esther hesitated. Did that mean Vectra knew who she was? Or was she just referring to herself?

"I, er, we didn't really meet properly back there—" Esther began.

"I'm Otto!" Thesaurus Boy said brightly, waving.

"Hi, Otto. I'm Esther."

"Yeah, we know. You said." Vectra could walk fast for someone with such short legs. "You're the Gothic Pixie Dream Girl all the boys have been wetting themselves over."

"Gothic Pixie Dream Girl" didn't sound like a compliment.

Vectra carried on purposefully along the pavement, hands jammed deeply into the pockets of her jacket. The rest of the group had all turned the same way, as if operating as part of a unified hive mind.

When Vectra stopped and half turned back, Esther worried that she'd finally identified Esther as a threat and the rest of the hive would swarm around and sting her to death with sarcastic comments about her academic abilities.

"Are you coming for a post-critique group drink or what?"

When her phone went off, Daisy pounced on it so quickly that the last of her fruit tea jumped out of her mug and splashed across her thigh.

Sorry, Daisy, going to have to bail on yoga tonight. Please send photos of Susan humiliating herself. xxx

Doubt, long buried and dormant, unfurled inside her chest, the same feeling that had nudged her toward seeking a social life in the first place. A fear that maybe the friends she loved so much didn't quite feel the same way. She'd barely stood up before someone swiped the chair from under her, banging the back of her knees. Ruffled, Daisy shouldered her yoga mat and stepped out into the night, drizzle settling in her hair and on her glasses, dusting the screen of her phone as she tapped out a cheerful reply letting Esther know that it was fine. All fine.

It really was fine. Susan was going to meet her there.

Esther wasn't to know that Daisy had been hoping to take her two best friends out for a celebratory milkshake after yoga to thank them for everything they'd done for her this last week. She'd utilized some of the skills she'd picked up from the various crafting groups she'd left and had made them both badges that said *Best Mum Ever*.

She could always do it another time.

The address Daisy had given her wasn't what Susan had envisioned. This was not the sort of suburb where one might locate a chilly church hall, or a dance studio above a parade of dingy shops. It was the sort of place one found Neighborhood Watch stickers on the windows and artisanal pizza boxes in the recycling bins. The houses here were detached, the gardens mature, and the trees leafy—or they would have been if all the leaves weren't on the pavement.

Half the driveways had fancy gravel leading up to porches whose leaded glass nestled between casement windows.

Stopping as she turned off the main road, Susan double-checked that she'd typed the address in correctly, wiping the rain-flecked screen dry on her chest to frown down at the map.

Two roads along and turn left. Number 21 . . .

Before she'd had a chance to move, Susan saw someone approaching who very definitely didn't belong there.

McGraw.

There was nowhere here for him to get keys cut or buy a lathe or a spirit level or a . . . protractor. (Susan hadn't exactly excelled when it came to Design and Tech class.)

Old habits died hard, and Susan slipped into the shadows cast by an ostentatious topiary before her target could see her. Hands in pockets, McGraw passed the hedge she was lurking behind with a muted rustle of damp leaves and a faint cheerful hum.

It had been a long day. Milo had already exhausted what little patience Susan had ever possessed, and she was cold and tired and had a backlog of lecture notes to catch up on, and instead she was out in the wilds of suburbia looking at McGraw being *happy*.

This was too much.

McGraw had effectively ruined Susan's life by turning up in Sheffield. Now here he was ruining Daisy's yoga session?

The fiend needed taking down. Right. Now. Self-righteous rage catapulted Susan from behind the tree into a brisk walk behind McGraw, determined to find whatever it was that had put him in such a cheerful mood and destroy it. The road came to a dead end, but there was a short footpath leading to a street that was a lot less affluent than the one Susan had come from. Here the houses were in terraces of four, the sort with as many doorbells as floors and cars parked on the road—student territory.

Seeing no sign of her quarry, Susan drew to a halt just long enough to catch the faintest sound of McGraw's tenor a short distance away. She saw him then, standing several car lengths down the pavement, phone to his ear, before he turned decisively toward one of the houses and pressed the bell. Fast as a ferret, Susan darted along the road just in time to see the door shut.

Had she been on the job, there were several things Susan would have considered doing next. Check the name on the bell and run a search through the university intranet. Peer in through the window. Concoct a quick disguise, nab a pizza box out of one of the recycling bins, and ring the bell for a wrong delivery.

But no one was paying her to do this. She wasn't on the tail of a known criminal—McGraw, for all his many flaws, was an honest man—and it was she, Susan, who was in breach of contract.

Following her enemy had been a mistake. But Susan barely had a chance to consider her own foolishness, because there, looming in wobbly silhouette through the glass pane of the front door, was McGraw.

Not having anticipated that he'd come out so soon, Susan had no escape plan. There were no walls to duck behind, no trees—but there, parked behind her on the road, was a van, with one back door open to accommodate the long beams of wood that were sticking out. Out of options and out of time, Susan scooted around the open door and thrust herself into a gap not designed for someone with hips. With a bit of a wriggle, it was enough. Her fingers hooked onto the cord that held the planks together. Chest squashed against the wood, Susan glanced back, confident that by crooking her knees, she'd remain safely out of sight.

There was no sound from outside. No footsteps. Head twisted around, Susan stared out into the night, wondering how long she'd have to wait before she could get out and get to yoga.

At which point the van rumbled to life and pulled away from the curb.

With Esther having cried off and an absent Susan, Daisy could feel the familiar breath of anxiety whispering in her ear as she made her way up the drive. *Esther doesn't think yoga is proper exercise . . . Susan hates relaxing . . . They're tired after spending so much time doing all your ridiculous clubs . . . They're bored with you . . .*

Enough of this. Susan had probably arrived already. Having waited for Esther, Daisy was a little later than she'd planned.

The smile with which Elise greeted Daisy when she opened the door was enough to push back even the darkest of thoughts. "Daisy! Zoise embraces you. Welcome, Sister."

She offered Daisy a cookie from the plate in her hand and peered over Daisy's shoulder at the shadowed driveway. "Didn't you say we'd be welcoming some of your friends?"

There was no hiding the effect the question had on her, and Daisy drooped as she let go of the final flutter of hope. "You mean Susan's not here?"

Elise shook her head and put a solicitous arm around Daisy's waist, guiding her through the house.

"I'm so sorry, Daisy. Sometimes friends let us down." She walked ahead of Daisy down the stone steps toward the welcoming warmth of the basement, turning to talk over her shoulder. "That's why we need our family . . ."

There was already a semicircle on the mats, everyone in their robes, Brother Jasper at the lectern ready to deliver the Voice of Zoise that would lead them into meditation. As one, the Brethren turned to Daisy, standing up in welcome and waving her into their midst.

"We'd just wrapped up the Ceremony of Sharing," Jasper said once she was settled. "Having attended your first few sessions, it is time for you to make a commitment to Zoise and pursue the path of enlightenment."

"Oh, er, of course . . ."

When she glanced over to where Elise stood at the bottom of the steps, the young woman nodded with encouragement, and without her friends there to stop her, Daisy couldn't really think of a good reason why she shouldn't participate. Only she hadn't brought anything with her . . .

"That's a very pretty necklace." Jasper nodded to where Daisy's hand had automatically gone to the delicate gold bird pendant that Granny had given her for her sixteenth birthday.

"Oh. Right. Yes." Reaching up, Daisy undid the clasp and handed over the necklace.

A gift from her old family so that she might join a new one.

There are more dignified ways to travel through Sheffield than with one's top half wedged in a van, a yoga-suitable bottom sticking out the back door. A situation made all the worse by the fact that there was no way Susan could reach for her phone without risking life and limb as the van swung round one of the city's many roundabouts. Fingers bloodlessly hooked over the cord, Susan thought of Esther and Daisy waiting for her to join them, assuming that she'd let them down yet again.

Which she had.

Wedged in the back of a van with only her guilt for company was not ideal, and by the time the vehicle pulled up at its destination, Susan's mood had grown so black that there was no telling exactly what manner of retribution she would inflict upon the driver once she found out who it was.

Futility had that effect on her.

When the engine died, Susan did her best to shuffle out of the van, feet kicking wildly as she tried to find purchase on something—*anything*—to help extract her shoulders so she could wreak vengeance on the idiot who'd started up the van without checking that the load was secure.

"Do you need a hand?"

The question stilled Susan's thrashing, her limbs momentarily incapable of activity, as every ounce of energy was required to comprehend what was happening.

That voice belonged to McGraw. But . . . McGraw was supposed to be making his laborious way back to campus via the public transportion network, as was his custom. He wasn't supposed to have . . . *driven here in this van.*

"What? *No!*" Susan yelled. Although whether in rejection of the offer of help or as a simple declaration of horror wasn't clear.

"If you're sure . . ."

"Touch me, and I will *end* you." Her thrashing resumed, all the more ineffectual for the amount of rage channeled into it. Eventually, Susan's efforts shifted things so that she was able to slide out, but her top caught on the rough surface of the beams and rolled up. Her skin scraped along the wood, splinters grazing her.

Emerging red-faced and fuming, Susan tugged her top down to face McGraw, sitting patiently on the car park wall by F-block, his mustache impassive, eyes hinting at mirth.

"Hello, Susan," he said.

Susan couldn't say anything. Her body couldn't process the level of rage she'd ascended to.

"Is there a reason you were hitching a ride in the back of my van?"

"*Your* van?" That was what she was going to lead with? Apparently so.

McGraw shrugged. "Technically the van belongs to Allan Cho, a third-year Mechanical Engineering student whose uncle runs a roofing company and had some unused—"

"Ugh. Stop talking!" Susan clutched her head, trying to claw all this unwanted information from her brain.

". . . good for a project I'm—"

"No! Not interested."

". . . said I could borrow the van while—"

"Stop!" In desperation, Susan lunged forward and slammed both hands across McGraw's mouth. Startled, the two of them stared at each other for a second, frozen in a horrifying tableau, McGraw's mustache strangely soft against her fingertips, his eyes no longer hinting at mirth so much as . . .

"*Ugh*." Susan sprang back, wiping her hands on McGraw's sleeve rather than contaminating her own clothes, ignoring the shape his muscles made under the material and the smell of metal shavings and sawdust and soap.

Turning her back, Susan stormed away as McGraw called after her, "You do know you're in direct violation of Clause 4 of our contract?"

Her response was in direct violation of basic human decency.

There is nothing quite so unsatisfactory as finding your soul mate and her not even noticing you exist.

That had been what it was like in the pub. Whenever Esther tried to talk to Vectra Featherstone (even her surname was cool!), one of the other Lit students would join in, dominating the conversation. And on the rare occasions Vectra said anything, Esther had barely been able to hear her. Vectra's throaty crackle was exactly the wrong frequency for a Friday night in a busy pub.

Every time Esther edged close enough to maybe say something, the group would shift, and she would find herself watching as someone else caught Vectra's attention, her heavily kohled eyes turned in their direction as Vectra chewed disinterestedly on her straw.

Oh, for such disinterest to be directed at *Esther* . . .

They would be friends. Of this Esther was utterly, completely convinced. There was no one Esther had ever met who hadn't warmed to her eventually, and she knew, deep in the chambers of her heart, that Vectra and she would be the best friends ever.

If only they talked to each other.

Stomping up the stairs, weighed down with creative writing ephemera and disappointment, Esther hoped that Daisy wouldn't mind what had happened. After all, she'd had Susan for company, and she didn't *really* need two of them to go with her to this club. It wasn't as if Esther had *abandoned* her. She'd sent a message. She'd been to all the other clubs. And Daisy had said she was fine . . .

Turning onto the landing, Esther walked into a wall of smoke. Once she'd stopped coughing, she wiped away tears to see Susan standing moodily by an open window, ash dusting the tops of her shoes and regret shadowing her eyes.

Yoga must have been *really* bad.

"I'm so sorry—"

"I feel terrible—"

They stopped as quickly as they started.

"You first," Esther said, tucking away a tight, guilty smile.

Susan sighed, flicked the butt of her cigarette out the window, and recrossed her ankles. "If I'm going to be apologizing, I'd prefer to do it only the once. Where's Daisy?"

"Isn't she with you?" Alarm flooded through Esther. She'd assumed Susan had been waiting there as vanguard for the recriminations she deserved for bailing on the two of them, but . . .

"What?" Susan frowned. "No, I thought she was with you."

The two of them stared at each other in shame, Susan's guilt multiplying Esther's tenfold. If she'd thought there was the slimmest chance of Daisy being on her own, she never would have contemplated going to the pub with Vectra.

"I only flaked out because I thought she'd have you there." The excuse sounded even more flimsy when Esther said it out loud.

"I was—should have been." Susan shook her head in irritation and looked down at her phone, running her thumb over the screen. "I got waylaid and couldn't use my phone until it was too late. Daisy's not replied to any of the messages I sent her."

Faintly, like a siren song a desperate sailor might cling to, there came a familiar hum from the bowels of the stairwell, echoing up to the fourth-floor landing. Instinctively, Esther drew closer to Susan, adopting a similar hangdog pose and penitent expression, facing the stairs and waiting for judgment.

A halo of golden curls edged into view, then the rims of Daisy's owlish glasses, and . . . her smile?

"Hello, friends!" Daisy beamed at them. "Is this a welcoming committee?"

The force with which they flung themselves at her nearly resulted in a twelve-limb tumble back down the stairs. It was worth the risk to smother Daisy in love and apologies and promises not to let her down ever again.

Susan drew away first with an awkward cough and a mumble about popping the kettle on. As the three of them walked along the corridor to the kitchen, Esther asked how the club had gone.

"How did you manage to disentangle yourself?"

"Did you declare a preference for Pilates?" Susan suggested.

"Ooh, or did you make all your poses weirdly provocative?" Esther stretched into Tree Pose and cast a coquettish pout over her shoulder.

"Actually." Daisy cleared her throat and gave a defiant tilt of the chin. "I decided to join up for good. It's the only club I've been to where I feel like I really belong. I'm going again on Monday."

Esther cast a cautious glance in Susan's direction. "Well, you do really like yoga . . ."

". . . and if these people make you feel at home . . ." Susan shrugged.

"What harm can *one* club do?" Esther finished, and she gave Daisy an affectionate squeeze.

7

THE PATH TO ENLIGHTENMENT

At home, there had always been someone to make stuff happen. Clothes would get washed, meals cooked, bills paid. Esther would write what brand of shampoo she wanted on the shopping list, and it would turn up in the bathroom. She never had to know how much it cost, the same way she never had to pay for the hairdresser or the dentist. There was no admin required for being someone's daughter.

But there was an overwhelming amount of it for being a student.

"Susan. Help me. I'm DYING." Esther staggered in through the door and collapsed face-first on the bed.

"You should see a doctor about that. A qualified one." Susan's voice had the distinct air of someone who hadn't bothered to look up.

"That's exactly what's killing me." Turning her head to one side, Esther smiled at Daisy, who was sitting on the floor, back resting against the bed.

"This is a very confusing conversation, Es. Is there any chance you could dial down the dramatics and actually make sense?" Susan remained intent on her laptop. From the look of it, she was browsing poisons on Wikipedia.

"The admin!" Esther rolled onto her back, specifically so she could fling an arm across her forehead and stare miserably at the ceiling. "There's so much of it."

"Ah." For the first time, she had Susan's attention. "I'm guessing someone has failed to register for a doctor and needs"—Susan turned from the laptop, eyes narrowed in calculation—"something that isn't life threatening enough to qualify as a medical emergency but is sufficiently urgent that you need the matter resolved sooner rather than later."

A pause followed, long enough for Daisy and Esther to hold their breath in anticipation.

"Someone forgot to renew her prescription for the pill," Susan pronounced.

Esther shot up in surprise. "Am I really that predictable?"

"Well, Susan's very perceptive . . ." Daisy began.

"Yes. You absolutely are." Susan said.

"Right. Well, have you got any I can borrow?"

Susan shook her head and tapped her arm. "Implant. Even though I like to think my womb naturally provides a toxic environment so that anything resembling sperm would shrivel and die on entry."

Esther leaned over the edge of the bed hopefully. "Daisy?"

"Providing a hostile environment for sperm hasn't been much of a priority for me." She blushed. "Sorry."

A moment later, Susan had the web page for the university health service up on her laptop, open to the registration form. "Here."

Esther pecked with distaste at the graying keys. "It says it'll take two days. That's forty-eight hours I don't have."

"I'd never have taken you for someone who took being prepared so seriously." Respect battled doubt in Daisy's voice.

"My moods are finely adapted to the hormone levels in my body. Do you want to mess with those? DO YOU, DAISY?"

Daisy shuffled so that she was pressed against Susan's shins. Her voice trembled a little as she said, "No?"

"Yet for all your fine-tuning, you've only just noticed that you've run out of contraception," Susan said levelly.

"WHY IS THE UNIVERSE CONSPIRING TO MAKE MY LIFE SO DIFFICULT?"

"You say 'the universe,' but I think we can all agree this is mostly down to you. And it's definitely not down to me or Daisy." Susan patted Daisy's shoulder much the way she might a nervous dog. "Personal responsibility."

"Is a ruse invented by those seeking to argue their way out of the problem of evil in the face of an omnipotent, omniscient, benign god." After filling out her home address, Esther looked up to see her friends staring in shock. "What? So I retained some information from one of the seminars I went to last week."

"Did you attend it because it was about the problem of evil?" Daisy asked.

Esther's gaze darkened gleefully. "They say problem, I say solution."

"But not to the problem of managing your hormones through birth control." Susan's tone was scathing, but the look she gave Esther was one of grudging capitulation. "I don't think the world needs to see how far your mood can swing without the restraining influence of added estrogen. Tell me what brand you need, and come meet me after lectures tomorrow. Daisy, you want in?"

Daisy worried her lip a moment. "When Granny warned me about drug deals, I don't think this was what she meant."

"Not unless she's Catholic," Esther reasoned.

"She isn't."

Esther studied the calendar on her phone, trying to work out what—if any—lectures she had on. "I've a lecture that finishes at eleven."

Susan glanced at Daisy. "Twelve noon up at the hospital? We can all go for lunch in the medical school canteen afterward. They do excellent potato wedges."

A large amount of Esther's time in her Prose lecture was spent on planning her exit. Not in the way Daisy might mentally prepare for a fire drill, or the way Susan fantasized about biting someone's arm with a blood capsule in her mouth to see what 250 medical students would do in the event of a zombie apocalypse. Esther's plans had a very specific aim: to orchestrate leaving the lecture theater at the same time as Vectra *and* to sustain some kind of conversation.

After the disastrous Creative Writing seminar, Esther knew she had to make this one count. Rather than blunder in and get it all wrong, she was adopting the Susan Ptolemy approved method of observing her target. The list in her notebook was coming along nicely.

Don't sit too close

No compliments

Don't rush out

Don't stay too long

Stay away from any lecture talk

No eye contact

Ed Gemmell reached across and scribbled in the margin of her notebook: *No bright light, no water, don't feed after midnight???*

After reading it through twice, Esther was still none the wiser and gave Ed a helpless shrug.

"You've never seen *Gremlins*?" he whispered. "It's a classic . . . in a so bad, it's good kind of way. There's these, er, gremlins . . ." His eyebrows knitted together, and he trailed off with a sigh. "Never mind."

"No! I love how you have faith that one day I'll understand one of your nerdy references." The lecturer was wrapping up. "Keep trying. One day we'll find some common ground other than Endings, Closure, and Narrative Ambiguity in the 1920s."

While Ed Gemmell packed away his things and hurried down to the front of the lecture hall to talk to the professor who'd given the lecture, Esther waved hello to Noor as she passed by, then twanged the elastic band around her notebook and buried her plans in the bottom of her bag. If there was one thing she could do now to ensure Vectra never spoke to her again, it would be to expose just how hard she was trying to impress her.

There was a message on her phone from Daisy saying

she was waiting down in reception, and Esther smiled at the picture she'd sent with it: a hand reaching for one of the little wooden models of faculty buildings on display with the caption *Giant Daisy!*

"All right?" A husky rustle of syllables, like bats emerging from a catacomb.

Startled, Esther did her best to arrange her face into something suitably cool and distant as she looked up to where Vectra had fallen into step next to her and nodded, biting back her inclination to ask where Vectra's boots came from or what online tutorial she'd used to get that perfect ripple effect going on her eyeshadow.

Six steps of silence, and it was Vectra who broke it.

"So. Your friend. Glasses too small, hair too big, tries too hard."

"Ed Gemmell?"

"Yeah. He's doing Introduction to Cinema, right?"

"I—er—maybe." With a guilty flush, Esther realized she had no idea which optional modules Ed Gemmell took—she only knew they weren't the same as hers.

"Yeah. So. Could you ask him for his notes from the last couple of seminars? I'm still trying to catch up after my throat infection, and that one's always scribbling away."

"He's just back there." Esther paused on the stairs and raised a hesitant thumb back toward the lecture theater. "You could ask him yourself."

"I'm asking *you* to ask him." For a second it looked as if she might have been smiling. "Because I think he'll say yes to you."

Bewildered, flattered, and a little uncomfortable, Esther carried on down the stairs, trying to decode the subtext of their interaction.

At the bottom of the steps, Vectra turned and arched her eyebrows at Esther.

"Let me know about the notes, yeah?"

"Yes, umm . . ." Esther did a quick sweep of the foyer, relieved when she saw that Daisy was preoccupied with reading the Postcard Poems display. "How? E-mail? Phone?"

"Or you could just bring them to the next Creative Writing seminar."

Of course. Esther was still getting used to her new schedule—and the fact that she was supposed to be sticking to it. Vectra gave Esther's outfit an impenetrable head-to-toe assessment.

"Nice belt."

And then she was out the door, turning her collar up against the wind and pulling her headphones on.

"Esther?" Daisy stood at Esther's shoulder, following her gaze to Vectra, who glanced back with another enigmatic half smile before disappearing.

"Vectra Featherstone liked my belt."

"That's good . . . well done for having a nice belt." She petted Esther much as she would Baby Gordon. "Shall we go and see Susan now?"

There was a gentle touch at her elbow, and Esther felt herself steered gently outdoors, someone zipping up her top and pulling her devil-horn hat down over her ears. (Daisy, presumably.)

"Do you know what a compliment like that means in the universal language of the outcast?" Esther turned, wide-eyed with conviction. "It means we're *friends*."

The walk from the English building to the hospital wasn't so long—not compared to how long it took to walk all the way up the hill to Catterick Hall—but the conversation made it feel an awful lot longer to Daisy. Although it was less of a conversation and more like listening to a monologue on Vectra Featherstone and all the ways in which she was some kind of super race of human brought forth into the world under a moonless night, anointed with sacrificial blood and destined for darkness.

When Esther liked something, she really went all in, something that Daisy admired. It took conviction and confidence in one's own judgment to make such strong proclamations about something—or someone—about which she knew so little. Daisy always felt that knowing what she liked took time, a seed planted and tended and watered, nourished under many suns, watched and cherished until it blossomed into something true and beautiful or withered away to create more fertile soil for something else. One of the many reasons she'd found her Social Period so stressful was because she'd planted too many seeds for her to keep track of.

With only Zoise to think about, her passions had taken on a certain clarity, her energies focused in a single direction.

"So, are you going to ask her for a coffee after tomorrow's seminar?" Daisy interjected as Esther drew breath.

From the reaction, Daisy might as well have suggested

Esther locate Vectra's room, try on all her clothes, and sit at the end of her bed, braiding loose hairs plucked from Vectra's brush while watching her sleep. Once Esther had recovered from all the theatrical gasping, she replied, "I don't want to look too keen."

"But if someone wants to be your friend, then . . . keen is? *Not* good?" Did Daisy have this all wrong? Was that *not* how to be friends?

Esther soothed her, standing on tiptoe so she could pat the top of Daisy's head, hand bouncing on her curls. *Pat, pat, pat.* Usually Daisy liked being fussed at by Esther. It made her feel safe and loved. Today, though, she felt patronized.

"You innocent little homeschooled flower. The path to true friendship is fraught with tests. Herculean tasks of logic overcoming emotion, a chessboard of moves to baffle your opponent."

Which bore no resemblance to how Daisy and Susan and Esther had come to be friends. Emerging from the depths came the thought that maybe this had all been too easy: One did not make friends for life by accident of university accommodation allocation.

Daisy was just a temporary associate, not a *friend* to whom Esther had to prove herself.

At least Daisy could be consoled that if the worst happened and Esther moved on, she had somewhere else to go. She knew exactly where she stood with the Brethren of Zoise. Or rather, where she sat, or lay, which was how everyone spent most of the time in the basement.

There was, however, the small issue of the Ceremony of

Sharing. Unlike everyone else, Daisy didn't have an inexhaustible supply of worldly possessions. Daisy had never found her life with Granny tarnished by a lack of wealth, but the two of them had always been frugal. It had required some adapting for Daisy to take Esther's extravagant spending habits in her stride, but looking around, Daisy saw that university life was rife with fiscal exuberance.

There was always the option of introducing someone else to the joys of Zoise yoga, but who? Susan's skepticism was insurmountable, and Esther was even less likely to give yoga a go now that she had Vectra to obsess over.

Daisy needed to come up with some ideas of what to share, or she wouldn't belong with the Brethren, either.

As Esther and Daisy passed the reception area for the hospital and made for the doors marked MEDICAL SCHOOL, Esther's phone blooped in her pocket.

Over the road.

Esther looked up, and another message came in.

Around the corner from the cash machine.

The two of them followed the directions and the thin trail of smoke that wafted past the queue at the cash machine to find Susan slouched against a wall, cigarette between her fingers, leg crooked so one foot rested flat on the bricks. Her head was tipped back, smoke leaking from her lips, eyes closed in bliss.

Esther cast a revolted look at the enormous trash container right next to where Susan was standing and wondered whether students had to pass some kind of basic hygiene test before they made the Hippocratic oath. On current evidence, Susan would fail. "So, is this where he's meeting us?" she asked.

"Him who?" Susan pushed her way off the wall and stubbed out her cigarette.

"*The man*," Esther whispered, but her friends looked nonplussed. "You know. The one we're seeing about a dog?"

"I wish we were seeing a man about a dog," Daisy said wistfully. "Do you think there's a black market for students who just want to pet a puppy for an hour?"

"Definitely." Susan nodded.

"It's a *euphemism*." Esther tried again.

"No, I think Daisy really does want to pet puppies . . ."

"I do."

"I MEAN THAT WE'RE HERE TO SCORE SOME DRUGS."

There followed the sort of silence that only occurs when lots of people have heard something they shouldn't, and Esther became acutely aware that the line of people waiting for the cash machine was peering at her from around the corner.

One of them, a middle-aged lady with a crutch in one hand and a cash card in the other said, "Aren't we all, pet? Aren't we all . . ."

The man in front of her nodded. "Came in here for some antibiotics, and now I'm waiting for a bloody X-ray." Others in the queue murmured in sympathy. "I told them, it's just a gammy foot. Google it, mate. All I need is a bit of penicillin."

Next to her, Esther felt Susan tense, but with everyone

distracted by comparing and contrasting Google diagnoses with the treatment they were waiting for, it was the perfect time for them to edge deeper into the shadows. As they did, an indistinct form emerged from behind one of the bins.

"Ptolemy," the figure said.

"Walters."

Their dealer was female, medium height, wearing office-style civilian clothing rather than the scrubs Esther had been expecting. Maybe thirty? As far as Esther was concerned, there were only five ages of human: child, her age, thirty, parent age, ghost.

"You got the goods?" Walters asked, and from the capacious pocket of her cable-knit cardigan, Susan produced a handful of small syringes still in their sealed bags.

Esther's eyes widened in horror as Susan exchanged syringes for a single slim foil pack of pills. Before she had a chance to protest, to fling herself between the two and prevent Susan from enabling this poor woman's addiction, the deal was done, and Walters was gone.

"Here you go." Susan pressed a blister pack into Esther's palm. Had it really been worth Susan jeopardizing her degree for *this*? Worth another woman's good health?

"Susan," Esther croaked. "Did you just aid and abet Walters's next heroin session?"

Daisy gasped in alarm. "Susan!"

"What are you going on about?"

"The syringes . . ." Esther mimed rolling her sleeve up and injecting something, eyes rolling back for effect.

Her charade was met with a burst of laughter. "*Penny Walters*? A junkie? She volunteers at a hedgehog rescue center. They use syringes for feeding the babies."

"But the pills . . ."

Susan clamped a hand on each of her friends' shoulders, steering them toward the entrance to the medical school.

"I put a call out on the phase 1 group chat asking if anyone else used Microgynon 30 and if I could have a pack. It's not been filched from Family Planning or anything."

"Do you have any more of those syringes?" Daisy asked. "They might be handy for Baby Gordon."

The medical school canteen had the same whiff of industrialized catering about it as the dining hall in Catterick Hall, but Susan assured them the food was better—she was positively evangelical about the potato wedges.

"So . . . better than halls, then?" Esther teased.

"Believe me, there's no way I'd be able to eat that crap for three meals a day. I'd make a sandwich or something."

"No, you wouldn't," Esther said with complete conviction. "You'd find some unsuspecting sap and steal their lunch instead."

"You make me sound like a bully."

"That makes it sound like it's not true."

"Daisy!" Susan reeled her into the conversation. "Tell Esther I'm not a bully."

"Well . . ."

"Say it! 'Susan Ptolemy is not a bully.'"

But someone from three places down in the queue leaned out and said, "You took my phone and deleted the number of the guy who'd sent me a photo of his penis."

"That penis was *diseased*. And unsolicited," Susan protested.

"Did you say Susan Ptolemy?" came a shout from a few paces back. "She spent the whole of Introduction to Embryology flicking me in the back of the head with a rubber band because I'd accidentally mistaken her for my friend Matt."

"Hey!" A shorter, slightly swarthy, mop-topped young man wearing a red-checked shirt scowled up at him. "I look nothing like her!"

"She dumped a bottle of water over my head."

"*Your hair was on fire!*"

"She told me I looked like my face had athlete's foot."

"I said you should see a doctor!"

"She made me repeat to my reflection that I have terrible taste in men and deserve better."

"*How is that bullying?!*"

"There, there." Esther put a condescending arm over Susan's shoulders. "It can't be easy admitting I'm right."

Susan issued a noise that a vat of blood might make just as it reached boiling point and practically flung her tray in the direction of the till. Esther asked for a portion of wedges, and the man serving leaned forward, glancing fearfully to where Susan was growling at the card machine. "I give that one extra helpings because I'm frightened of the way she looks at me." He lowered his voice further. "And you can have some extra for being so brave as to challenge her tyranny."

Smugness emanating from her pores, Esther pushed her tray containing a triple helping of wedges toward the till.

"May I have potato wedges too, please?" Daisy asked, but the man shot her an apologetic look and gestured at the empty tray. Choosing a bagel instead, Daisy contemplated the nature of injustice—how Susan got appeasement wedges and Esther got gratitude wedges and Daisy, who only wanted her lawfully appointed volume of wedges, got none at all.

Despite an inauspicious start, lunch was pleasant enough. With Esther spending more time updating Susan on the many virtues of Vectra than eating, Daisy was able to sneak the occasional wedge from her plate.

"What's everyone got on this afternoon?" Daisy asked.

"I'm going to get these notes for Vectra," Esther said, not looking up from her phone, where she was relentlessly wearing down Ed Gemmell into giving them to her.

"Something called 'Street Medicine,'" Susan said.

"Ooh, that sounds exciting. Do you have to use cool-sounding slang for all your procedures?" Esther made a complicated arrangement with her fingers and crossed her arms, pouting as she said, "Hey, doc, hit me up with some 'slin for my 'betes."

Daisy and Susan stared at her for a full second before bursting out laughing, collapsing into each other, Susan slapping the table as Daisy doubled over, clutching her friend's arm, barely able to draw breath, she was laughing so hard.

Susan did an uncannily accurate impression of Esther's pose, reaching around to snatch an orange from the person eating at the next table. "My girl, Daisy-Woo? How 'bout some Vit-C to boost that immuno-sys?"

Susan tossed the orange at Daisy, who could barely see it through her tears.

But something was wrong with Esther. Usually the first to laugh at herself, her expression had turned from light to dark as fast as if she were a shiny penny dropped into the mud at the bottom of a well.

"I'm sorry for not immediately understanding what you meant by 'street' medicine and trying to make a joke."

"You were a joke, all right." Susan fired a finger gun across the table and blew away the imaginary smoke, winding Esther up so much that she actually stood to leave.

"Oh, Esther, we're only playing!" Daisy called after her, but Esther ignored her, sashaying off across the room and tipping the remains of her wedges, which Daisy had been hoping to eat, into the waste bin. She didn't even glance back before she left the room entirely.

Daisy looked across at Susan, who tipped back the dregs of her soda can and set it on her tray with a clatter. "In my not-yet-professional medical opinion, I suspect that Esther's new Goth friend has infected her with a sense-of-humor failure. A common malady among the macabre community."

"But . . . Esther's never been like that!"

"No, but this Vectra will expect our Es to take herself seriously. Trust me."

Daisy didn't much like the thought of that.

After parting ways with Susan, Daisy started to make her way out of the building, wondering how her friends would have reacted to her afternoon plans. Not that either of them had shown any interest in asking about them . . .

Which might be for the best, given that she was attending another session with the Brethren. Her previous commitments had limited Daisy to attending the Tuesday evening sessions, but now that she had more time, she thought she might attend a drop-in session that afternoon. Provided she could think of something to share.

Deep in thought, Daisy missed her turn in the corridor and found herself exiting the building via the medical school. It wasn't especially illuminating. As in any other university building, all one got to see of the lectures were the doors. There were bulletin boards, of course, as well as screens displaying information that might as well have been written in a different language, for all Daisy could make of them. It wasn't until she passed the reception desk that she saw something familiar. Or, rather, someone.

"Grace!" Daisy brightened, raising her hand in a half wave as their paths were about to cross.

"Hey, Daisy," Grace said. Her smile was real, but there was a nervous edge to the way she dodged eye contact.

"How've you been?" Daisy did her best to sound like someone who cared, but not so much that Grace would pull away. The kind of delicate line Daisy trod when feeding Baby Gordon.

"Oh. You know. Same." Grace shrugged. "Start every morning with a shot of coffee and an energy drink to get me through the day, then stay up all night worrying what I'm doing with my life."

Daisy took a second to check she'd heard correctly. "That's a lot more truthful than I was expecting."

Grace squinted at her as if she wasn't sure Daisy was being honest. "Most people assume it's a joke."

"Oh. Well, is it?"

Although she half expected Grace to try to convince her it was, the girl's shoulders drooped, and she collapsed into a chair. Taking Grace's cue, Daisy perched on the edge of the chair next to her, hands tucked between her knees as she looked on solicitously, hoping that whatever Grace was going to say, Daisy would somehow be able to help.

"I'm homesick. That's all. My course is tough, I miss my boyfriend, and yet all I do when he calls is shout at him. I'm tired. *So* tired. All I want is to sleep, and all I end up doing is staying out." Grace looked at her then, properly, as if she was seeing Daisy as someone she could trust. "I just feel so lost, you know?"

What Grace needed wasn't night after night out. What she needed was a family.

"This is a weird question," Daisy said, "but do you like yoga?"

8

DESPERATE MEASURES

So many weeks of sleepless nights and a relentless schedule of lectures was starting to take its toll.

"Susan! Wake up!" Kully hissed.

"Not asleep," Susan groaned. She wished she was. She'd fallen forward, head pressed on the warm glass over the hot-breakfast section in the dining hall. "I am the waking dead."

"Wake a little further. You're holding up the breakfast queue."

Reluctantly, Susan slid her cheek along the glass.

Last night Susan had stayed up hate-watching every Richard Curtis film she could illegally stream onto her laptop. It had been the only way to distract her from the merry-go-round of anxieties arising from Esther's new infatuation with this weirdo Goth Girl added to the standard simmering rage regarding McGraw. She'd had to drag herself out of the nadir she'd reached when she found herself contemplating a "Buy It Now" option for *About Time*, after which point she'd stared at her ceiling until the birds had started singing and she'd eventually fallen into a fitful doze that proved less restful than the things she'd been doing while awake.

"Carbs . . . sugar . . ." Susan muttered, slathering butter and jam onto her toast, once they sat down.

Kully gave Susan's breakfast a dismissive sniff as he sliced an apple over a bow of muesli. "You need vitamins and protein."

"I NEED SLEEP."

Susan's snarl echoed around a suddenly silent canteen before everyone returned to their own conversations.

"So sleep, then." Kully shrugged. "Snatch a power nap in a bathroom stall between lectures."

"A nap will disrupt my diurnal rhythm."

"You diurnal rhythm is about as consistent as the Internet connection in F-block." Kully eyed Susan's hands, which were now smeared in grease and sugar, such was the accuracy of her jam application. "Are you sure you're going to be OK to lead today's Anatomy practical?"

"What? No!" Susan tried to read the timetable she'd scrawled on her hand before realizing that was left over from yesterday. Pulling up her sleeve, she found faded ink detailing last week's schedule. No sign of today: Monday. Susan tipped her head back and howled at the ceiling, "Curse you, Richard Curtis, and your inability to distribute gender-balanced speaking roles!"

Opposite, Kully gave her a mild raise of an eyebrow before reaching into his monogrammed leather satchel and pulling out a can so bright, it could cause a migraine from fifty paces.

"Desperate times call for desperate measures," he said, sliding it across the table.

"What's this?"

"You haven't ever pepped up with a little ENN-ARR-GEE?" Kully's face was the picture of astonishment. "Late-night Physics revision? Partying till three when you're the designated driver?"

"I have never done either of these things," Susan said, picking up the can and looking at the label. The colors alone made her eyes buzz, and try as she might to find the ingredients list, the typeface was impossible to read.

Cracking the lid, Susan downed the lot.

Since Vectra had talked to her, Esther had upped her sartorial efforts in an attempt to prompt further interaction. Today she was wearing red leather shorts, fishnets, and a "top" that was essentially nothing more than a complex array of stretchy bandages that had taken her half an hour to put on that morning.

Although Ed Gemmell said he liked it, his expression was one of terror, and he kept casting Esther anxious glances as she spent the lecture calculating the perfect trajectory from bench to door. When the lecture ended, Esther's plotted course intercepted that of Vectra Featherstone's exactly three paces from the main door.

Ever polite, Ed Gemmell held it open for both of them.

"What? You want a cookie?" Vectra shot him a wry look before doubling back to confuse him with a compliment. "Those notes on how the camera angles encourage a mainstream audience were pretty intense. Thanks for letting me copy."

Ed Gemmell started, darting a confused glance in Esther's direction. She'd not exactly been truthful as to why she'd wanted the notes, feigning an interest in swapping modules for the next semester.

Never one to let a silence remain uncomfortable, Ed Gemmell cleared his throat and pointed nervously to the necklace Vectra wore.

"I, um, that's cool. Is it real?"

"What do you think?"

He swallowed, eyes flitting nervously from Esther to Vectra, voice trembling with the kind of tension you'd expect from a finalist on *The X Factor*. "I think wearing a real razor blade that close to your throat would be very unwise?"

Vectra rolled her eyes and met Esther's gaze. "The company we're forced to keep."

We! So delighted at being included in the same pronoun as Vectra, Esther decided to overlook the fact that this comment had come at her friend's expense, choosing instead to focus on the excitement of discovering that Vectra, too, was heading from lectures to the S.U. With every step bringing them closer, Esther allowed herself the excitement of imagining a coffee together. A straight-out invitation wouldn't work, but maybe if she casually mentioned needing a drink . . .

As they stepped toward the glass doors of the S.U., Esther opened her mouth, ready to deploy her plan.

"Er, hi, sorry, excuse me, are you Esther?"

Alarmed at the sound of her name, Esther turned to find herself face-to-face with a young man with a closely shaved head and tortoiseshell glasses. When he raised his eyebrows above the round frames, he looked a little like an owl.

"Back off, stalker." Vectra stepped between them. Half a head shorter than either of them, she held the same threat as a cocked hand grenade.

The boy backed off a couple of steps, arms up in surrender.

"Whoa there! I'm not trying to be creepy. My name's Anthony—Tony—Grace's boyfriend. From back home?" He shot Esther a pleading look across Vectra's head. "I recognized you from one of the photos she posted."

"Yes! She told me all about you." Which was a bit of an exaggeration. "I thought you were down in Plymouth?"

"I am. I was." He glanced at Vectra and lowered his hands. "I got the train up today to surprise her, only she's not around. Her housemates said to try the Union." He pointed through the doors. "Which I'm assuming is right there?"

"Why don't you just call her?" Ed Gemmell said.

"Her phone's been off for the last couple of days—that's kind of why I'm here. I was worried."

Just as Esther was about to say how sweet that was, Vectra gagged and said, "Or maybe take a hint?"

There was an awkward pause in which none of them really knew what to say.

"You could try up at the hospital. I'll message my friend Susan—they're on the same course." Although lectures were over, and Esther had no idea whether Grace and Susan were rostered to do any of the other weird things on their course together. A dull nudge of guilt elbowed her in the stomach when Esther realized that in the unlikely event of some tenacious paramour looking for a phoneless Susan, Esther wouldn't be able to say where to find her, either.

"Something like this happened in an episode of *Buffy the Vampire Slayer*," Ed Gemmell said, eyebrows knotted as they watched Tony stride away to find his lost girlfriend. "It didn't end well."

"My *mum* goes on about that show." Vectra gave him a disdainful look. "You really need to get a life."

"I, er, yup . . ." Ed Gemmell fiddled with the straps of his backpack. "Heh. Can't really argue with that."

"Can you imagine being so naive as to start university already in a relationship?" Vectra returned to the Grace issue.

Esther was very aware of Ed Gemmell looking at her when she said, "I know. What a chump."

Vectra shrugged. "Screw love."

"Yeah, screw it. Hammer it. Sand it down like a dodgy plank." Esther stopped herself. Would Vectra respect this level of DIY puns? It was a risk . . . but Vectra gave her an indecipherable look before nodding toward the S.U.

"Want to come bitch about love with me over a disappointing panini?"

"Sure!" Esther beamed, dialing it down a bit when she saw Vectra's expression.

"I . . . er . . ." Ed Gemmell looked wildly about and pointed in the opposite direction. "Just got to go do a thing."

They watched him scurry off toward the English faculty.

"You should keep him around." Vectra nodded after him. "Virgins make excellent sacrifices."

Already, the walk up to the House of Zoise was starting to feel less like a journey to a yoga session and more like coming home. It helped that the walk between the Archaeology Department and the suburb in which Jasper and Elise lived took Daisy through one of Sheffield's many parks. Sometimes, if she closed her eyes and held her breath, she could imagine she was back in Crickleton, the *ploop* of an upended duck in the pond, a breeze riffling the last of the leaves, the damp grass turning the toes of her shoes soggy . . .

The hiss of tires from an oncoming cyclist, about to knock her over.

You didn't get *that* in Crickleton. No one there was ever in enough of a hurry.

When Daisy knocked on the door, Sister Chloe opened it. Sister Chloe had been inducted into the Brethren the week before Daisy and wore a cyan belt around her robe.

"Hi, Daisy—no, wait." She stopped Daisy from coming in. "Zoise embraces you. Welcome, Sister."

Chloe grinned as she opened the door wide. She held a duster in her free hand, and a can of furniture polish peeped out of the pocket of her robe. Noticing the direction of Daisy's glance, Chloe shrugged. "So, I couldn't get any of my friends to come, and I don't want to just *hand over* all my stuff, but, like, I want to progress. Get the goods and the belts. So I had a word with Jasper, and he's put in this scheme where you can volunteer to share your *time* with the Brethren. So if I come here, sleep in Mei's barely occupied bedroom, and do all the housework for a week, bing, bang, bosh, I've paved my path to the next level."

"You sleep here?" Envy nipped at Daisy's insides; how lucky Chloe was to spend more time with Elise.

Chloe's shine faded a little. "Yeah, well, more than I do in my own house . . . my housemates are pretty hard to be around at the moment."

"I know what you mean," Daisy tried to empathize. "One of the people on my corridor plays really loud heavy metal when I'm trying to study."

"I'd take that over obnoxiously loud sex and finding chocolate body paint in with the Nutella."

"Oh." Daisy backpedaled. "Yours sounds much worse."

"Winning the nightmare-accommodation lottery!" A comment Chloe accompanied with a tight-lipped smile and a thumbs-up.

Daisy wondered why it was that she'd felt a need to grumble about Esther, when really, she quite liked listening to her angry music through the walls. There was something reassuring about Esther's undying allegiance to her own tastes in spite of all the ways in which university life could tempt you into something new. She hoped her friend's sense-of-humor failure in the hospital the other day had just been a blip, not a sign of changes to come. Daisy liked Esther exactly the way she was.

As always on initiation night, there were a couple of people looking distinctly uncertain about being in a room full of robed yoga fans. Grace had been the same when she'd come here last week, but when Daisy scanned the room, she saw her slouched back in the beanbags by the windows, a plate of cookies balanced on her tummy, wearing what looked suspiciously like the same clothes she'd been wearing when the two of them had dropped in for an afternoon session two days ago.

A sunburst of pride waxed in Daisy's chest at the thought of being the one to introduce Grace to the family, and she wondered whether she knew anyone else who might benefit from joining the Brethren . . .

Moving among the groups of people, taking the fresh cups to where Elise was reading chakras and dispensing infusions, Daisy smiled, uttering words of welcome to fellow Brethren, enjoying the alien sensation of being the one to reassure the newcomers, to feel that quiet confidence that comes from knowing you belong.

The sound of a gong washed over the gathered crowd, and they turned to face the front. Jasper was standing there, robe hanging open, hands resting casually in the pockets of his jogging bottoms. As when he'd opened the door to Daisy, he gave off an air of bemusement, as if he weren't quite sure how everyone had gotten there. There was some-thing disarmingly charming about it.

"Welcome, Brethren, and friends of the family." Seeing the nervous glances on the newcomers' faces, he laughed, flapping a casual hand in their direction. "Ah, don't worry about it. You'll get used to it. It's just the way we talk."

The inducted Brethren nodded, and the people responsible for their friends laid a comforting hand on their arms. Daisy tried to share a moment with Grace, but her head was tilted back, eyes closed. She appeared to be snoring.

Taking a sip of her own herbal tea, Daisy breathed in the calming scent of jasmine and chamomile, enjoying the warmth rolling down her throat and into her tummy, a satisfying glow spreading out from her center and relaxing her mind.

Jasper was still talking, explaining the structure of Zoise, the concept of sharing, and the pursuit of worldly peace.

"So we start the session by forming a semicircle around the lectern, get comfy, there's beanbags and tea—no, take as many cookies as you want. No guest of the Brethren leaves here hungry . . ." Jasper was gently guiding everyone to sit. Pretty, vulnerable girls and pretty, vulnerable boys swooned a little as the tea and cookies dismantled their inhibitions, and they felt comfortable enough to let their eyes linger a little longer than strictly necessary on Jasper's offhand smile and soft auburn curls.

Elise passed the bowl around, each person putting their phone inside.

"The world will turn without me," Daisy said, intoning the chant as she put her phone in. It was a shame that phones were forbidden from these sessions—a photo of Jasper would be a persuasive argument in recruiting Esther.

He was standing now by the lectern, the belt he would be awarding hanging around his neck, giving the impression of a rakish society gentleman returning home in the early hours of the morning. With a thrill, Daisy noticed it was cyan, the first belt of achievement, and she wondered who it was for.

"As always, before the Ceremony of Sharing, Zoise opens the door to those of us who have opened ourselves to Zoise." He smiled then, self-deprecating, taking the weight of the words he was saying lightly, inviting everyone in on the joke. "Step forward please, Sister Daisy."

"Me?" Daisy's heart fluttered up into her throat as she took a tentative step forward. "But I've yet to master the Nodding Dog . . ."

Jasper waved her closer, and Daisy's feet seemed to have decided this was where she was going. The tea had worked its magic, and the world was turning fuzzy.

"No one works harder on their yoga moves than you, Daisy. Zoise thanks you for your efforts, and for bringing unto us Sister Grace." Who was asleep in the corner. As family members went, she wasn't particularly active. "You are now a Cyan Sister."

The others applauded as Jasper carefully threaded Daisy's new bright blue belt through the loops of her gown. Overwhelmed by so much attention, Daisy gazed down at her toes. She'd let Esther paint her toes a few weeks ago, and they were still mostly a pretty pearly pink.

"Your belt and your cookies." Jasper handed her a prettily packaged little bag of Zoise cookies. "Share only with those you trust."

And he winked at her, a conspiratorial twist to the way he was smiling.

"Take a place on the mat. You've earned it." Jasper gestured to Elise, who gave Daisy a fresh brew with a kiss on the forehead. After just one sip, Daisy felt the warmth of confidence flow through her body. Today she would master the Nodding Dog.

She would honor her position as a Cyan Sister.

Over uneaten paninis (Vectra had declared hers inedible after the first bite, and Esther talked too much to manage more than three mouthfuls), Esther learned that the harder one tried to impress Vectra Featherstone, the less she liked you.

The conversation had taken a swerve toward disastrous when she'd told Vectra that her piece they were critiquing in Creative Writing that week was "an inspired exercise in manipulating clichés into tortured falsehoods." Vectra had rolled her eyes and uncrossed her legs as if about to leave.

"Actually, I wrote the whole thing using predictive text, so, like, you're really just complimenting an algorithm."

Panicked, Esther's response was, "Well, that algorithm writes better prose than me!" Followed by a bit of borderline hysterical laughter and a not-entirely untrue, "Everything I write ends up like catharsis through public humiliation."

For the first time since they'd sat down, Vectra's interest shifted from their surroundings to Esther as she leaned forward and said, "Cathartic *how*?"

And so began the debasement. Esther's attempt at long-distance love ("So *you* were the chump?!") to the ill-considered one-nighter ("What? *Him* with the baseball caps? How drunk *were* you, Grooty?"). Somehow it all came pouring out, Vectra's watchful silence and dry interventions the perfect receptacle for all of Esther's romantic woes. All the things she'd held back from anyone else, for fear they were already bored of hearing about it, but Vectra was new, and the more Esther talked down her terrible choices, the more Vectra warmed to her company.

Well, *thawed*, might have been more accurate, as if her affection had been taken out of the freezer to defrost in the fridge.

Eventually, a congealed panini and two cups of coffee later, Vectra actually *laughed*, revealing rows of such perfect little white teeth that it seemed a shame she so rarely showed them off in a smile.

Esther couldn't have felt a greater sense of achievement if she'd rewritten *The Canterbury Tales* in dactylic hexameter.

The conversation edged away from Esther's failures to Vectra's relative triumphs—the time the drummer from Gravedust sent her love letters written in what turned out to be chicken's blood, the deliciously doomed affair she'd conducted with her married Art teacher who'd wooed her with his one-stroke watercolor brush technique, and the lost love of her life who'd moved to the other side of the world and turned away from the dark.

"Every picture he posts is disgustingly wholesome. We fell out when his sister got a kitten. Didn't take it too kindly when I made a joke about shaving off its fur so he'd be less tempted to post so many photos."

Mentally reviewing her own Instagram feed, Esther

decided she was safe. Dark nail art, graveyards . . . the closest thing to cute that she'd ever posted was a picture of an owl pellet. If Esther had slumped any farther forward in her eagerness to listen, she'd have ended up sprawled on the table. As it was, just as she was reaching the tipping point, they were interrupted by an approaching lad, who stopped a foot away and cleared his throat.

"Hello, you lovely—"

"No." Vectra sneered and wafted the boy away like a bad smell in a gesture reminiscent of one that Susan used on many an occasion. God, those two would get on *brilliantly* . . .

" —Japanese—"

"Leave."

"—horror?" But Vectra had turned the full force of her formidable glare in his direction, and he dropped a flyer on their table before scuttling off as fast as possible to the other side of the seating area.

Esther leaned forward and picked up the flyer. There was a line of Japanese script and underneath:

A connoisseur's collection of films by Kōji Shiraishi

(Expect subtitles. Obviously.)

Her eyes widened. A test! Japanese horror was the only genre of film she cared about. Creepy, long-haired women; vengeful videocassettes; unbridled violence . . . what wasn't to love?

Cautious, not wanting to reveal how much this mattered, Esther held the flyer up to show Vectra, eyebrows raised in a suitably ambivalent manner, allowing Vectra to draw what she would from the expression. Vectra's gaze flickered over the words before meeting Esther's.

"Kōji Shiraishi? As if googling Japanese horror directors and not bothering to look beyond the first page makes you a 'connoisseur.'" Even her air quotes were half-hearted as her eyes rolled back in contempt.

Esther could barely breathe for excitement. Vectra knew who Kōji Shiraishi was. More to the point, she knew so much about the genre that she considered him *mainstream*. This was it.

"Shall we go anyway?" Too hopeful. Vectra needed her plans peppered with cynicism. "It's not like there's anything better to do."

There was a long, pin-drop moment in which Esther felt like a gladiator waiting for the emperor's verdict.

Vectra shrugged. "Whatever."

Someone was singing Daisy's name. She was a daisy in a field, and all the daisies were complimenting one another on how soft their petals were, how cheerful their smiles; they called one another "Brother" and "Sister," and the sun was reading to them, and Daisy blossomed, throwing her face to the sky and . . .

"Daisy!"

A dark weed was in their midst. The flowers started to panic as the moon shoved the sun from the sky and hissed angrily at the meadow below.

"Daisy Wooton, this is an emergency!"

The moon had brought with it a storm! A shower of drops

spattered across Daisy's face as she lifted her petal hands to protect herself . . . and realized she wasn't wearing her glasses.

She was not a flower in the meadow. She was dreaming.

When Daisy managed to drag her eyes open, the beautiful moon revealed itself to be Esther, who was holding a water bottle with a sports cap, poised to squirt Daisy in the face again. Words floated through Daisy's brain, but her mouth was too slow to catch them. So she blinked, lashes a little gummy from sleep, and tried to converse with Esther through the power of her mind.

Esther simply stared back, waiting for a response.

"Daisy?" she said eventually. "Are you awake? Your eyes are open, but I've watched far too much Japanese horror this evening to cope with anything other than some very specific confirmation that you're not a somnambulant serial killer."

Daisy went for it. "Whmupmhsmblumkllerrrr."

"Brilliant. You're plotting my untimely and violent death, aren't you?" This fact didn't seem to bother Esther as much as one might expect. "Between you and whatever's scavenging in our kitchen, I'm done for."

Groping for her glasses, Daisy managed to poke herself in the eye with the stem before pushing them onto her nose, so that the room, and an edgy-looking Esther, clad in what looked like gaffer's tape and pleather, came into focus.

"There's something in the kitchen," Esther whispered. Then she added, "You should really lock your door at night, Daisy. Anyone could just wander in here, you know."

The lights were off in the hall, but when Daisy reached for the switch, Esther stopped her with a quick shake of her head.

"Listen!"

There were, indeed, noises coming from the kitchen.

As they crept carefully along the corridor, Esther's grasp dug so deeply into the flesh of Daisy's arm that Daisy wondered whether she shouldn't be more afraid of Esther than of whatever lay ahead. On reaching the door, the two exchanged looks: Esther's gallows-grim determination met Daisy's cautious curiosity.

They stepped into the kitchen doorway—and stared.

Every single cupboard was open, the contents heaped on the table. Stray lentils and noodle fragments dusted the spaces between packets and boxes and nine tins of supermarket-brand beans.

Stacked on the seat of each chair sat a tower of bowls, plates, mugs, and glasses, with the toaster, kettle, and new microwave on the floor underneath.

Over by the sink, in striped pajama bottoms and an over-size T-shirt, feet bare, hands clad in the familiar yellow of Daisy's rubber gloves, stood . . .

"Susan?" Esther's grip relaxed, and she stepped from behind Daisy to stare in shock at the horror before them.

"Help me," Susan said, face haggard, eyes practically vibrating in their sockets.

"Sure!" Daisy said. "Hand me the spray and some kitchen towels."

"Not with the kitchen!" A muscle in Susan's cheek spasmed. "I've been awake for *fifty-two hours.*"

"That's an awfully long time to be awake . . ."

"YOU THINK?" Susan howled, waving at her surroundings. "Look at what it's reduced me to."

"Becoming someone conscientious enough to understand that communal areas are the responsibility of those who use them and not just the person with the lowest tolerance for mess?" Daisy asked. It was a bit of a reach.

"I. Can't. Sleep." Susan wildly misjudged the location of her limbs in relation to the recycling bin. As the bin toppled over, the contents spilled out across the floor, empty can upon empty can of ENN-ARR-GEE with flavors like Lawless Lychee, Lemonade Can Grenade, Berserker Boysenberry . . . Esther picked one up. Pineapoplectic. There was a label in the smallest possible print. CAUTION: DO NOT CONSUME MORE THAN 500ML IN ANY 24-HOUR PERIOD.

"How many of these have you had?" Esther said, looking up from the label. There were ten cans scattered at their feet.

"Didn't you read the label?" Daisy asked.

"I can't. The letters are all blurry." Something strange had happened to Susan's face.

"Susan . . . are you *crying*?"

"These are not tears. This is what happens when you consume so much caffeine that your eyeballs melt." Susan put her finger to her pulse. "Either my heart's beating so fast that my pulse is nothing more than a single continuous beat, or I'm dead."

Time for some drastic action.

"You stay here . . ." Daisy whispered to Esther before hurrying back to her room. Pushing the door shut, just to be safe, Daisy leaned over the box on the windowsill that contained Baby Gordon's nest. It was a big, sprawling affair—an old box of printer paper in which Daisy had tucked an old towel, before layering shredded paper and leaves to form a soft, nestlike bed. Gently lifting the corners of the towel, she transferred the sleeping chick from box to bed, revealing what was hidden underneath.

A lockbox with a combination padlock that opened to reveal Daisy's passport, a photo of Daisy and her parents taken on her second birthday, a watch whose battery needed replacing, and her bag of Zoise cookies. Cyan belts were given only three cookies, but with the state Susan was in, she'd need all of them. Taking the tin out, she popped Gordon back where he belonged and returned to the kitchen.

If Daisy wanted more, she'd just have to work hard to make it up to magenta belt.

Daisy had been gone *forever*. Of this, Susan was convinced. How else could she have had the time to descale the kettle, clean inside every cupboard, put everything back, and itemize the contents alphabetically? Esther wasn't helping. All she kept doing was following Susan and taking everything she put in the cupboards back out and muttering that no one would be able to find anything.

"Susan?" Daisy shimmered in and out of focus, as

substantial as a mirage. "Why don't you take the gloves off and come with me?"

"What gloves?" Susan stared down at her hands and watched as Daisy held her wrists still and Esther appeared to peel off a layer of jaundiced skin to reveal neonatally pink fingers.

"Come on now . . ."

Susan buzzed along the corridor and back into her room, where Esther folded her into a seated position on the bed and Daisy handed her a plate with a cookie on it and a cup of warmed milk.

"No one can sleep when they're hungry."

Susan couldn't remember the last time she'd eaten. She now functioned on a plane beyond the physical. She was a wormhole.

"Eat the cookie, Susan."

When Daisy returned from the library, something very strange happened.

Susan Ptolemy hugged her.

It was like being slowly consumed by an affectionate steamroller, and Daisy wasn't sure whether she would survive.

"I slept for two days straight, Daisy Wooton, and I love you."

"Could you maybe let go of me?"

Susan released her, and air rushed to fill the vacuum in Daisy's lungs. She found it hard to believe this was the same person she'd seen in the kitchen at three A.M. the other night. Susan's hair was glossy, her eyes bright, and her skin shone with something other than the sheen of sweat that emerged when she was forced to walk at the same pace as her friends. She looked so like a freshly groomed spaniel that it was tempting to pat her on the head.

Daisy resisted.

"Didn't you have lectures to go to? Cadavers to dissect?"

Susan flapped it all away. "Kully took notes. And the only other thing was a session at the medical center yesterday afternoon, but I've already e-mailed an elaborate yet plausible reason for missing that one."

As Susan spoke, Daisy unlocked her door, remembering just in time that she'd been doing some yoga earlier and had yet to put her robe away. Faced with the possibility of Susan seeing this, Daisy felt a sudden stab of pain in the middle of her forehead.

"I suppose this means I'll have to go back to keeping the kitchen clean on my own," Daisy managed, bringing her fingers up to massage the growing ache in her third eye.

"Not if you give me your magic soporific cookie recipe."

Share only with those you trust, Jasper's voice intoned inside her head. Surely Daisy could trust Susan. She was one of Daisy's best friends.

But when she opened her mouth to suggest she come to the next meeting of the Yogic Brethren of Zoise, the words that formed were not the ones she intended to say.

"Some things should only be shared with those who wish to walk the path."

Even Daisy was taken aback at how flat and strange her intonation was, but after a second, Susan seemed to shrug it off.

"Fair point. It's not like I'm going to do any baking, is it?" She patted Daisy on the arm. "Make sure you bake double the number in your next batch."

"Of course!" Daisy nodded a little too fervently, but in her beatific state, Susan didn't seem to notice, drifting contentedly back to her room. Unsettled, Daisy hurried through the door and, dropping her bag on the floor, immediately assumed Listening Pose and pressed the buds of her earphones into her ears, starting the calming cycle of the latest Zounds of Zoise.

9

VERIFICATION

Esther had been talking nonstop for the last hour.

English students.

During their conversation, Susan had successfully completed a practice paper, read an article on gestational diabetes and compared it with notes she'd taken from Mrs. Doherty, watched the last fifteen minutes of the *My Little Brony* documentary she'd started watching the previous night, and posted a cathartic rant under the angrier of her Reddit pseudonyms in response to an accusation of so-called reverse racism.

Esther, it seemed, hadn't even managed to finish her cup of tea.

A paper airplane cruised lazily over Susan's shoulder and landed on her keyboard.

Pay me attention.

"I am paying you attention," Susan said without looking up.

"Then what have I been talking about?"

In response, Susan held up her phone and played back the last ten seconds of the voice memo.

"*You'd really like her. I really like her. I'm not sure whether she likes me. I'm going to need independent verification. So how about it?"*

"You want me to come to the pub with you this evening so I can meet your wonderful new friend Vectra, assuage your insecurities, and receive free drinks all evening for services rendered." Susan turned in her chair and grinned. "I'll be drinking the finest whisky Wetherspoons has to offer, thanks."

"Actually, Vectra thinks pubs are a rip-off."

"*Wetherspoons*? That famously cheap chain of drinking establishments?"

But Esther ignored the objection. "I'm meeting her in the S.U. The Stand-up Comedy Club is running an open mic night."

"No." Susan turned back around in her seat and waved the idea away. "Take Daisy."

"Can't. She's got yoga tonight."

"Again? Seems like she's got yoga every bloody night. What about Ed Gemmell, then?"

"He's playing pool with McGraw." Susan could *feel* the look in Esther's eyes as she added, "They might come along later."

"That's nice. Leave them a seat at the front, and whoever's onstage can destroy their self-esteem with comments about their appearances." The thought of this made it almost tempting . . .

"*Pleeeeeeease.*" Esther draped herself across the desk and pouted hopefully. "I really think the two of you will get along."

× × × × ×

Daisy always enjoyed the bone lab. There was something deeply satisfying about studying bone fragments. It was like piecing together a skeletal jigsaw to tell a story about the past.

"What've you got there?" Reggie peered over Daisy's shoulder.

"Fibula. Left. According to the carbon-dating record, it's placed between 345 and 420 AD. Dug up in St. Albans."

"Roman. Snap."

"Mine's female. I think she looks like a Metella. What do you think?"

"I think she looks like a bone fragment." Reggie sounded far from enthusiastic, and Daisy noticed he was wearing the same T-shirt he'd been wearing yesterday. And the day before. It said *(Carbon) date me?* And there were soil stains on the hem and something that looked like toothpaste smudged above the *C* of *Carbon*.

Professor Jones walked past to cast an eye over their work.

"At some point, you're going to have to learn your arse bone from your elbow, Reginald. That's a jawbone, and you're looking at it upside down. You've got to think around your specimens in more than a single plane. When one discovers something buried in the earth, it is rarely the right way up."

Daisy held her breath while Professor Jones scrutinized her work, but the older woman let out a grudging sort of grunt, nodded, and moved on.

Trying not to bask in the glory of what was tantamount to praise, Daisy gave Reggie a sympathetic smile.

"Don't take it to heart."

"Every time, Daisy, every time." Reggie rotated his bone somewhat despondently and leaned in, gaze flitting around as he lowered his voice. "I think I'm doing the wrong course. I'm starting to get 'The Fear.' Like, what am I even doing with my life?"

"Don't say that—you've got all the makings of an archaeologist." Daisy nodded at his chest. "Look at your T-shirts!"

"I feel like such a fraud! People know me as Archaeology Dude—"

"They do?"

"—and if I left this course, then who would I be?"

The middle of the bone lab was not the best place to have an existential crisis, but it seemed now that Reggie had opened the trapdoor to the void, he was determined to hurtle through it.

"I'm no one!"

"That's not true."

"What would I wear? Who would I be? You don't know—*I* don't even know."

Daisy snapped her fingers sharply in front of Reggie's face. It was a trick she'd learned during Girl Guides whenever one of the younger members started to panic in the middle of camp.

"That's enough. You need to calm down."

"How? How can I calm down when everything is chaos?"

Daisy closed her eyes, and when she opened them, she knew what to do.

"Reggie. Have you ever tried yoga?"

✳ ✳ ✳ ✳ ✳

"Is that what you're wearing?" Esther gave a critical up-down sweep of Susan's attempt at an outfit.

"You mean clothes?" Susan crossed her arms and adopted the kind of glare that Esther knew better than to challenge. And yet . . . this was important. She needed Susan to make a good impression. For all Esther wanted to believe that it should be enough for her to like people for them to like each other, these were two tricky customers. All the variables had to be right.

Reflecting that it was a shame she hadn't been able to persuade Susan to buy something more than a coat when they went shopping, Esther selected a better ensemble: black T-shirt, black cardigan, gray jeans, cuffed to look a lot less tattered and a little more fashionable. To drown out Susan's grumbles about cold ankles as they trudged their way down the hill, Esther filled her in on the rules of engagement when interacting with Vectra, even more elaborate than the ones she'd written in her notebook just over a week ago.

". . . and whatever you do, don't try to pretend you know anything about music."

"Is that something I do?"

"You pretend you know everything."

"Because I do." Susan's voice had lowered to a growl, but Esther was resolute.

"Not music. You think just because you've been to one or two gigs—"

"Seventeen gigs and two festivals."

"—that you're entitled to an opinion."

"It's art, Esther. The whole point is to have an opinion."

"I can't risk you having a wrong opinion. Stow it."

They'd arrived at the S.U., and Esther stopped to check everything over. Black lipstick, best boots, leather trousers, massacred T-shirt . . .

"Hang on. How come I'm not allowed to have an opinion on music, but you're wearing this?" Susan jabbed her in the chest, right in Marilyn Manson's googly white eye. Or what was left of it. This was a seriously vintage article of clothing, a memento of Esther's days as an innocent baby goth. She'd been practically an *embryo* when she went to her first Marilyn Manson gig.

"Unlike you, I have the credentials," Esther said. This declaration of taste was a calculated risk. A tribute band called Charles Munroe had a gig in one of the local pubs next week—a strategic T-shirt was the perfect way to invite conversation and casually suggest that she and Vectra go.

It wasn't like Susan or Daisy would be interested.

Vectra took a long time getting to the bar, and Susan had to endure Esther's constant fidgeting, her attention bouncing back and forth between the door and her phone while Susan made her way steadily through her first drink. From Esther's description, she was about to meet either a kindred spirit of sarcasm or a total nightmare.

"There she is!" Esther hissed, then immediately added, "Don't look!"

"I wasn't."

Vectra saw Esther a moment later, but it took her a long

while to actually make it over to their little table. Maybe it was because of her tiny legs and frail little bones?

"What are you drinking?" Esther sprang up, knocking the table. Susan was interested in the disdainful flicker in Vectra's hooded eyes and the way Esther immediately downgraded her wide beam to a polite smile.

"Vodka, lime, and soda. Double. Fresh lime."

As Esther skipped off, seeming to forget Susan's existence, Susan took it upon herself to initiate contact.

"Fresh lime is a bit optimistic for a student bar," she said, raising a hand in a casual wave of welcome. "Hi. I'm Susan."

"I'm Vectra."

Once it was clear that was all she was going to say, Susan went on, "Vectra's an interesting name."

"Susan . . . is not."

The two looked at each other for a very long moment, each measuring the other to discover she came up short.

Susan was going to need that second whisky.

The basement was always warm. Not like "hot yoga" warm, but the sweet spot between sweater off and air-conditioning on. It was the equivalent of a pleasantly snug duvet on a morning you didn't have anything to get up for. The kind of place that, once you were in, you didn't want to leave.

"What do you think?" Daisy asked, sticking close to Reggie to make sure he didn't feel intimidated. She needn't have worried.

"I think that cookie was the best thing I've ever eaten." Reggie held his hand in front of his face. "I feel like I'm melting."

A new acolyte had answered the door for them tonight. Daisy was starting to lose count of all the different fresh young faces she'd seen in the house recently. There seemed to be a never-ending carousel of Brethren, some staying for days; some who came once, never to return; and some regulars with colorful belts and a casual attitude to yogic meditation, who seemed more interested in cookies and socializing than in discovering new poses.

Some of the more affluent initiates opted to hand over possessions in the Ceremony of Sharing rather than bringing friends or helping with housework. Brother Jacob seemed to have an infinite supply of console-related nonsense to hand over to the Brethren, but Daisy's supply of goods was running low. Last session she'd brought in her favorite mug, hoping that the emotional value was significant enough to be considered worthy of Zoise, but Jasper had quietly taken her aside as she was leaving and explained that while worldly worth mattered not on the meditative plane, he felt that perhaps Daisy was not as committed to the Brethren as he had first thought.

Pressing the mug back into her hands, Jasper had given her a sorrowful look.

"If we cannot share, we cannot belong."

"But what of the emotional value of my transaction?" Daisy had looked down at the rejected mug, the wonky daisy she'd painted on it as a little girl and the speech bubble that didn't quite fit the words *I'm a flower!* "Doesn't that count for something?"

Jasper had looked long and hard at the mug.

"I'll be honest with you, Daisy. Emotional value usually corresponds to something more . . . appealing. Zoise desires more than a kid's mug."

Today, with Reggie by her side, some of that fear was assuaged. She was sharing. She belonged . . . but for how long?

When Elise sounded the gong, and the Pathway Unlocked, Daisy presented Reggie as her gift to the Brethren.

"This is Reggie. We study Archaeology together. I don't think he's alone in having anxiety about what course he's on—"

There was a murmur of agreement among some of the others in the room.

"—but I know Zoise has helped release my anxieties, and it might help yours," Daisy finished, looking hopefully up at Reggie.

The rest of the Brethren came into the circle to introduce themselves, exactly how it had been the first time she came. Warm and welcoming. A place that felt part of the university but safer somehow. Smaller and friendlier. And with really good cookies. Daisy smiled as Grace stepped forward and enveloped Reggie in a hug as if they'd known each other for weeks. Reggie's hands flapped at his sides, but then he hugged her, too.

"You'll love it here." Grace pulled back and gave both

Reggie and Daisy a fond look. "I'm so pleased Daisy asked me along. I never want to leave."

Once everyone had welcomed Reggie, Jasper took over.

"The Yogic Brethren of Zoise is all about finding inner calm by alternating between meditation and intense stretching. Take everything at your own pace. The important thing is to stay hydrated. Has Elise given you plenty of tea?"

Reggie held up his empty cup, and almost instantly one of the other Brothers emerged to fill it up.

"And so our circle grows. Zoise thanks you, Sister Daisy. Step forward and receive your bounty. You are now a . . ." Jasper pulled a tangle of belts out of the pocket of his gown, frowned briefly at the pink belt that Daisy had acquired the week before, and selected a bright yellow belt. "You are now a Yellow Sister."

But rather than thread the belt through the loops as he had with so many of the other Brethren, Jasper handed the belt over for Daisy to do herself, adding in a low voice, "You're the most dedicated of the Brethren, Daisy. No one's made it up to silver yet, but if that's what you want, you're going to have to sacrifice a little more of yourself. Zoise has other needs. Perhaps you could help restock the kitchen shelves—we're running a bit low on ingredients. Or can you reinstall Windows 10 on a laptop?"

Daisy shook her head. "I use Apple."

Jasper sighed. "Think on it, Daisy. What more can you give to Zoise? What sacrifice are you willing to make for your family?"

It was impossible to say anything right—unless the person saying it was Vectra. Even if Susan agreed with her, she still ended up wrong. So far she'd had been wrong about:

Her favorite ale.

Who was the best Mr. Darcy.

What flavor a white jellybean was.

Where the North started.

Whether you could get a ginger female cat. (WHICH YOU COULD, BECAUSE TIBBLES, WHO LIVED NEXT DOOR TO MRS. DOHERTY, WAS BOTH OF THOSE THINGS . . . but when Susan reached for her phone to show Vectra a picture, Vectra had shown such derision for people who used their phones to settle an argument that Susan had been distracted by thoughts of smashing the phone repeatedly into Vectra's face and settling things that way.)

"None of these people are very funny, are they?" Esther said as the last stand-up left the stage, giving up halfway through his set and leaving the audience with a blissful twenty minutes before the next.

Vectra nodded. "I've seen black holes that sucked less."

"See a lot of those, do you?" Susan was three drinks down and had stopped trying to be nice.

"Sarcasm. How droll."

Susan's rage was so intense that suppressing it must have caused her to black out, because the next thing she knew, she was tipping the contents of her purse out onto the bar and praying for enough change to buy a double shot.

"I don't think they take this here."

McGraw was next to her, long fingers holding something circular and shiny. The souvenir coin of St. Matthew that Susan had kept in a succession of wallets and purses since her yaya gave it to her when she was six years old.

"Thank you." She took it carefully, making sure there was no contact between her fingers and McGraw's.

"Since I'm ordering one for me and Ed, would you like me to buy you a drink?" he offered.

Such an offer directly contravened the ever-breachable Clause 4, but the flames of rage reserved for McGraw were losing their heat. In the last two nights, dwelling on her grudge had barely kept her awake long enough to see her alarm clock tip over into single digits. With Vectra on the scene, Susan's enmity toward McGraw seemed a little . . . unnecessary.

Besides, in accepting a drink from her old enemy, she could avoid further engagement with her new one.

"That would be great. Thank you."

"Still drinking Lagavulin? Single measure? Neat?"

"I am . . ." Susan looked him in the eye, waiting for a familiar stab of hostility. "But make it a double."

She was still waiting for it when he turned to summon the woman behind the bar.

Five whole minutes Susan had been speaking to McGraw, and Esther had yet to see blood. What was happening over there?

"I see Susan's ditched us for a guy." Vectra followed Esther's gaze. "Typical."

"No, I don't think—"

"Make that two guys. Richard Branson's arrived."

"Richard Branson?" Esther was confused—the only other person she could see talking to them was Ed Gemmell.

"You know. *Virgin*."

"Of course. Ha, ha, ha." Esther didn't like the sound of her laugh any more than she liked the joke. "We could always go up and—"

"No." Vectra turned her back on the bar. "Susan doesn't like me."

"She's like this with everyone."

"Then you should really get some better friends."

Esther wilted. Sure, Susan could be a bit caustic at times, and sarcasm was her first language, but Esther had never really seen that as a problem.

"Well, you've not yet met Daisy," she began, but Vectra was losing interest, and Esther decided against pursuing it. The amount of time Daisy spent doing yoga would make it impossible to arrange a meet-up anyway.

They needed something else to talk about, and Esther looked down at her T-shirt. Vectra was wearing a sweatband with the familiar Marilyn Manson logo stitched white on black, but she'd not mentioned Esther's outfit, and if Esther wanted to steer the conversation toward music, then she was the one who needed to take the wheel.

"Um . . . so . . . you like Marilyn Manson, too?"

"What gave you that idea?" Vectra frowned.

"Your um . . . this." Esther tapped Vectra's wrist, taken aback at how fast her friend recoiled from the contact. "Sorry."

"It's called irony, Grooty." Vectra swung the band around her wrist and then pointed to the print of the T-shirt she wore underneath her hoodie. "You really think I look like a *Star Wars* fan?"

Esther had no reference as to what a *Star Wars* fan looked like. Box office numbers suggested they were everywhere, lurking under perfectly normal facades.

"I, er, so you don't want to go and see an MM tribute band with me?"

Vectra curled her perfect, plum-tinted lips. "And party with the fat forty-year-olds who still think that kind of thing is current? No thanks."

When the next person walked into the spotlight, Vectra turned back to the front, while Esther stared up at the bar where Susan, McGraw, and Ed Gemmell were all laughing at something far funnier than student stand-up.

Walking back from the House of Zoise, Daisy scrolled through her phone, frowning at just how many missed calls from Granny she'd accrued. Weeks ago, such a thing would have been unfathomable. Voicemails were listened to, calls returned by a diligent granddaughter who missed her home.

Perhaps it was an indication of just how far she'd come since she signed up with the Brethren. She had a new family, with cookies and tea and yoga. She didn't need Granny anymore, in the same way she didn't need Susan and Esther. The Brethren of Zoise was where she belonged.

At least . . . it was supposed to be.

If we cannot share, we cannot belong.

What else was she supposed to share? She'd recruited two new members and gutted the contents of her bedroom. The only thing she'd yet to do was move in to do the cleaning and—judging by Jasper's comments—do all the things that the residents would expect from a parent.

When Daisy had yearned for a family, she hadn't envisioned that *she* would be the parent.

As she shoved her hands deeply into the pockets of her coat, Daisy's fingers closed around the two badges she'd made for Susan and Esther that she'd never had the chance to give them. Once she'd thought they were the best mums ever . . . but would they even notice if she moved out?

Needing the reassurance that the Zounds of Zoise provided, Daisy slipped on her headphones as she trudged back toward her dorm.

". . . *move through the physical, on through the emotional and into the spiritual . . . 100g of dark chocolate (at least 70 percent cocoa), two tablespoons of golden syrup . . . groceries delivered to 21 Tuttlebury Avenue would be great . . . mix the dry ingredients in a bowl . . . don't trust your friends, trust your Brethren . . .*"

When Daisy reached her room, she sat down in the dark, still in her coat, and opened her laptop to order groceries to be delivered to the House of Zoise.

Once the last comic died onstage, Susan asked the two boys if they'd come and sit with her.

"You mean . . . sit with Vectra?" Ed Gemmell glanced fearfully over his shoulder. "I'd rather not."

"Me neither," Susan whispered. "But Esther would like it."

"Come on, she can't be that bad . . ." McGraw said.

But Ed Gemmell and Susan gave McGraw equally grave looks. Still. Susan loved Esther, and she didn't want to upset her. Girding her loins of tolerance, she herded the other two away from the bar.

"If you're really so into music, why don't you support some of the bands that are just starting out?" Vectra was saying to Esther. She took a sheaf of flyers from her bag, and when she saw Susan, Ed Gemmell, and McGraw, she handed one to each of them. Underneath the logo of the pub was the tagline: *One night, thirteen must-see bands.*

"Thirteen?" Susan said. "That sounds like an unfeasibly large number to fit into one pub."

"Or one evening . . ." McGraw's slight frown spoke of frenzied mental calculation. "Fifteen minutes per band, allowing five-minute interludes for logistical stage management."

There was something exceptionally pleasurable in seeing the effect McGraw's comment had on Vectra.

"Am I supposed to be impressed by your mathematical agility?"

The spite in her voice was enough for McGraw to exchange a sympathetic glance with Susan before saying, "Only if simple arithmetic is something you find impressive."

Correction: *That* was exceptionally pleasurable.

There was an awkward pause into which Esther leaped with an optimistic, "I guess it's, like, a really short festival?"

"Grooty's got it." Somehow, even when agreeable, Vectra managed to be obnoxious. "This is the sort of thing you've got to do when you're starting out. Some of us have to take the opportunity where we can get it."

Each of them clocked the "us" at the same time, and Esther scanned the flyer for a clue. If she asked Susan later for independent verification on whether Vectra considered Esther a close friend, there was the evidence: absolutely not.

McGraw beat the rest of them to it. "Which band is yours?"

"Rutting Corpse." Vectra pointed to a band listed halfway down the page. "It was supposed to be Rotting Corps, but they got it wrong on the flyer, so we're leaning into it. Kevin's stenciled a logo of someone having sex on a gravestone onto his bass drum, and we're all going onstage dressed as sexy zombies."

Somehow, Susan managed to refrain from displaying her allergic reaction to the phrase "sexy zombies." It didn't matter how little she liked Vectra; Esther liked her, and for one night only, Susan could keep a lid on it.

"So, what are your influences?" Esther's inquiry was too keen, and Susan watched the exact second Vectra disengaged.

"No one you'd know," Vectra said dismissively. "Your taste is too mainstream."

At that moment, Esther knew what Susan was expecting, because she'd already witnessed the storm that words like this summoned. Susan was braced for it, drawing closer to McGraw, breath held, eyes wide. When Esther opened her mouth, Susan would expect hail and fire, as if Vectra had, in fact, opened a vortex to the underworld and a beast of fury were about to claw its way out from within Esther's skin.

Instead, Esther said, "Maybe you could send me some links?"

"Whatever. No need to pretend, Grooty." Vectra shrugged and looked past them to the far side of the room, as if scouting for someone better to talk to. "I don't really expect you to come. Gotta go."

"I'll see you at your gig!" Esther called out in desperation.

"Er . . . that's a week away. You'll see her tomorrow in lectures," Ed Gemmell said, looking confused.

"AND AT LECTURES!" Esther bellowed across the room, waving as Vectra turned and rolled her eyes before leaving.

That night, Susan had a think. A proper one. The kind that brought with it some perspective. It had been fun tonight—not with Vectra—but with McGraw and Ed Gemmell. Easy, almost, as if . . . well, as if they were friends. All the things she'd done, all the running away and the backfired acts of vengeance: the contract, the stalking, leaving a party where she'd been enjoying herself, the sleepless nights spent resenting his very existence. These were not the actions of someone who'd put the past behind her. It was the behavior of someone who was dragging it with her.

Maybe it was time to let things go.

And so, in the deadest hour of the night, when only foxes and insomniacs roamed the campus, Susan cut across the barren patch of grass between J-block and F-block. The door opened more smoothly than the other blocks', the hinges better oiled, the bottom of the door sanded to swish a little smoother over the bristles of the doormat.

Avoiding the sensors that would turn the lights on to illuminate the communal hallway, Susan weaved her way upstairs to number 15. There, she took an envelope from her pocket and slid it silently under the door.

It was done.

The next morning, McGraw woke up in a timely manner by willpower alone. In nothing more than a pair of jogging bottoms, he did some cursory sit-ups and push-ups, just a few to get him moving while he toyed with the idea of testing his new soldering iron . . .

Once he was dressed and about to leave for the first hearty meal of the day, McGraw saw a stark white envelope edged under his door. Plain, businesslike, with no hint of who had put it there. An eddy of torn paper spiraled out when he opened it. Inside, he found a page from a notebook, torn off and folded in half, on which was written a single word.

Truce.

McGraw picked up a piece of the shredded contract and smiled.

10

OPENING UP

Brewing a cup of the latest herbal infusion that Elise had blended for her, Daisy sat on her bed, a plate of Zoise cookies next to her, and dialed Granny's number.

"Daisy!" Joy came flooding down the phone, and Daisy felt an itch of guilt, as if her heart were wearing a slightly scratchy shirt. She should have called sooner.

"Hey, Granny, how's things?"

"Oh, you don't want to hear about things this end—well, I mean, apart from the fact that you know the Tailor brothers who own the village shop? Well, they've fallen out again, and now no one knows when the damn thing's supposed to be open or closed. Everyone's started getting their things delivered from Avocado or whatever it's called. All a bit la-di-da." Granny was in the kitchen—Daisy could tell by the slight echo around her voice and the rattle of the drawers as she opened and closed them. Granny had never been one for sitting still during a phone call. "But as I said, nothing interesting. You know Crickleton. The most exciting thing that happens here is a duck wandering into the pub. Sounds like the start of a joke, doesn't it?"

"Uh-huh," Daisy "mmphed" around a mouthful of cookie.

"Speaking of birds, how's that little pigeon of yours doing?"

Daisy leaned over to peer into the box in which Baby Gordon was residing. As if sensing Daisy's presence, the chick opened its mouth, and not wanting to disappoint, Daisy dropped a cookie crumb inside.

The second the crumb was gone, the little bird went straight back to sleep.

"He or she seems to be doing fine. I think." Time seemed gluey these days, splodged unevenly between Zoise sessions, not quite making the same sense it once did. So many of her memories these days seemed like things that had happened to someone else entirely. Trying to dredge them up to pass on to Granny was like reporting back a film she'd watched of someone else's life.

"And how's the yoga coming along?"

Yoga—the word triggered something in Daisy, a switch flicking on in a dimly lit cellar. "What do you mean?"

"You said you were doing yoga with those Zeus—"

"Zoise."

"Whatever. Those other students. Last time we talked about it, you were very excited about progressing through their belt system."

Had Daisy been talking to Granny about the Brethren? Fragments of warnings fluttered through her mind. *Share only with those you trust . . . The branches of one family should not cross with the other . . . They don't understand you like Zoise does . . .*

She needed to be careful. "Oh. Yes. Well, I'm on yellow belt now. Fourth level."

"That's fast."

"I'm very good at meditating!" Daisy snapped. A heavy lid slammed down on her instinct to reveal more. The Ceremony of Sharing was sacred and not to be discussed with anyone outside the Brethren.

"All right, Daisy, no need to take that tone with me." Granny huffed, then added, "Sounds like you could do with a bit of meditation now, if you ask me."

"Yes, well, I didn't."

"Daisy!" There was a crash, as if a drawer had been slammed shut on the other end of the phone.

Neither of them spoke for a moment. Normally Daisy would have been the one to break the deadlock. She didn't like confrontation, especially not when it came to Granny, with whom she'd always had a very peaceful relationship. But she didn't like anyone questioning her too much about the Brethren of Zoise.

Reaching out, Daisy knocked twice on the wall.

"That's Susan!" she said in a forcibly bright voice. "I'd better be going . . ."

"Daisy, is everything all—"

"Love you, Granny. Bye!" Daisy tapped the end call button as fast as she could and stared straight ahead at her yoga robe hanging on her wardrobe door, the magical Eyes of Zoise staring right back at her. Reaching into the nearby bag, Daisy shoveled in a second cookie.

When Granny's number flashed back up on her phone,

Daisy was in Xena Warrior Pose, earbuds in, bathed in the Zounds of Zoise. After three more calls, Granny gave up.

"Do you think Daisy's acting a bit . . . weird?" Susan asked when she and Esther were walking back from the supermarket.

"Yes." There was no arguing it, really. The times Esther had seen Daisy over the last few days, her behavior had been distinctly odd. For a start, she'd stopped cleaning the communal kitchen, which meant Esther had picked up the slack, and now no one knew where anything was—including Esther. Then there was all the chanting that Esther heard through the walls and so much herbal tea . . .

"I think it's all that yoga," Susan said.

Esther snorted. "You think any form of exercise is suspicious."

"Yeah, well . . ."

They lapsed into an uncomfortable silence. It wasn't just things with Daisy that were awkward. After open mic night, Esther had the impression that Susan was holding something back. Not that Esther wasn't holding something back, too: a desperate need to gossip about McGraw. Was their feud really forgotten? Was he . . . *forgiven*?

But she didn't want to ask; she wanted to be told. She was giving Susan a chance to prove that things really had changed since the home-friends debacle. That Susan was allowing Esther and Daisy to get to know her on her own terms.

Sometimes, Esther wasn't so sure.

It was with great relief that they finally entered the kitchen, the task of putting the shopping away drawing attention from the absence of any meaningful conversation. Just as they'd set the bags down on the table, Daisy burst into the room.

"WHY HAVE YOU BEEN SHOPPING?!" she asked.

United against a common enemy, Esther and Susan shrank closer together, keeping the table between them and a very angry Daisy.

"We? . . . needed? . . . food?" Esther whimpered.

"I only did my online shopping yesterday!"

Susan and Esther exchanged a glance. They'd been through all the cupboards after lectures and written a list of all the things that weren't in there. Essentials such as instant noodles and hummus and beef jerky and pesto.

"Maybe the delivery hasn't arrived yet?" Susan sounded as nervous as Esther felt.

"I ORDERED IT TO BE DELIVERED BEFORE NOON."

"Maybe someone ate it?" Esther's voice got smaller with each word, so fiercely was Daisy scowling at them.

"MAYBE THAT PERSON WAS YOU?"

"I don't think Esther was—"

"OR YOU?"

With the full beam of Daisy's rage focused on her, Susan reached out and gently pushed one of the shopping bags toward Daisy. "We bought you some crumpets."

And as if someone had flicked a switch, Daisy returned to normal. "Ooh, crumpets. Thank you."

Then she left the room.

Once they'd heard the click of her door, Susan whispered, "Definitely acting weird."

Susan and Esther were acting weird. Why had they eaten all the food Daisy had ordered, then replaced it with all the wrong things? So Daisy decided the best thing to do was to encourage them to fill up at breakfast, so that the next time she ordered food to be delivered from the supermarket, she'd actually get to eat some of it.

"But, Daisy, I don't *like* muesli . . ."

"No one does, Susan. But things that are good for us aren't always nice. You know that. You're training to be a doctor."

"I—what . . . ?"

But Daisy did not have time for this, and she simply pushed her tray purposefully along, taking Susan's with it. Potatoes, bacon, beans, nuts, fruit . . .

"I can't eat all this!"

"You didn't have a problem eating all these things yesterday."

Susan cast her a desperately bewildered look, which Daisy ignored, because Esther hadn't put enough eggs on her plate. They were like children, these two.

This thought aroused something deep and precious within Daisy's brain, and there was the briefest flicker of something . . . but as with so many of Daisy's thoughts these days, it got sucked back into a formless fog.

"Come on." Daisy marched across the room to where she'd spied a lovely big space for the three of them.

Just as she'd set her tray down, someone else did the same. Big, jovial, familiar.

"Poppy!"

"Jonathan." Her response was a lot less enthused than his. "I'm afraid this seat's taken."

"Yes, by me and the lads. You'll have to find somewhere else. Sorry and all that."

He did not look sorry. But he would be. Jonathan's lack of manners was just the last straw in the haystack piling up on Daisy's back—Granny's inquisition, her friends' duplicity on the shopping front . . . the creeping fear that she no longer had a place waiting for her with Zoise.

Daisy had had enough.

"I will be sitting here." Daisy leaned forward across the table, raising one hand high into the air and pressing all her fingers to the tip of her thumb to make an eye shape. Silently, from all around the room, people started standing up and walking over to where Daisy was, until a quiet, disparate herd gathered to stare at Jonathan.

"Please move," Daisy said, and the Brethren whom she'd summoned crossed their arms and looked at Jonathan.

A minute later, he'd left the canteen entirely.

"What just happened?" Esther whispered to Susan as they watched a load of people they'd never seen Daisy talk to return to their seats.

"I don't know, Esther, but let's not anger them."

The two of them walked meekly over and sat with Daisy.

Daisy's behavior had awoken Susan's dormant investigative instincts. What had happened at breakfast was *not* normal, and Susan had the uneasy sensation that she had taken her eye off the ball. First the McGraw-inspired insomnia, now Esther sucking up so much of her attention with the Vectra obsession . . . Susan realized with shame that it had been far too long since she'd last seen Daisy's willowy figure standing in the doorway to number 13, offering a cup of tea and sitting on Susan's bed, peaceably flipping through a magazine or reading up on something for her course or chatting gently and unobtrusively about her professors.

Almost as soon as she realized this, Susan realized that she missed it. Where Esther jostled, Daisy soothed. No wonder she was left feeling so prickly about the ridiculous Vectra situation . . .

Susan paused, a cushion of air between the knuckles of her raised fist and the door of number 11. Leaning in a little closer, she tried to catch the sounds beyond, which were murmured voices, pan pipes, and what was either whale song or the cry of a woman in labor.

Enya's creative direction had certainly taken a turn for the worse.

Following updated protocol, Susan knocked three times, and the music stopped.

"What is it?" Daisy called.

"It's Susan. I'm a who, not a what." Susan twisted the handle. "Er . . . Daisy—have you *locked* your room?"

"I must have done it by accident."

Susan found that hard to believe. The locks on J-block doors were so temperamental that it required careful alignment; a whispered prayer to Portunus, the Roman god of locks; and the precision of a master surgeon to get the key to work.

There were more muffled sounds behind the door, and Susan fervently hoped that she hadn't just interrupted someone else's masturbreak. Although doing that while listening to Enya seemed a bit . . . niche.

"I can go away if you want some private time?" Susan called through the door.

"No! It's fine! Just doing some meditation . . ."

If that's what she wants to call it . . . an imaginary Esther muttered, nudging Susan in the side and winking suggestively. Susan's smile soured at the thought of Esther wasting all her terrible innuendos on someone as humorless as Vectra.

When Daisy finally opened the door, she was breathless and shifty.

"Hi . . ." Susan raised a wary eyebrow. "Meditating, you say?"

But when she tried to peer over Daisy's shoulder, the door shifted to block her view.

"I'm meeting the Brethren later, so I was just getting in the zone . . ."

"You mean your yoga friends? All those people we saw at breakfast?" She leaned an elbow on the doorframe, fingers ruffling her hair as she studied Daisy intently, watching for a reaction that didn't come. "Those Zoise guys see more of you than we do."

"I like yoga."

"Obviously." Something was wrong here, but it was hard to know what. "I was wondering if you had time for a cuppa and catch up? Esther's driving me nuts with this whole Vectra thing—"

"Who?"

"Vectra. The goth girl Esther hasn't shut up about for the last two weeks." Susan faltered. "You've . . . talked to Esther in the last two weeks, though. Right? I mean, about more than what she's having for breakfast."

"Of course! I've just been busy with—"

"Yoga. Right." Susan tapped a fingernail on the jamb. *Click, click, click.* "Say, why don't I come to your next session? Find my inner calm."

But instead of the wide-eyed enthusiasm she'd been expecting, the shutters came down, and Daisy shook her head rapidly.

"No! That's not good. Jasper said I'm not to recruit any more members."

"Recruiting?" Susan pounced, her fingernail tapping more insistently on the wood of the frame.

"New members drive. That's all." Daisy had grasped too quickly for something that sounded plausible, something inconsistent with her original story. The kind of error the naturally truthful made.

"Except, presumably, the opposite of that? Since you don't want me to come along . . ." It wasn't like Daisy to make so little sense. She seemed ruffled and unfocused and a little dazed, her gaze darting around, looking for an escape.

"We're oversubscribed."

Click, click, click!

As Susan watched, Daisy closed her eyes and took a deep breath. When she opened them, all the haziness was gone, and in a firm, final tone, she said, "You missed the chance to join, I'm afraid. Now, if you'll excuse me, I've got to go, or I'll be late for my session."

Daisy reached back into the room for a bag and slipped out to join Susan in the corridor before waving cheerily and walking off rapidly. Once she was out of sight, Susan eyed the door to Daisy's room thoughtfully.

"Who have you been recruiting, Daisy Wooton . . . and why?"

As a result of her brush with Ptolemy P.I., Daisy had been so flustered that she'd practically run all the way to the House of Zoise and arrived half an hour early to the drop-in session. Someone Daisy had never seen before opened the door— Jasper's older brother, judging by the family resemblance— and led her into the hall. He stuck his head into the lounge and called, "Jasper? El? One of your acolytes is here."

It was strange, sitting in the kitchen with just Elise and Jasper, neither of whom was dressed for a session. Out of his billowing black robe, Jasper looked somewhat unremark-able, a typical boy next door. Still, the way he was standing by the sink, arms crossed and chin tipped back, gave him an air of authority.

Sitting in the chair that Elise had pulled out for her, hands warming on a standard brew of English Breakfast, Daisy did her best to get a grip.

"I think one of my friends is suspicious," she said.

"Of what?" Elise said calmly.

"The Brethren."

"We're just a yoga club. There's nothing to be suspicious about." Elise forced out a breathless laugh that didn't quite mask the look she shared with Jasper.

"Is this about what happened in the dining hall this morn-ing?" Jasper stepped forward and took a seat next to Elise so that Daisy felt a lot like she might be in an interview. Jas-per took his phone out of his pocket, setting it face up to play a video of Daisy calling the Brethren to arms. When the video finished, Daisy kept staring at the screen.

"The Zummoning isn't something for someone of your level to attempt on their own." Elise's voice was gentle, and she patted Daisy's hand consolingly. "We all make mistakes, Daisy."

"And we all face the consequences," Jasper added.

Daisy looked up in horror at Jasper. "What consequences?"

"Maybe it's time you reconsidered your place within the group."

"But I've been to every meeting and mastered all the

moves—I've recruited new members! You can't punish me for this!"

All the while, Jasper merely watched her, leaning casually back in his seat, still wearing his disarmingly baffled grin as if it was Daisy who was being unreasonable.

"There's no need to get worked up," Elise said. "No one's saying you have to *leave*."

Weren't they? Surely it wasn't just Daisy's anxiety at work here.

"It just . . . it feels like you're trying to get rid of me."

"Of course not." Again, it was Elise who was the one to soothe. "But we need to find a way of dealing with this—Jasper? A word." Elise jabbed a thumb in the direction of the hallway. "We'll be back in a minute."

Jasper's air of cool, calm confidence disappeared as Elise dragged him by the collar of his polo shirt out into the hall, pulling the door shut behind them.

Daisy blew across the surface of her tea. The situation didn't look good. Her Zummoning of the Brethren had backfired horribly, and instead of drawing her closer into the group, she was looking at being expelled. Was this what had happened with the other retired members? All the people who'd been there to welcome Daisy into the group had faded away and been replaced by new members. She'd thought it was because they weren't really committed to yoga, but now . . .

The creak of the door being opened interrupted her thoughts as Elise and Jasper came to sit back down.

"Every acolyte reaches a crossroad, and we think you've arrived at yours." Elise was very businesslike in her delivery as she drew a line on the tabletop from where Daisy was sitting and paused in the middle. "Many of our Brethren have chosen to leave the fold." Elise's finger swerved off to one side. "They feel they've realized their full potential, and they leave because, um . . . they have . . . er . . ." She glanced at Jasper for an answer.

"Zoise has bestowed upon them the confidence of knowing that they have outgrown the place where they once belonged, that they are ready to set root in the wider world."

"You really are good at this," murmured Elise.

Jasper shrugged off the compliment and directed Elise's attention to Daisy.

"Oh. Right. Yes. Well. There's the other path." Elise swooped her finger back toward where she and Jasper were and stubbed it meaningfully on the wood. "There is the option of *staying*. Here."

"Here?"

This time it was Jasper who answered. "Your enthusiasm is a powerful force. It's time you harnessed that energy for the greater good. Come and stay with us for a few days, Daisy. Help run the house."

Although Daisy was intrigued by the promise of spending more time in the house—perhaps getting to know Elise on a more personal level—as a friend, even—something had always held her back from actually offering her time. There was still a part of Daisy that worried she'd be missed.

"Could I still go back to my room at night?"

"We wouldn't *force* you to stay!" Jasper said with a laugh. "But . . ."

"As experienced instructors, we'd suggest time away from other worldly distractions," Elise said. "Like a yoga retreat."

Daisy's doubts must have been writ clearly across her face, because Elise leaned forward then, her expression as gentle and persuasive as her voice. "Remember, Daisy, the world will turn without you. Sometimes we need to walk away from our responsibilities to truly discover what matters."

"You want to commit, Daisy? Then commit. If you don't want to . . ." Jasper splayed his hands open, and Daisy watched her last shreds of hope evaporate into thin air. "Maybe your path leads elsewhere."

Susan needed a break. There was only so much time she could spend reading up on vascular supply to the stomach before the words swam together and she started playing vertical word searches within the text. Daisy's door was shut, and when Susan knocked, there was no response. Again.

Susan hadn't seen her after she'd gone to yoga the night before, and today, despite Daisy's insistence that they all breakfast together, there had been no sign of her.

How healthy was it to spend all your time with your body in someone else's basement and your mind on another plane?

Susan could hear the music even before she opened Esther's door.

"Ah." Susan stared at the scene before her.

Opening the door had pushed an arc of clear space on a floor covered with clothes. Esther was sitting on the bed wearing a camisole, her long white limbs and chest giving the impression of an albatross hunting above a sea of black silk. Treading carefully, Susan made it the short distance from door to desk without anything coming at her from within the depths. Since the chair was otherwise occupied as a display rack for an assortment of tights, Susan nudged the laptop over and shimmied up onto the desktop.

"And what prompted this?" she asked, eyeing the empty hangers dangling forlornly in the wardrobe and wondering how Esther had ever managed to fit everything in there.

"I'm trying to work out what to wear."

"To what?"

"Vectra's gig. Tomorrow."

Susan's face contorted in confusion with such force that she pulled a muscle. "What? You're actually going to that?"

"Of course! I'm someone who supports my friends."

"Undeniably true. You are relentlessly supportive. Like a sexy bra that surprises you by actually being functional." Susan paused. "But Vectra. Does she really fall into the friend category? Isn't she more of a . . ." Susan wanted to say "noxious arsehole," but if Esther really was delusional about Vectra being her friend, that might not go down so well. ". . . course buddy? You know, like—"

"You and Kully?" Esther said brightly.

"No!" Susan was faintly insulted on Kully's behalf. "Like,

umm . . . I don't know, me and someone I've never spoken to who sits in the same lecture as me sometimes."

"What are you getting at?" Esther lowered the top she'd been holding up to stare at Susan in suspicion. "Me and Vectra talk all the time."

"Really? Because you've been so-called 'friends' for weeks, and she didn't even tell you she was in a band. Friends tell friends things."

"You don't." Esther looked smug, like she'd scored a point in a playful debate.

"I—" Susan floundered for a moment; it was as if Esther had just pushed her off a diving board, not realizing that there were sharks circling below, and Susan had forgotten how to swim. "Well. But, I will. I *do*. I told you about McGraw."

"Eventually." Esther was concentrating on folding her clothes, lips pursed primly, eyes down, so that there was no way she could see the effect her words were having.

"Opening up . . . emotionally"—the word tasted so strange, Susan had to spit it out—"is not the same as not even bothering to tell you about my hobbies."

"You don't talk to me about those, either."

"Because I don't have any!" The desperate edge that had crept into Susan's voice finally caught Esther's attention. "I talk to you about important things. I let you take me shopping, and I carry you back from Halloween parties, and I make sure you don't run out of birth control. Those are friend things. Things that someone who cares about you would do."

Susan didn't do those things for just anyone. She did them for Esther, and she'd do them for Daisy.

"Vectra would do those things!"

"You unwholesome loaf! Vectra *wouldn't*. You wanted independent verification of whether or not Vectra likes you. Well, she doesn't. She doesn't like anyone or anything—the woman is *awful*. She's mean to everyone around her, she calls you 'Grooty,' and I've never heard her say so much as *one* single nice thing to you."

"You're one to talk!"

Neither of them said anything then. Something screamy and sad was playing in the background, and there was a creak from the floorboards of the room above. The lacy purple top in Esther's hand was scrunched into a tight little ball, her eyes blazing angrily across the room at Susan.

"What was that supposed to—" Susan began before knowing that she didn't want to hear the answer. "No. Actually. Don't say anything."

Susan slid from the desk and stepped carefully back to the door.

"I've Anatomy to be studying, anyway. Did you want anything from the kitchen?"

"No, thank you." Esther's voice was cold and hard, each word a rock dropped in Susan's stomach, making every movement that much heavier.

"Right. Well, if you wanted someone to come to the gig with you . . ."

"I think Ed Gemmell's going."

Out in the corridor, Susan stared at Esther's door, then at

Daisy's, before retiring back to the safety of solitude and a sarcastic skeleton.

Hey, EG. I need to ask a favor.

Anything.

Would you come with me to Vectra's gig tomorrow?

Well, I did say "anything" . . . but can we please not call it "Vectra's gig"? With 13 bands, that seems like a bit of a misnomer.

Sure. You're a good friend, Ed.

That's very nice of you to say.

11

BARRY MANILOW SINGS

"Did you see that Grace is back?" Kully asked when he and Susan were coming out of Anatomy.

"Hadn't noticed she'd gone." Susan's stride was heavy, heart so leaden, that it felt as if she was trying to drag an unconscious rhinoceros around. In a lecture, or a tutorial, or dissecting a pancreas, there was something to focus on. It was during this dead time, after one session was over and another about to start, that discontent leaked in.

"Yeah, well, she was. Now she's back. Saw her in lectures this morning."

"Keep her away from me, or she'll bugger off again because I'm so mean and hateful."

Kully stopped in his tracks to give her a startled look. "Will she?"

"Of course. That's how I drive all my friends away, apparently."

"Not this one." He flashed out his hand and ruffled her hair none too gently.

"Don't touch me."

"Sorry." The hand retracted.

It was as if she couldn't help it. "See? Mean and hateful."

Out in the stairwell, Susan left Kully behind the way she always did during a break. Normally she bolted for fresh air and the promise of nicotine, but her rhino-shaped heart made everything sluggish. By the time she actually got outside, Susan doubted there was time for a full cigarette before she'd have to make her way back for whatever integrated learning activity she had next. It had just tipped into December and was still dark when she'd arrived that morning. The night had long since closed around the hospital building, darkness pooling in Susan's spot by the bins. She'd just lit up, head back, eyes closed, back braced against the wall, when she heard someone say her name.

Kully was standing at the corner, a steaming cup in each hand and a bright red scarf looped elegantly around his neck as a nod to the cold that Susan could feel gnawing at her knees and creeping beneath her clothes.

"You moved fast," Susan said, almost impressed.

"Don't get too excited. These are from the vending machine in reception. Here, twenty sugars, right?"

Susan took the cup with a grunt of gratitude. "Why are you bringing me coffee? What is it you said? 'Smoke clings to cashmere like snot to a toddler.'"

"I'm here because I care more about my friends than I do about my clothes." He dodged a fleck of ash drifting in his direction. "Just."

It was probably the nicest thing anyone had ever said to her, so obviously it needed questioning.

"Even though I'm mean and hateful?"

"Stop saying that." Kully sipped his coffee, gagged, and swapped cups. "Sure, you're cynical and blunt and the angriest person I've ever met . . ." Something Susan would usually have taken as a compliment. "You're petty, you're grumpy, and you're so sarcastic, it's hard to know if you ever mean what you say . . ."

A truly uplifting pep talk.

". . . but, Susan, I've only ever heard you be mean to people who deserve it. Besides, I kind of thought this anarchic rage vibe was your shtick. I'm your friend *because* of who you are—not in spite of that."

"Thanks, Kully." Susan bumped her cup to his, a small smile escaping from her lips. "I'm glad we're mates."

"Me, too. It's good to know there's someone who'd come looking for me if I went missing." As soon as he said it, concern crept across his expression, weighing down the corners of his mouth and wrinkling his brow. "It's been happening a lot you know."

"What has?"

"Students disappearing for a few days before popping back up, the way Grace has." He sipped his coffee and frowned at Susan. "Have you really not noticed? She was gone for a week—her boyfriend came to visit and couldn't find her, and all her housemates were really worried. Turns out she'd just been doing yoga in some guy's basement and forgot to come home."

"Grace Latter, famously the hardest of partyers, forgot to come home because she was doing *yoga*?"

"Apparently so."

"And we're sure that's not a euphemism?"

"Positive. It was your friend Daisy who set her up."

Susan almost sucked the cigarette into her mouth, such was the force of her shocked gasp. *I'm not to recruit any more members . . .* that's what Daisy had said. Was Grace one of those members?

Kully was saying something, but Susan's vision had become a film reel, splicing together all the strange interactions she'd had with Daisy since she started going to yoga: the shifty way she'd stopped letting anyone come into her room, the breakfast incident . . . the locked door that had been shut every time Susan walked past it in the last twenty-four hours.

All of a sudden, it became *very* important that she find Daisy Wooton.

Vectra's band was playing in a pub called the Obscure Breed of Sheep, and it cost thirteen pounds to get in.

"A pound per band!" the guy on the door had said, taking their money and stamping their hands. "A bargain."

Something that Esther—had she been feeling herself— would have contested. In all her years of supporting local bands and weird acts, standing on pub carpets saturated with sweat and stale beer, or in basements with questionable health and safety standards, Esther had *never* paid more than a tenner for entry.

Feeling guilty for dragging Ed Gemmell along, she marched right up to the bar that ran the full length of the room and waved furiously at the man behind it, who seemed preoccupied by poking the material of his T-shirt into his belly button.

She turned to Ed Gemmell. "What do you want? My treat."

"Oh, er, thanks, but can I just have tap water? Maybe with a bit of ice and lemon? Treat myself and all that."

The bar didn't have any lemon. Or ice. But it did have a tap.

"Are you sure that's all you want?" Esther said, handing him a not entirely cold glass.

"Yes, thanks." Ed Gemmell took his drink and eyed the limescale still clouding the contents. "Water's good for you. Plus I need to stay up and finish reading *A Portrait of the Artist as a Young Man* ahead of tomorrow's seminar."

"You work too hard." Esther sipped her drink and pulled a face. She wasn't even sure why she'd ordered it. Stout had never been her thing, but Vectra had gone on about how Northern breweries were suffering from the influx of London-based microbreweries. "The first year of university is about life experiences like these . . ."

She waved a hand at the sparsely populated room. The venue was a function room at the back of the pub, with peeling wallpaper and mirrored pictures mottled with age. A bit like the patrons. The people there looked less like enthusiastic music fans and more like people who'd arrived early for a town hall meeting about parking restrictions.

"Do you think there's more people here to perform than to watch?" Ed Gemmell speculated, tugging his coat tighter as another couple of people swept in through the side door.

Neither of them was Vectra. If she was already there, then Esther couldn't see her. Which meant that Vectra wouldn't know she was there.

"What are you doing?" Ed squawked as Esther put an arm around his neck and yanked him so close, her nose ended up in his ear.

"Taking a picture."

Ed Gemmell twisted as if trying to free himself. "Can't I put my drink down?"

"What are you, an amateur? Incorporate it into your pose." Esther clamped him tightly enough to prevent further wriggling. He let out a pained wheeze as Esther held her phone up to catch them at the perfect angle. She took a few, cycling through all the appropriate poses—excited, moody, ready to rock. Ed Gemmell stuck with terrified.

Five minutes after she'd posted the best one, sixty-two people had liked the picture . . . but none of them was Vectra.

"Watch out." Ed Gemmell nudged her. "First band's up."

They were predictably awful. A mandolin, a xylophone, and a singer who sounded like a blue whale impersonating Michael Stipe. By the end of their ten-minute set, Esther's picture was up to eighty-four likes. No Vectra.

If anything, the second band was worse. So bad that Esther caught Ed Gemmell trying to stuff his hair into his ears.

"Can't we go for a drink somewhere else and come back? Rutting Corpse isn't on till nine."

"No."

"Why not?" he said plaintively.

"In case Vectra's here." When his face indicated a missing of the point, Esther clarified. "I don't want her thinking we're not going to show."

"No offense, Esther, but Vectra doesn't strike me as the sort of person to worry about something like that." He waved at the door. "We could just . . ."

"We are going to stand here until Vectra Featherstone gets up on that stage and sees how cool and brilliant a person I really am in my limited edition Bleeding Orifices '06 tour T-shirt as I mosh along to"—she checked the list she'd written on the palm of her hand—"The Devil Rode a Unicycle and . . . er . . . Washing Machine Head Duck."

"Are you sure it says 'duck'?"

"Yes, Edward, I'm not bloody autocorrect. DUCK. Look!" She pushed her palm into his face.

Esther's voice had risen with every syllable, a pressure building in her chest that she didn't know how to release. Maybe if she could thrash about, expend it through energetic flailing to something fast and angry and . . .

The man who walked onstage held an acoustic guitar, and when he cleared his throat, he announced to the room that he liked to rewrite cheerful nursery rhymes into mellow tunes.

Without realizing, Esther had started shaking. She felt a gentle hand resting on her shoulder, Ed Gemmell's voice coming to her as if through a thick veil woven together by stress and anxiety and the out-of-tune twang of a melancholy rendition of "Humpty Dumpty."

"Esther. We're going to go and sit in the beer garden, and you are going to tell me what's wrong. OK?"

"OK," she whispered.

Breaking and entering was immoral. Susan knew this. She also knew that the immorality of breaking and entering doubled when the victim was a friend, and the crime moved from a violation of privacy to a violation of trust.

She waited for the skeleton to object.

Ach. No jury's going to convict you.

"Because I won't get caught," Susan pointed out.

Well, then. What are you waiting for?

Shoving some balled socks, a bra, and some medical textbooks out of the way, Susan shimmied under the bed to where a grease-stained pizza box lurked in a far corner. Pulling it out, she flipped the lid to reveal a plastic bag containing a roll of fifties, a signet ring that had once belonged to a man referred to only as "Big Papa," a crime-scene kit, and a selection of fake IDs for *Mr. Sufjan Tolemy, Ms. Suzanne Pottolemy*, and (Susan's personal favorite) *Miss Susin P. T. Olemy*. Taped to the lid of the box were several smaller bags containing an assortment of useful tools, and it was from one of these that Susan selected a black velvet pouch.

The locks in J-block might have been temperamental when it came to keys, but when it came to picking, the simple pin tumbler should prove a breeze. As Susan crouched in the hallway, she cast an eye over the lock and selected her tools from the black pouch.

A pick and a torque wrench, a one-of-a-kind tool hand-made by a man who knew locks the way a nun knew the Bible.

"May Jesus bless you, McGraw," Susan said, her smile an echo of adventures past: breaking into the sealed cabinet in the headmaster's office to steal the skeleton that now resided in her room (and replace it with a tower of sarcastic-looking cuddly toys), rearranging all the mannequins in the windows of the local department store to look like they were performing "Y.M.C.A.," gathering evidence against that notorious Northampton reprobate Logan Hogan.

Ah, youth . . .

In her more fanciful moments, Susan had anticipated a den of chaos, as if Daisy had been taken in the night and her room trashed by men in balaclavas looking for a USB stick filled with state secrets. There was also a dark, entirely implausible scenario in which Susan opened the door to find Daisy unconscious, with Baby Gordon pecking at her glasses in an attempt to feast on her eyeballs.

What she got was something else entirely.

Daisy's room was bare.

Not the stripped bare of the recently departed drop-out, but more like a room that had been on a faddish diet and lost all its weight too quickly. Gone was the flesh—and with it, the soul. There was no Anglepoise desk lamp, no glitter lamp, not even any photo frames—the photos themselves were pinned haphazardly on the university-issue bulletin board. Even poor Enya had been stripped of her frame, left to curl at the corners under the bed, and the speakers through which she had once warbled were gone.

It didn't make any sense. Based on what remained, it was inconceivable that Daisy had moved out. But then . . . where had all her stuff gone? And *why*?

No wonder she'd been so shifty about letting anyone in here.

But still, a bare room and an absent Daisy weren't any reason to panic . . . only wherever she'd gone, she'd taken Baby Gordon with her. Smothering a bubble of worry with reassurances that Daisy had often taken the chick with her to lectures, Susan went to inspect the desk.

Sitting in the middle of the desk was a patchily highlighted handout: *Pottery in the Neolithic Era—An Overview.*

"Thrilling . . ." Susan muttered, noting that Daisy had written the date of the lecture at the top. Two days ago. Unlike Esther, Daisy was diligent in her class attendance. According to the timetable pinned to her board, she'd had two more lectures since. There were no handouts, but there was a selection of primary-colored exercise books—the sort Susan had used in junior school—lined up in a neat little row along the back of the desk. Each one had a topic written on the front, which Susan checked against the timetable.

Renaissance, Reformation, European Colonialism . . .

Lecture match!

Flipping that particular book open, Susan nodded in appreciation at the opening page of methodical color-coding and bullet points, carried on throughout . . .

Until more recently.

Here the notes were fragmented, doodles of what looked like a flower emerging in the margins, a motif repeated over and over with increasing intricacy. As the occurrences of the flower motif increased, the quality of Daisy's note-taking deteriorated to the point where the notes barely made sense.

The path to enlightenment is paved by sharing . . . Zoise opens the door to those of us who have opened ourselves to Zoise . . . Share the sanctuary only with those who wish to embrace it . . . Zoise desires more . . .

And then, on the next page, a single question: *What sacrifice are you willing to make for your family?*

Beneath, in capitals, the answer: *THE WORLD WILL TURN WITHOUT ME.*

Susan slammed the book shut in horror. Daisy hadn't joined a yoga group. She'd joined a cult.

"I don't think Vectra likes me," Esther said, bum resting on the bottom step leading down to the beer garden, feet planted wide enough that there was a nice big patch of paving for her to stare at while she avoided Ed Gemmell's gaze.

"I don't think she likes anyone."

"Really?" Esther was surprised.

"I think that's why she makes herself kind of hard to like."

"Oh, you mean the whole . . ." Esther indicated her own attire with a wave of her hand.

"No, actually . . ." It was Ed Gemmell's turn to stare at the pavement, brushing his fingers through his hair, then evening out the toggles on his hoodie as he said, "All that's really quite appealing." His voice broke a little on "appealing," and he took a sip of water. "It's more about her personality."

"But she's just like me! Sisters of the dark, kindred black souls, rebels in the night, united against a world that hates us."

"No, Esther—she really isn't. She might like the same music and wear the same clothes. She might have a cool piercing and sing in a band—*which*, by the way, is probably going to be terrible, because they've been together for all of twenty seconds, and my friend Shelley says she's heard Vectra singing in her room and she's *not* good . . ."

"Have you made enough noise for your sonar to have located the point yet?"

"Sorry. My point is, Esther, that you are a ray of human sunshine, and Vectra is a joyless vortex sucking all that is good and pure out of the world because she can't bear the thought of anyone else experiencing happiness. You are pretty much opposites."

"But she's my dark twin, exiled to the void—"

"That might have been the case before you came here. Kids are mean. But in Sheffield? Everyone you meet loves you."

"Except Vectra."

"I don't want to dig too deep into this one, but take it from me, you really need to not focus on the one person who doesn't like you and focus on the ones who do. Why would you pay thirteen pounds to come and watch someone who loathes you when you could be in your room playing Communist Monopoly with two people who think you're brilliant?"

But Esther was pretty sure Susan didn't think she was brilliant, and Daisy . . . well Daisy had all but disappeared.

"Communist Monopoly takes ages," Esther said, not sure she was capable of any more heart-to-hearts until she'd gotten hold of another drink. One she actually liked. "Besides, no one ever wins."

"Spoken like a true capitalist," said a familiar voice from behind them.

"SUSAN!" Esther shot off the step and launched into a hug with the sort of force that could take down a tower block. And when she did, Susan didn't tell her to get off. She hugged her back. Grudges were for people who didn't care that they'd wronged you, not for people like Esther. Not for friends.

The hug was broken up almost immediately by the bouncer from the front door.

"I warned you. No fee, no entry." He tightened his grip on Susan's shoulder and held his other hand out. "Pay up or shove off."

"Unhand her, you tenacious ape!" Esther said imperiously. "We were about to leave."

"We were?" In a moment of joyous abandon, Ed Gemmell sprang up and flung the contents of his cup over his shoulder—just as the stage door opened.

The scream that rent the air tore through the city of Sheffield with all the force of a sonic boom.

"What. The. Actual. *Hell?*" Vectra stormed toward the

group by the steps, rage burning so hot that it was almost a surprise that the water hadn't evaporated on impact.

"Sorry," said Ed Gemmell, looking sheepishly at his glass. "Didn't fancy the rest of it. It was only water . . ."

"*Only* water?" It appeared Vectra wasn't the sort of person to accept an apology. Her fingers dug so deeply into the material of Ed Gemmell's hoodie that when she yanked him closer, it was clear she'd grabbed a few chest hairs. "You ruined my makeup."

"That's enough!" Esther edged into the gap between the two of them, and Ed Gemmell stumbled back so fast that if Susan hadn't caught him, he'd have hit the ground. "He paid *thirteen pounds* to come and see you tonight—"

"Please note that I did *not*." Susan didn't want Vectra to get the wrong impression.

"—and the first thing you do is have a go at him?"

"He wrecked—"

"You and I both know it's waterproof."

Vectra met Esther's challenge with a dismissive sneer. "Whatever, Grooty. If you're here to watch us play, better get back inside. Someone dropped out, and we've been bumped up the list to go next."

Susan wasn't convinced this was a bumping up so much as a dropping down—support bands came on *before* headliners—but there was no time to argue the point as Esther moved things along.

"As I was saying to this gentleman, we were just leaving."

"Frightened of finding out what real metal sounds like

when you finally hear it played live?" But even as Vectra's lip curled in disgust, her eyes dropped down to the top Esther was wearing. "Wait . . . is that a Bleeding Orifices tour T-shirt?"

"It is." Esther propped her hands on her hips to better display the weeping skull. "I bought it in Berlin during their secret summer tour, where only super fans were e-mailed the location of the gig twenty-four hours beforehand. Fans like me."

Vectra's jaw had dropped with every word and now hung there as if the ventriloquist working her had fallen asleep on the job.

"You can have it if you want?" Esther slipped it off over her head, revealing a cropped singlet underneath. She held the T-shirt out to Vectra, who touched it with the kind of reverence befitting an unholy relic.

"What . . . why? If you don't want it, you could sell it on eBay for over a hundred quid."

"I think you're missing the point," Susan said, stepping up so she was shoulder to shoulder with Esther. "It's not that this sexy saucer of milk doesn't want the T-shirt—it's that she likes making people happy. If someone with a shriveled little pellet of a heart like me can love her for it, what does that say about you?"

Ed Gemmell didn't say anything, but he held out his hand and mimed a mic drop.

"Come on, gothy," Susan said, nodding to where the bouncer had opened the side gate for them. "Time to go save Daisy from the grips of an evil yogic cult."

"What?!"

"I'll fill you in on the way . . ."

But as the three of them turned their backs on Vectra, she let out an astonished gasp.

"Grooty! Your back . . . that tattoo . . . is that . . . did you . . . are you a member of the *Black Metal Society*?"

Esther glanced back and gave her a secretive smile and a devil-horn salute. "Not anymore. Some of us are too metal to be tamed . . ."

Two paces down the road, Ed Gemmell cleared his throat. "Esther . . . didn't you say your tattoo stood for 'Barry Manilow Sings'?"

12

A VAN, A PLAN, AND TWO MANS

So what's this about Daisy being abducted by a cult?" Ed Gemmell asked as they walked down the road from the Obscure Breed of Sheep.

"And if that's the case, why aren't we marching straight there?" Esther said. Her confrontation with Vectra had left her with an excess of adrenaline, and Susan and Ed Gemmell were having to trot to keep up the pace she'd set.

"And do what, exactly?" Susan said mildly.

"Bust her out and burn the place to the ground!" On seeing the look Ed Gemmell was giving her, she added, "Metaphorically."

For all that Susan was pleased to have Esther back on her side and out of the thrall of that toxic pixie witch, it was going to take more than an overabundance of enthusiasm to take down the Brethren.

Slowing her pace so that walking and talking became viable, Susan filled the others in.

"So Daisy's been absent of late, and whenever we've seen her, she's been pretty weird. That much we already know."

"Right."

"Right." Ed Gemmell frowned. "Last time I saw her, it was like she'd been hypnotized."

"Either that—or *drugged*."

Susan unfolded the paper bag she'd found when rummaging in Daisy's wastebasket for more clues about the Brethren of Zoise. The flower motif was stamped on the outside of the bag, but it wasn't that in which Susan was interested. "Open that and give it a sniff."

It was immediately clear that both Esther and Ed Gemmell were familiar with the scent of hash.

"When I had my energy-drink episode, Daisy gave me some cookies, and I passed out for forty-eight hours. When I ate them, I was buzzing too much to know what they were, but afterward, when I asked for the recipe, Daisy turned extremely cagey." Susan paused to flip off a car that sounded its horn when she stepped into the pedestrian crossing.

"Like she *knew*?" Esther was aghast.

"I don't think so, but she doubled down on the cageiness when I suggested I come with her to yoga."

"You volunteered to do exercise?" Esther stopped in the middle of the crossing, oblivious to the futile honking of the driver waiting for her to cross. "Were *you* on drugs?"

"I was suspicious." Susan dragged her to safety. "As I should have been. Look at this."

She held out her phone to show them the photo of the notes she'd found on Daisy's desk. Esther's hand went to her mouth.

"Drugs and psycho writing—are you sure it's the yoga and not that she's fallen in with some rebel archaeologists set on opening a cursed tomb?"

"Always with the curses." Susan rolled her eyes. "I'm sure it's the yoga. Those archaeologists are hardly a bad crowd. Have you *met* her friend Reggie?"

"You know, Archaeology Dude?" Ed Gemmell interjected. "Big guy, goatee, punny T-shirts. He was out for Daisy's birthday. Nice chap. No social skills." There was a very self-aware pause. "Which I think says a lot, coming from me."

Esther looped her arm in his and pulled him close. "We love you, anyway."

As Ed Gemmell turned crimson, Susan carried on. "There's more to it than that. See this symbol?"

"The flower?"

"Something far more sinister . . ." Susan said darkly. "These petals are the Eyes of Zoise."

"So what are we going to do?" Ed Gemmell asked. They'd reached the gates leading to Catterick Hall, and dusk had darkened to night. "Considering it's just a stoner yoga group, they seem remarkably organized."

"We're going to do exactly what Esther said: bust Daisy out and (metaphorically) burn the place to the ground." Susan grinned wickedly as she took her phone out and scrolled down to McGraw's number. "And for that, we need a very big box, a van, and a plan."

"And a man?" Esther nudged her in the ribs, and Susan allowed herself a rueful smile.

"Yeah, all right. We'll get us one of those."

"I mean, I'm right here . . ." Ed Gemmell muttered.

Man(s) and van secured, they moved on to the plan.

Hey, Grace. Good to have you back.

Who dis?

Susan (Ptolemy)

Sorry. Hi. Yeah. All my contacts got deleted while I was up at the house.

What house?

THE OUTSIDE SHALL NOT SEE THE INSIDE.

OK . . .

Sorry. Just read that back. Not sure what came over me.

Too much Zoise yoga, presumably?

NO ONE CAN DEFEAT ZOISE.

Good to know. About that . . . who, exactly, is Zoise?

ZOISE IS ALL AND NOTHING. LOVE AND HATE. ACTION AND INACTION.

Is Zoise contradiction and consistency? Hot and cold? Knife and fork?

"Knife and fork aren't opposites," Esther said, reading over her friend's shoulder as the two of them sat scheming on Susan's bed.

"Stow it, gothball."

God. I'm really sorry about this. Every time I see the word Zoise: TRUST NOT THE UNTESTED, TEST NOT THE TRUSTED.

"Screw it." Susan put her phone down and cracked her knuckles. "There are better ways to get answers."

Reaching for her laptop, she set to work—and Esther went to get ready.

It was possible that Esther had invested in her role a little more than was strictly necessary. On opening the door to Susan's knock, Esther was met with a nonplussed sweep of her outfit and a sardonic, "You know we're not actually going to do any yoga, don't you?"

Esther was wearing three-quarter-length leggings and a lotus flower–printed tunic she'd accessorized with a yin-yang pendant and a hemp hairband, which pushed a long black plait off her face. Never in her life had Esther looked quite so wholesome, and she could envision the scorn this would prompt from Vectra. So much time spent contorting herself to meet someone else's impossibly evasive standards, when she already had two friends who loved her just the way she was.

In trying to prove herself to Vectra, Esther had lost sight of herself. *This* was who she was. Someone who could change how she looked without worrying it would change how she felt.

Just because it *looked* like she enjoyed yoga didn't mean that she actually *did*.

"I'm sorry about what I said before," Esther said quietly while the two of them waited in the car park, both resting their weight against one of the bike racks. She'd wanted to say this sooner, but there hadn't been a chance.

"I know," Susan said, leaning against her slightly. It wasn't a hug, but from Susan, it was close enough. "But I grudgingly admire the way you're able to blurt out whatever it is you're thinking—even if I don't like what those thoughts are. So don't let your penitence change you. OK?"

That was the difference between Susan and Vectra: Susan didn't need to like something to respect it. And Esther kind of loved her for it.

"Ach! Get off me, you she-demon." Susan struggled ineffectually as Esther smothered her in an enormous hug.

There came the sound of an engine from down the lane. When the headlights swept across the forecourt, lighting Susan's face, she was looking at Esther with something approaching affection. Pushing away from the bike rack, she approached the van, casting a glance back over her shoulder to wave Esther forward.

"Come on, gothy. Let's go save our friend from these amoral fiends."

There wasn't really enough room for four people in the front of the van, and Susan found herself straddling the central console, Esther's legs hooked over one thigh. Her other leg pressed tightly up against that of the driver.

She held out her phone for McGraw to read the address Daisy had sent her all those weeks ago.

"It's near where you picked up this van."

"Of course." There was a smile buried deep in his voice as McGraw keyed in the address on his sat nav.

"Thanks for doing this." Awkwardness had rusted Susan's social skills sufficiently enough that even forcing out that platitude had been painful.

"Anything for a friend."

"Yeah, Daisy's a special one."

"I wasn't solely referring to Daisy."

For a moment, Susan's eyes flickered up to meet those of McGraw.

"Everyone ready?" he asked, leaning across to Ed Gemmell, who was looking exactly as uncomfortable as he was delighted, sandwiched between Esther and the passenger door. Both Ed and Esther gave McGraw a thumbs-up. His gaze returned to Susan, who replied with a single curt nod.

McGraw's leg shifted as he pressed the accelerator, jeans brushing denim against denim for a moment, his arm reaching out to shift from first to second. Susan swallowed. She should have chosen to sit in the back.

As McGraw navigated the streets of Sheffield, the other three ran through the plan. Using her intrepid computer skills, Susan had hacked into the university system to reveal what they were up against: Jasper Tooley and Elise Fournier—a deadly combination of charisma and competence. Final-year students with perfectly respectable academic records who'd chosen to go rogue. Deep-diving into e-mail accounts she shouldn't have access to, Susan had unearthed a slightly wobbly video someone had accidentally taken during something called the "Ceremony of Sharing." Their phone had been placed in a bowl that Elise had carried around the circle and taken upstairs to the kitchen, where there was interminably long footage of her faffing about mixing herbal infusions and baking, presumably while Jasper did nefarious things in the basement.

It wasn't much to go on, but it was enough.

When the van pulled up a little way along from number 21, the avengers assembled outside the vehicle for a debrief.

"Phones on silent." Susan watched them all switch off the sound. "Yogi Bear?"

"Check." Esther.

"Deliverance?"

"Check." Ed Gemmell.

"Dry Old Stick?" No response. "McGraw. That's you." Still no response. "Fine. How about . . . Vengeful Kindling?"

McGraw twitched a smile. "Copy that, Ragnarök and Roll."

They were ready.

A lifetime of practice had Esther well prepared for lurking in the shadows, watching as McGraw and Ed Gemmell, posing as Danube Delivery drivers, rang the doorbell to number 21. The whole operation hinged on someone answering the door. There was no Plan B.

The door opened, and Esther's heart gave an extra little pump at the sight of the boy who'd opened it. Ginger, freckly . . . he'd fill out a Superdry polo shirt nicely, that one. As it was, his outfit was hidden by a black robe.

"Hello there, we've a delivery for Jasper Tooley," McGraw said.

Target acquired, Esther fired off to Susan before scurrying out from the shadows and aiming for the house.

"Hi! I'm so sorry I'm late. My friend said there was this amazing yoga group?" She approached Jasper and deployed her most charming smile.

"Your friend?" Jasper paused on the front step, blocking Esther's access.

"Yeah—shall I just go in? You look kind of busy . . ."

McGraw had the back doors of the van open and chose that moment to call to Jasper, "It's quite a sizeable delivery. Not sure we can get it through the front there. Do you have another entrance?"

"I—er—" Jasper looked from Esther to the van and back, his adorable freckled face screwed up in indecision. "Sure. I guess, go through to the kitchen. Elise can help you," he told Esther.

Although they had downloaded a floor plan from Rightmove from when Zoise HQ had been on the market three years earlier, Esther took a second to match the blueprint in her brain to her surroundings. Stairs to the right, sitting room to the left—kitchen straight ahead, where she would find . . .

"Er, hello?" A young woman, petite and perfectly turned out in Lululemon leggings and a flowing T-shirt dress, set a tray of cookies down on the kitchen table and fixed Esther with an appraising look. "Have we met?"

"I don't think so," Esther said, adopting an entirely unnecessary American accent. "How y'all doing? I'm Fenella."

She held her hand out and beamed enthusiastically as the young woman took it.

"I'm Elise."

"What a cute name!" Esther ambushed her with a hug. Elise smelled like the cookies she'd been baking. "Now, can y'all tell me where I'm supposed to be going?"

"Where's Jasper? He usually introduces the new initiates."

"You mean that handsome young man who let me in?" Her accent had melded into something from the Deep South. Or rather, Esther's approximation of such an accent. Fanning herself seemed entirely in keeping when she said, "My, my, what a fine specimen. There were some gentlemen here with a delivery—he told me to come on in."

"Yes. Right, well . . ." Esther's arrival had flustered her, and it took a moment for Elise to remember what she'd been in the middle of doing. On the table was a tray of expensive-looking cups—stoneware gray with colorful enamel rims. No handles. "If you could take this tray of tea and cookies down with you, I'm sure Jasper will be along shortly."

"Aren't you comin'?"

"No." Elise dusted crumbs off her leggings. "I've things to do. The session started ten minutes ago. I'm sure Jasper can catch you up, but if you could leave your mobile phone in the bowl . . . ?" She gestured to a bowl in the center of the table—a cheerful Buddha smiling down on a bounty of mobile phones. "Here at the Brethren of Zoise we find a complete disengagement from the material world really helps you get into the zone."

No way was Esther about to hand over her phone.

She glanced down at the tray of steaming mugs and the plate of warm cookies.

That could work.

When the doorbell rang, Daisy had already taken several steps along her meditative path. The herbal tea had seeped through her system, slowing her pulse, lulling her body into a slow and steady thrum of relaxed anticipation.

Slow is the air in my lungs, the beat of my heart, the blood in my veins.

Arteries, Susan would have corrected her. That's what's taking the oxygenated blood *from* your heart.

Daisy shook her head to clear it, but there was too much disturbance in the room. People milling about by the bottom of the stairs—or, rather, those still capable of milling. There was a tangled heap of robes and smoke in a corner, where some of the other Brethren had transcended from the waking plane to commune with their dreams.

Daisy gave up and opened her eyes to see Jasper rapping on the glass doors at the back of the studio that led out onto the garden.

What now?

When Daisy had first joined the Brethren, she'd seen Jasper as some kind of pied piper, leading the lost into a warm and welcoming cave. Forty-eight hours of living in his cave, and she was starting to think he was nothing more than a charismatic child. All the decisions, the planning, the preparation was Elise.

Elise was the taskmaster, Jasper the spin doctor, and together they had wrung every ounce of energy from Daisy's aura.

"Sister Daisy!" Jasper banged on the window again. "A little help here. Can you unlock these? We've a delivery that's too big to fit through the front."

Dragging herself down from a higher plane and across the room, tripping over casually placed limbs and heaps of robes, Daisy unlatched the doors and pulled them wide to admit two delivery men as they wrestled a huge wooden crate into the middle of the room. The two were mismatched in height and—judging by the tilt of the box—in strength. It couldn't have been easy, negotiating their way in the dark with those Danube Delivery caps pulled down so low over their eyes.

The same logo was stenciled in red across the crate, and Daisy wondered what was inside. There were a lot of deliveries sent to the house—groceries ordered by grateful acolytes and the occasional case of wine, Blu-rays, games, and other essentials. It seemed Elise only had to add something to the chalkboard in the kitchen and it would magically appear at the door.

But Daisy couldn't think of anything on there that would necessitate such a big crate. It looked as if it could house a washing machine.

"Are you sure you've got the right house?" Jasper made as if to approach the box, but the taller of the two delivery men stepped in front of him, pulling an order form from the back pocket of his jeans.

"Says here to deliver to Jasper Tooley, 21 Tuttlebury Avenue."

Jasper didn't look convinced. "And it's company policy to deliver exercise balls preinflated?"

"Absolutely. It's . . . special heavy air. Better for stretching." That voice sounded dimly familiar, but with his cap pulled down, Daisy couldn't see his face. "If you wouldn't mind coming to sign for it. The paperwork's back in the van . . ."

Grumbling, Jasper retreated through the doors, pulling them shut behind him, and Daisy settled back into her meditation on the mat.

Susan shouldered her bag of supplies—a family-size bag of pickled onion crisps and a sports bottle loaded with ice water—and counted to twenty. When she clicked the spring-loaded lock inside the crate, the side swung open like a giant door to reveal . . .

A perfectly respectable basement. Recently renovated by the looks of it, with exposed brick walls and expensive spotlights. Squishy sofas and beanbag chairs skirted the edge of the room, and on top of them all, in varying stages of dozing to flat-out unconscious, slouched maybe ten or so acolytes of Zoise. Anyone conscious enough to notice the intruder in their midst clearly couldn't be bothered to do anything about it. Three of the Brethren were sitting facing the wall and sipping tea, giggling at patterns in the bricks, while a small cluster near the middle of the room appeared to be attempting actual yoga, albeit of the sitting variety.

At the sound of feet on the stairs, Susan drew back inside the box, but it was only Esther.

"Yogi Bear reporting for duty," she said, an elated expression on her face. "Hostile two is down. Repeat, hostile two is down."

She was positively buzzing with pride, and Susan was feeling indulgent.

"Full debrief, soldier."

"I sprayed a load of half-chewed cookie and herbal tea into her hair."

"You didn't."

"I did. Pretended to sneeze." Esther looked very pleased with herself. "She'll be showering that out for a week."

Susan clamped a hand onto her shoulder and gave her a reassuring shake. "You are equal parts revolting and resourceful. I'm proud of you. Now, on to hostage extraction . . ."

The two stepped over the Brethren on the mat—Esther stopping to poke one of them in the nose and marvel at the lack of response—and paused next to where Daisy was lying flat on her back, hands folded gently on her chest in a position Susan would have called the Cadaver.

Esther crouched down, concerned. "You don't think she's sacrificed herself already, do you?"

13

TRUST EXERCISES

There was a lot of talk about finding one's center in yoga. Daisy imagined that hers was made of caramel. Golden and lazy, as if her whole body was melting from the inside out, as if she were a chocolate left too long in the sun. During Zoise yoga, that was certainly how she felt—meditating turned her warm and oozy. She was the human embodiment of not wanting to get out of bed on a cold morning. That was the name of one of the moves, actually, now that she came to think of it, where you were supposed to curl up underneath one of the blankets. A lot of the moves had oddly mundane names. There were no trees or mountains or warriors here; it was all much more relaxed than that. There was Pretending It's Nighttime, when you lay on your back and folded your arms over your eyes, and Feigning Interest, where you sat cross-legged, resting an elbow on one leg and propping your chin in your hand.

Daisy's favorite was Staring at Dreams, where she lay on her back with her eyes closed.

It was the easiest position in which to transcend meditative planes, and it just so happened to be the position from which someone was trying to rouse her.

"Daisy . . ." Someone was patting her cheek gently. "You need to wake up."

I'm meditating, Daisy corrected the usurper. Only it didn't work, because she wasn't awake enough to form words.

"Seriously. How many of those cookies have you had?"

Before she could answer, freezing spray hit her skin, and Daisy's mind was yanked back into her body. A sharp tang of chemicals wafted up her nose, and her eyes snapped open, but what she saw must have been a meditative vision. There, looming over her, like two warring airships, were Susan and Esther. Which made no sense whatsoever. Esther despised yoga almost as much as Susan despised exercise.

Squeezing her eyes shut, Daisy willed herself to consciousness, but when she opened them, her friends remained.

"Hello," Esther said, rustling an open bag of crisps. "We've come to rescue you."

"From what?"

"The Brethren." Susan frowned. "And also yourself. You know everyone here's on drugs—including you, right?"

"What?" This was too much. "But it's just a yoga social . . ."

Susan snapped her fingers in front of Daisy's slightly wobbly vision. "Get with it, Wooton. Look: weird robes, passed-out students—*all* of whom are first-years. That's not even a little bit suspicious?"

Carefully, as if helping a foal stand for the first time, Esther pulled Daisy to her feet, muttering to Susan, "We need to open those doors, get some fresh air in here."

"What's wrong with the air that's already in here?" Daisy asked, breathing in the familiar waxy scent of the candles, the warm, toasty infusion of freshly baked cookies. The next moment, Esther was pulling on her arm, because Daisy had drifted back down onto her mat, halfway into assuming Pretending It's Nighttime.

"There are some things a home-based educational system doesn't cater to, and one of them is learning what weed smells like," Susan said. "Everyone in this room is totally baked."

"No, that's just the cookies."

"*Yes—it's the cookies*," Esther hissed, shoving the open bag of crisps right under Daisy's nose and muttering, "Let's see how strong the munchies are . . ."

Overwhelmed by need, Daisy let out a desperate groan and fell on the bag of crisps. Esther opened the back doors and pushed them wide. The fresh air and mouth-shriveling properties of a pickled onion crisp had an immediate impact on Daisy's cognitive functions.

"How did you get in here?"

"Long story." Esther wrestled with supporting Daisy, who was swaying about and feverishly tearing through the packet of crisps. "Susan?"

But Susan was standing very still, body tensed as if tuning in to a signal only she could receive.

You don't spend a summer working as a private investigator without honing your instincts, and Susan's told her that there was more to Zoise than stoner yoga. The operation was too slick for that. Besides, drugs cost money, so why would you give them away for free?

Unless you could make *more* money by doing so.

"Tell me, Daisy. Exactly what sacrifices have you been making to the Brethren?"

They'd gotten her as far as the bench outside the back of the house, the doors pushed wide in the hopes of rousing some of the others to consciousness.

"You can bring a friend. I introduced Grace and Reggie to the group." She looked over her shoulder to where Reggie was sprawled on a settee inside, robe open to expose a T-shirt with a T-rex holding a hacksaw and the word *Dino-saw*. He looked peaceful, but that peace had come as a direct result of avoiding thinking about his problems. Jasper and Elise preached about leaving the world behind, but now that the world had hurried to catch up with her, Daisy realized that "leaving it behind" was nothing more than running away—and since when was that a solution?

"Anything else?" Susan prompted, dragging Daisy's attention back to the matter at hand.

"You're supposed to share worldly possessions."

A dark look passed between her friends.

"Like your Anglepoise and glitter lamps and your photo frames and your speakers?" Susan asked.

Daisy nodded, remembering the way she'd snuck those items out of her room when she was sure neither of the others would see, knowing on some level that it wasn't something she should be doing.

"Jewelry, too." Her hand drifted up to touch the hollow in her collarbone, where the gold pendant Granny had given her should have sat. "But I don't have much of that—just a necklace and a watch. Everyone else seems to have so much more stuff than I do. When I couldn't give any more, they asked if I'd give myself."

"What? Like a *sex* thing?!"

"No!" Daisy flushed red from neck to hairline. "Just staying here for a few days to help around the house."

"You mean to do all the grunt work for them?" Esther looked outraged.

Daisy shrugged and caught Susan looking at her, that razorlike perception slicing through the remaining fog of the space bakes and seeing right into her heart.

"We missed you, Daisy. And not just because neither of us knows how to use the pizza setting on the microwave." She laid a hand on Daisy's arm. "You know that, don't you?"

The way Susan was looking at her, the penitent little gasp that escaped Esther's lips, Daisy wondered how she'd ever doubted it.

Susan rose, fists planted on her hips, head turned so that her purposeful profile was silhouetted against the glow of the studio's dim lighting. "Now. Let's reclaim your things and burn this place to the ground."

"Metaphorically!" Esther clarified.

Back inside, Daisy transferred Baby Gordon from his temporary nest in one of the many Buddha bowls to the breast pocket of her robe. That done, she showed her friends the enormous storage closet in a corner of the studio.

"There's hardly anything in here," Esther said blankly as the three of them stared at a few shelves of Blu-rays and odd little knickknacks—a blender, a funky little digital clock, and some books. No jewelry—nothing much at all, in fact.

"Ooh, the new Dan Brown!" Esther reached in to pick it up and flipped through it. "Wonder if it's any good . . ."

"Almost certainly not," Susan murmured.

"It's signed!" she squeaked.

"And yet remains without value. Put it back."

Susan stood back to study the half-filled shelves. They should have been filled to bursting with sacrificial offerings, but if they weren't here . . .

"Daisy, are there any places Elise has warned you away from?"

"Well, not exactly . . ." She glanced up at the ceiling. "But she did make a lot of jokes about how awful Jasper's bedroom was—that I didn't need to worry about cleaning it unless I had a hazmat suit handy."

"So, a room like Susan's?" Esther put in.

As the two of them shared a joke at Susan's expense, Susan smiled, thinking how easily manipulated fastidious people were into steering clear of any kind of mess. These two would never look inside her secret pizza box.

"If they're hiding anything, that's where we'll find it. Let's . . ."

But as they turned purposefully toward the stairs, they

were met with what appeared to be a wall of wavering zombies.

"Hey . . ." One of them raised an arm and pointed at the open closet. "Are you trying to steal all our stuff?"

"You handed all this stuff over to Zoise," Esther pointed out. "So, technically, we'd be stealing from . . . them? It? Her? Him?"

None of the Brethren looked like they knew the answer, either.

"Esther!" Susan let out in exasperation. "We're not stealing anything. Go back to gobbling your cookies . . ." She shooed them back, but with no Elise there to replenish the supply of tea and cookies, the acolytes were coming to their senses. And they weren't happy about finding the intruders. Casting a desperate glance at her friends, Susan saw Daisy set her jaw resolutely.

Raising her hands in the air, she touched thumb to fingers to make the Zign of Zoise.

"Esther, get to the lectern, Susan—the stairs. We've got this."

"What, exactly, am I doing?" Esther made for the lectern on which rested an inconceivably huge volume with ZOISE lettered on the front in gold leaf.

"Read from the book!" Daisy said, edging close, the Brethren focusing on them now that Susan had escaped up the stairs. "Jasper starts our meditating sessions that way. It should calm them down."

"Right . . ." Esther hauled open the front cover, confused at the title page inside.

"Esther . . ." Daisy sounded unnerved. "They're getting very close."

"I don't know what—"

"Anything! Look—some of the pages have tabs on them!"

"Yeah . . ." Esther flipped through to those pages. "That's not much help. This is . . . Daisy. This is just three of Nigella Lawson's cookbooks glued together with a bit of leather stuck around the outside. Look." She hefted the book into her arms and held it up for Daisy—and the rest of the Brethren—to see. "Did any of you actually listen to what Jasper was *saying*?"

There was a pause then, the crowd's mood shifting from accusatory to curious as they pressed in to have a closer look at a recipe for chocolate pear pudding.

The shower was still on. The adrenaline rush of freeing Daisy had altered the space-time continuum—Susan had emerged from the crate at 20:20 hours, and it was only 20:36. Still . . . for all Esther's predictions of Elise needing to shower for a week, Susan needed to pick up the pace.

There were four doors leading off the landing, all shut. A second staircase led up to the next floor, but there was a sign across the stairs that said Fintan's Lair. There had been no mention of a "Fintan" in any of the Brethren's e-mails—she'd try up there only if she struck out down here. Dismissing the door behind which the sound of the shower was loudest, Susan tried one that opened into a room clearly belonging to Elise. There was a rainbow row of nail polish along the mantelpiece, files and folders marked A–Z by subject on the shelves, and a desk by the window that looked as if it had been tidied with a set square. The only hint of disorder was the heap of clothes left in the middle of the floor. The next room barely looked lived in—although Susan recognized Daisy's pajamas on the bed and quickly shoved them into an empty backpack, found hanging on the back of the door, which she was at least 63 percent sure belonged to Daisy, too. Susan turned to the room at the front, feeling the steady build of triumph that came with knowing she was on to something. No lock. Jasper and Elise had relied on rumor alone as deterrent.

Paper chaos reigned inside—splayed books in French and Spanish lay facedown on almost every surface, sheaves of notes and magazines strewn across the floor. Clothes hung over the back of the desk chair, the end of the bed, and the corner of the wardrobe, from which a dinosaur onesie loomed into view. The place lived up to its reputation . . . apart from one area. There was a single tidy zone on the far wall. Someone had positioned an Anglepoise lamp (Daisy's!) to light a stack of wooden crates, upon which stood one of those obscenely expensive candles that wealthy, frivolous students used as a way of demonstrating a personality.

On the floor next to that, an assortment of oddities laid in a heap. Travel sets of branded toiletries, expensive stationery, a leather jacket, some pricey scarves, a stack of games and Blu-rays and hardback books . . . some barely worn shoes still in their boxes. And there, dangling off a student-issue mug tree, was a selection of necklaces and bracelets and bangles and rings.

Hurriedly, Susan pulled her phone from her bra and snapped photos of the things the Brethren had so willingly handed over, priced and ready to sell over the Internet. Then she crouched down and hunted for Daisy's missing necklace.

It was only when Susan knocked the pile of Blu-rays over and they clattered to the floor that she realized she could no longer hear the hiss of the water pipes.

When Esther's phone buzzed, her immediate reaction was to check it.

"Now's really not the best time . . ." Daisy said.

"It's the perfect time. Guys, look!" Esther held her phone out to show the gathered Brethren the series of pictures Susan had just sent of the treasure trove of goods up in Jasper's room. Esther swiped through the pictures. "We didn't take your stuff! It's all here in Jasper's room, ready to be sold for a profit."

"OK." Reggie shrugged, and the others exchanged somewhat resigned glances, mumbling apologies to Daisy and Esther before peering a little more closely at the bag in Esther's hand and asking if she had any more packets of crisps with her.

But Daisy wasn't done. Slamming the "Book of Zoise" shut with a clap, she straightened her spine, her gaze blazing out across the room.

"Are you just going to accept this?" When Daisy spoke, Esther gave her an admiring glance.

The Brethren stopped their shuffling about and arguing over crisps and turned to look up at her, and for a moment, Daisy felt the same heady surge of power that Jasper must have felt at the start of every session, faces turned toward him in hushed adoration, waiting for him to proclaim their fate.

"How many of us came here because we needed somewhere to belong?" There was an almost universal avoiding of her gaze. "Because it was hard fitting in, because we missed home, because we weren't sure we were doing the right thing? We're first-year students! That's how we're supposed to feel. Jasper and Elise know this—they were freshmen once, too. But instead of reassuring us, telling us that it's normal to feel like this, they took advantage."

"How is giving us free weed taking advantage?" someone piped up.

"You knew?" Daisy frowned, but her confusion was overshadowed by Esther's dramatics.

"IT'S NOT FREE! They're getting you to hand over all your stuff and selling it online. Zoise is nothing more than a front for a fencing ring! You're neck-deep in the criminal underworld!"

Technically they were comfortably seated in the basement of a well-to-do suburb of Sheffield, but Esther had never been one to let the facts get in the way of a good narrative. Which meant it was probably best not to let her control that narrative.

"The point is," Daisy persisted, "they knew we were

vulnerable, and they exploited us. The belt system is set up to encourage us to give and give and give, until we have nothing left and we're asked to leave. We might be numbed to the world while we're down here, high on cookies and meditation, but the reason we came here—to university—wasn't to avoid the rest of the world; it was to explore it. And I don't know about you, but I prefer my friends *not* to drug me without my consent."

The room erupted, crisps got tossed into the air, gowns were flung off in jubilation, and Daisy beamed out across the (not very impressive) crowd. As the group splintered into individuals once more, some went to look for their things in the closet—Reggie rejoicing in finding his signed Dan Brown book—while others ditched their robes and left through the back doors. This might be the end of Zoise, but it was the beginning of something better. Independence.

"I don't think they're going to need this anymore . . ." Esther said, picking up the Book of Zoise and flicking through the recipes as they followed the rest of the Brethren out the back doors and toward the front of the house. "There's some really good stuff in here."

Daisy slipped her arms around Esther and gave her a grateful squeeze.

"Thank you for rescuing me," she whispered into her friend's shoulder.

"We missed you, Daisy," Esther said quietly. "A lot."

"And who, exactly, are you?"

Susan scrunched up her face in frustration. Getting

caught by Elise hadn't been part of the plan. Time to improvise.

"Oh, er, hey." She turned to face the doorway and adopted a slightly sheepish expression, mussing her hair up as she rubbed the back of her head apologetically. "I'm Susie. Nice to meet you."

Elise wasn't so tall. Susan could take her if she had to. Probably best not to, though. Daisy wouldn't approve of bloodshed.

"I'm afraid I can't exactly say the same." Elise shifted her weight and crossed her arms, one eyebrow rising in challenge. Her hair was still slick from the shower, and her skin looked scrubbed clean, as if subjected to several rounds of exfoliation. "Why, exactly, are you rifling through Jasper's things?"

"I wouldn't say *rifling* . . ."

"I would, and I did."

Susan's attempt at a smile was as successful as a snowball fight in the Sahara. "Look . . ." She lowered her voice as if embarrassed. "I didn't even know his name. It was just one of those things, you know?"

Elise acted as if she did not.

"Both of us were so . . ." Susan let out a breathless, dreamy sigh. The kind that implied pleasures of the flesh. "We just had this *connection*. So intense."

Elise was tapping her foot.

"We barely even spoke. So wild." She glanced at the rumpled bedclothes, the discarded socks and shoes and clothes, letting her wistful gaze and disheveled appearance do the talking. When Susan glanced over at the girl in the doorway, it was clear they hadn't said enough. "I had hot sex with your housemate, and now I can't find my bra. OK?"

It came out a little more confrontational than intended. Which was on-brand, really. Susan waited, watching to see if her play worked. She *looked* like she might have awoken after a night of wild and sweaty sex. Dishevelled was her signature look.

"You know it's nine o'clock at night?" Elise said.

"Really? Is that the time?" Susan tried to look alarmed. "I must have slept in. Definitely time I got going." She moved toward the door.

"Without your bra?"

"It wasn't my best. I can get another."

"Or a shower?"

"Can have one of those when I get in . . ." She made a gentle "May I get past?" movement, but Elise remained still, blocking the exit and scrutinizing Susan up close.

"You're not exactly Jasper's type."

"That's pretty rude. I might not be *typical* . . ."

"His type don't usually wear bras."

Susan tugged her shirt tighter about her. "Some of us need a little more support."

Elise narrowed her eyes further, until they cut like knives into Susan's. "Jasper's type are usually men."

Ah.

Susan shrugged. "I mean . . . university's a time for experimenting, right?"

The two girls faced off for a second longer before Susan

gave it up entirely. She should really have done a bit more background work before going in like this.

"Oh, whatever. I'm here to expose the Brethren of Zoise for the fraudulent scoundrels that we both know you are. Now, are we going to have a rumble or what?"

There was a furious banging and hollering coming from inside the van upon which McGraw and Ed Gemmell were leaning, waiting for Esther and Daisy to arrive.

"Jasper didn't take it too kindly when we suggested he try meditating," Ed Gemmell said, cocking a thumb over his shoulder as McGraw grinned, slow and warm and wide, handing Daisy the thermos he'd been holding.

Daisy sniffed tentatively.

"Restorative hot chocolate," McGraw said. "No secret ingredients."

Daisy smiled, feeling a little wobbly at seeing the boys there, too. "Thanks. I don't seem to have the best of luck when it comes to my extracurricular activities."

"No, well, about that . . ." McGraw said. "Ed and I were wondering if you wanted to form a splinter pool group. Just us three."

"There's no official timetable. We just pay membership to the pool hall and play whenever we want." Ed Gemmell's eyes wrinkled kindly behind his glasses. "How about it?"

But before Daisy could respond, there was a thump from above their heads like a bird flying into a pane of glass. The four of them looked up to see Susan hammering on an upstairs window.

"SHE'S TRAPPED ME IN HERE!" Susan screamed through the glass, accompanying this with very elaborate hand gestures that presumably meant "Get me out."

Ed Gemmell rushed forward to find the front door locked.

"Around the back?" Esther suggested, but Daisy was looking up at the bay window with steel-strong determination. Handing Baby Gordon to Ed Gemmell, she sat down and dropped effortlessly into the briefest of meditations. The Brethren of Zoise might have been in this for the money, but that hadn't stopped Daisy from attaining some next-level yoga skills.

Snapping her eyes open, Daisy knew exactly what to do. Opening the van door, she fired the engine and steered the van so close to the house that one wheel ended up in the flower bed. Jasper's hammering on the partition behind her had reached a crescendo, but with this kind of focus, it was no more distracting than a gentle, continuous hum. Opening the door, Daisy levered herself onto the roof of the van and cupped her hands to shout.

"Open the window and jump down!"

Susan opened the window, but only so she could shout, "ARE YOU INSANE?"

"I'll catch you!"

"Why can't a few of you just come in through the back and open the door?" Susan looked helplessly at the group huddled below, McGraw's anxious frown, Ed Gemmell clutched up against Esther in concern. "This is a terrible idea."

"Susan Ptolemy, do you trust me to catch you?" Daisy said with marrow-deep conviction.

Susan's eyes met Daisy's. Susan Ptolemy trusted no one.

But maybe she should.

The sound of her two best friends hitting the van roof and screaming as they slid off was one Esther hadn't anticipated when she'd set out that night. As it was, she and the two boys hurtled to where Susan and Daisy were dangling down in front of the windshield.

With no great delicacy, Esther and Ed Gemmell helped maneuver Daisy off the roof and onto the ground. Only a couple of paces away, she noticed the tenderness with which McGraw guided Susan off the roof, arms sliding under hers to support her weight as she flopped from the roof and into his chest. Almost as soon as he'd lowered her to the ground, the two stepped apart, each looking in every direction except at each other.

A dull thud came from inside the van, followed by a faint, "Hello? Please . . . *please* can you let me out? Herbal tea is a diuretic. I'm *dying* for a pee."

EPILOGUE

In many ways, things had simply gone back to the way they were. Reggie returned to his course, Daisy to her routine, and Esther to relying upon Ed Gemmell's notes rather than attending lectures herself (anything good enough for the almost-impossible-to-please Vectra was good enough for Esther). Susan's hackles still rose when McGraw's name crept into conversation.

Except there were differences. No less important for being subtle. The ghost of Susan's grudge no longer haunted her sleep, and when she saw McGraw, Esther would swear that there was something like fondness in the way Susan insulted him. While Esther might have embraced a lax attitude to academia, she was the one most likely to be found cleaning the communal kitchen, descaling the kettle, or ordering the food—and when she cooked, she locked her phone in her room to avoid distraction. So far, she'd only set the smoke alarm off once. And for Daisy, a return to routine was welcome, but it no longer felt necessary. If one of the boys suggested a spontaneous game of pool when she'd planned a late-night library session, she would accept. She felt confident enough that changing her plans wasn't somehow letting other people down or even annoying them.

Still. That didn't mean she wanted to be late for her Wednesday hot lunch in the S.U. with Esther and Susan. As the three of them queued, Daisy chatted contentedly to Esther, but Susan seemed on edge, checking her phone. All through the meal she kept glancing around, her revolting, ketchup-covered panini growing cold.

"Keeping your eye out for McGraw?" Esther said, with so much waggling of her eyebrows, they were in danger of falling off.

"Hmm?" Susan turned back to her friends with a distracted frown. "No. Actually. I'm looking for someone much worse . . ."

Esther and Daisy exchanged a look of alarm.

". . . and there they are."

As one, the three women looked across the fixed tables of the cafe area of the S.U. to see Jasper and Elise standing there, scanning the room. When Susan raised her arm to make the Zign of Zoise, Daisy nearly toppled off her chair in shock.

"Hey. Miscreants. Over here."

Now that they had been exposed, Daisy struggled to see what it was that she'd liked about Elise. Sure, she was exceptionally pretty and well turned out, but as she approached, it seemed obvious to Daisy that her charm was an accessory she wore when someone was looking; it wasn't a kindness that rose from within. Even Jasper's boy-next-door vibe failed to raise so much as an eyebrow from Esther when he took the seat opposite hers.

"Daisy, we're sorry . . ." Elise began.

"Not good enough." Esther slammed a fist on the table, making the cutlery rattle on their plates.

But Susan shushed her before turning back to the erstwhile Brethren. "She's right. We're not interested in apologies."

Daisy pressed her lips together to stop herself from objecting. Apologies were nice, but it seemed there was something else at play, judging by the look Susan was giving Elise, who sighed and took a package from her bag, a small padded envelope with the Zoise address on the front.

She laid it on the table and slid it across to Daisy.

"This is your necklace. We bought it back from the person we sold it to."

A grateful little gasp escaped Daisy's lips as she opened the envelope and tipped the gold chain and pendant into her outstretched palm.

"And the rest?" Susan asked. Pleased as she was that the irreplaceable item had been replaced, Daisy had given the Brethren a lot more than that.

Jasper and Elise exchanged worried looks. This time it was Jasper who spoke.

"Look. We tried . . ."

"Not good enough."

"I know. Just listen—"

Susan uncrossed her arms and stood to lean over the table, so close that she could feel Jasper's panicked little breaths tickling her skin.

"I believe I made our terms clear."

Susan sat back down. Waiting.

Slowly, watching Susan as a French nobleman might eye a barely tethered guillotine, Jasper nudged Elise, who passed him an unremarkable brown envelope.

"We couldn't get everything back." Jasper held the envelope out. "So we're compensating you in cash."

"Esther. Please count it."

Snatching the envelope, Esther thumbed through the contents twice and let out a low whistle before confirming, "One hundred and seventy-five pounds."

Susan didn't break eye contact. A trickle of sweat worked its way from Jasper's hairline all the way to his left eyebrow. He swallowed.

"How about we make it an even two hundred?" he croaked.

Susan nodded. Once.

The transaction complete, Susan finally averted her gaze, breaking her eye lock with Jasper, who listed sideways onto Elise.

"You may go," Susan told them. "I believe you have a few more people who need compensating."

The two final-year students stood, Elise giving them a mutinous glare, a protective hand resting on Jasper's shoulder as if he were the victim in all this.

Before they took another step, however, Esther blurted out, "Why'd you do it? I mean, the gowns and the cookies and belt system. It was so . . . *organized*."

Elise brightened. "You were impressed?"

Giving Daisy a guilty look, Esther said, "Well . . . only in the same way I'm impressed that U2 still have a career. Reluctantly."

"Look. I'll be honest with you. It was for the CV." When the three of them failed to respond, Elise leaned across the table, a gleam of desperation in her eye. "Do you know how tough the job market is? A Philosophy degree means almost nothing to potential employers, but how many other graduates can put 'founded a profit-making yogic cult' on their job applications?"

"Hopefully very few!" Esther said in alarm.

This time it was Jasper who was settling Elise, tugging the strap of her handbag as if to pull her away. "Leave it, El. They're only freshmen. They'll understand when the time comes . . ."

Once they were gone, Esther reached into the envelope and pulled out all the notes, fanning them out like playing cards, her eyes alight with joy.

"Two. Hundred. Pounds. Do you know what this means?"

"That one of your closest friends was horribly ripped off by two self-serving criminals who have no moral currency?"

"That I can finally download all of Enya's back catalog?"

Esther shook her head, the gleam in her eyes growing brighter. "SHOPPING TRIP!"

ACKNOWLEDGMENTS

Not only did this project introduce me to my favorite series of comics, but I also had the joy of meeting their creator, John Allison, who is as dry and funny in real life as in his writing. Thank you so much for letting me hang out with Susan, Daisy, and Esther; it really was an honor.

Erica Finkel, my editor at Abrams, has been the Actual Best to work with, and I hope I may do so again one day. I'd like to thank both the team at Abrams and BOOM! for everything they've done to help the story along as well as Juliet Mahony for her admirable agenting.

Not having gone to Sheffield University, I needed some insider advice, which I got from Emma Hartick, the most excellent medical-student adviser I could possibly have asked for, and from Rachel Ellis, who didn't seem to mind how many times Susan insulted English Literature students. Thank you also to Mariam Khan and Patrice Lawrence for being patient with me, and to Grace Latter for tacitly giving me permission to nick your name, if not your personality.

Hugest of thanks to two people essential to the whole project: fellow Giant Days fan Robin Stevens, the first person I told about working on this and definitely the most enthusiastic, and my friend Molly Ker Hawn.

As always, thank you to my family, especially Pragmatic Dan, who offered McGraw's calm to my out-of-control Susanish tendencies.